JENNI DAICHES was born in Chicago, ed[...] England, and has lived in or near Edin[...] years of part-time teaching and freelan[...] in Kenya, she worked at the National M[...] to 2001, successively as education offi[...] editor for the Museum of Scotland, a[...] of Scotland International. In the latter capacity her main interest was in emigration and the Scottish diaspora. She has written and lectured widely on Scottish, English and American literary and historical subjects under the name of Jenni Calder and writes fiction and poetry as Jenni Daiches. She has two daughters, a son and a dog.

By the same author:

Chronicles of Conscience: A Study of Arthur Koestler and George Orwell,
Secker and Warburg, 1968
Scott (with Angus Calder), Evans, 1969
There Must be a Lone Ranger: The Myth and Reality of the American West,
Hamish Hamilton, 1974
Women and Marriage in Victorian Fiction, Thames and Hudson, 1976
Brave New World and Nineteen Eighty-Four, Edward Arnold, 1976
Heroes, from Byron to Guevara, Hamish Hamilton, 1977
The Victorian Home, Batsford, 1977
The Victorian and Edwardian Home in Old Photographs, Batsford, 1979
RLS: A Life Study, Hamish Hamilton, 1980
The Enterprising Scot (ed, with contributions), National Museums of
Scotland, 1986
Animal Farm and Nineteen Eighty-Four, Open University Press, 1987
The Wealth of a Nation (ed, with contributions), NMS Publishing, 1989
Scotland in Trust, Richard Drew, 1990
St Ives by RL Stevenson (new ending), Richard Drew, 1990
No Ordinary Journey: John Rae, Arctic Explorer (with Ian Bunyan, Dale
Idiens and Bryce Wilson), NMS Publishing, 1993
Mediterranean (poems, as Jenni Daiches), Scottish Cultural Press, 1995
The Nine Lives of Naomi Mitchison, Virago, 1997
Museum of Scotland (guidebook), NMS Publishing, 1998
Present Poets 1 (ed, poetry anthology), NMS Publishing, 1998
Translated Kingdoms (ed, poetry anthology), NMS Publishing, 1999
Robert Louis Stevenson, (poetry, ed), Everyman, 1999
Present Poets 2 (ed, poetry anthology), NMS Publishing, 2000
Scots in Canada, Luath Press, 2003
Not Nebuchadnezzar: In Search of Identities, Luath Press, 2005
Letters From the Great Wall, Luath Press, 2006
Frontier Scots: The Scots Who Won the West, Luath Press, 2010
Lost in the Backwoods: Scots and North American Wilderness, Edinburgh
University Press, 2013

With thanks, again, to Faith Pullin, and to Colin Manlove.

I

THE WINDOW WAS open. Larry watched her walk slowly, hands in her pockets, while the dog stravaiged in and out of the long grass. He often watched her. It was love, of a kind, but there was no urgency. He poured what was left of the bottle into the squat green glass he always drank from and returned to the window, holding the glass in both hands. It had been a warm day, a little cloudy until evening, when the sky had cleared. Now, after ten, it was still light. Ruth had reached the far end of the track, where it looped round a clump of rhododendrons and brambles, but he heard her voice. 'Dixie,' she called. 'Come here, Dix.' It was a low voice, slightly breathy, as if something were being held back.

Peter at his bedroom window also watched Ruth and Dixie as they came round the house past raspberry canes and currant bushes. He had just put on a clean shirt. He was going out. Peter often went out at this time. With both hands he smoothed gel into his thick brown hair.

In the kitchen Ros and Emma were making cocoa. Emma was seven and should have been in bed.

Larry hummed. *My Dixie darling, my Dixie belle.* He had sung it on the doorstep a year ago, a summer evening like this one. 'What's the dog's name?' he'd asked. He had a pleasant, gritty tenor voice. 'Okay,' Ruth had said. 'You'd better come in.' Now he heard the sound of Peter's motorbike revving and a moment later it was heading up the potholed track to the gate. He watched the tail light against the almost imperceptible graininess of the encroaching dusk.

Ruth walked up to the house, white and spectral in the last of the light. There was a new moon just visible, tilted and thin as a pencil line. The green of the garden and the fields beyond was darkening, and the stand of trees by the road was black. Headlights glimmered intermittently beyond them. Sometimes she thought, *how often have I done this, how often have I circled the house, watched the darkness creep in?* She went into the kitchen and the dog drank from her water bowl. The sleeves of Ruth's cardigan were pushed above her elbow, showing her tanned arms. Her face was tanned and her short-cropped brown hair freckled with grey. Larry had at once been compelled by her eyes, luminous, almost bronze in colour. He sensed her eyes now, emerging from the darkness into the lit kitchen.

Emma concentrated on the pan of milk on the Aga. 'We're making cocoa,' she said. 'I'm waiting for the bubbles.'

'Would you like some, Ruth?' Ros asked.

Ruth shook her head. She heard the roar of Peter's motorbike and caught Ros's eye. They both smiled. Ros looked tired, and the tiny scar on her upper lip was more prominent than usual. Her narrow, oval face never had much colour, and when she pulled back her dark hair, which she did for going to work, she had an enclosed, Victorian photograph look.

'Good day?' Ruth asked.

'So-so.'

Emma squealed. 'It's ready, mum.'

'Okay, pour it in then. Carefully.'

The two women watched the little girl pick up the pan with two hands and pour hot milk into a mug. Her curly hair flopped over her eyes.

'She couldn't sleep,' Ros said. 'Again.'

'It will take time.'

'It's been five months.'

Emma stirred her cocoa vigorously, dropped to her knees to hug Dixie, who had stretched out under the kitchen table, and then was up again wriggling onto a chair. She took a cautious sip from her mug.

In the attic Larry finished his wine, ran a hand over his scrubby beard and at last moved away from the window. He bought wine by the case when he sometimes had scarcely enough for food. Wine and memories. A restaurant by the ocean watching the grey Pacific rollers under a layer of mist, a Napa Valley cabernet cupped in his hands – he remembered the painting that bought that bottle. A sidewalk and garbage cans bought by a man in black-rimmed glasses and a button-down shirt. He settled in the frayed armchair and picked up the paper of the day before which lay on the floor beside it. News. He didn't much care for news. At the far end of the long, low room was a half-finished picture on an easel and a bench encrusted with colour and cluttered with brushes and tubes of paint and filthy rags. Sketches and photographs were pinned onto the walls. He had arrived with almost nothing: a few clothes, some tubes of paint, a camera.

Ruth went into the living room, which over the years had mutated into a work room. On her desk was a heap of typescript, which she contemplated for a moment, but no, she would do no more work now. Instead, she picked up a letter. Her boys, scattered. It was inevitable, she supposed. The letter was a rare communication from James, the middle son. On his occasional visits to Nairobi he sometimes phoned or sent an email if he had access to a computer, but he seldom put pen to paper and she had got used to his long silences. She sat in her favourite chair to read the letter again, a commodious armchair with room for books, papers, a pencil case, knitting, sometimes two cats, as well as herself. A dictionary rested on its broad arm. Dixie lay on the rug, her chin on her black and white paws, watchful at first, but then her eyes closed and she seemed to sleep. James wrote cheerfully that he had organised a sports day at the school upcountry where he was teaching, fun but exhausting. He suggested, not for the first time, that Ruth should come for a visit. *Come to Kenya and I'll show you elephants red from the African earth, the Great Rift Valley spread across the continent, Maasai warriors, a pink sea of flamingos.* Ruth put the letter down and smiled. 'Come to London, mum,' Ewan said when he phoned. 'Come to San Francisco,' from Sam. But the house anchored her. She did not necessarily want it that way, but that's the way it was.

Would she ever go to San Francisco, where Ed and Arlene and their two little girls looked out over the ocean? Ed and Arlene. Once it had been Ed and Ruth here in this house, and all these years later Ed in California with another wife seemed unreal.

She heard Ros and Emma go upstairs, and a few minutes later Larry coming down. Dixie's ears went up. He'd be making himself his late-night sandwich, while Peter, a dozen miles away, went into the Bailie with his helmet tucked under his arm. The bar was crowded, but Russell was there, his deep brown eyes smiling, and a pint was waiting for him. It was Friday night, but the next day Peter was setting up the lighting for a concert in Dunfermline. One drink and then back to Perth Street, to the flat that Russell shared with two girls who worked for the council. It wasn't very satisfactory, but it was the best they could do.

Larry held the fridge door open and contemplated its contents. Cheese, tomatoes, German salami, one gherkin in a jar. He longed sometimes for hot salt beef and good rye bread.

There was still a glimmer of light in the sky when Ruth locked up, but the new moon was etched a little more clearly. She opened the door for a moment to catch the smell of the honeysuckle that clambered over the old stable wall. She heard the creak of stairs as Larry returned to the attic. Peter wouldn't be home until late. How many times had she done that, paused at the open door, looked out into the near-dark, where the ridge beyond the house could still just be made out, and listened for the sound of the burn that gave the house its name? Only when there was no wind could she make out the ripple of water.

They would all hear Peter when he did return, all except Emma, who slept at last. Ruth was already awake, as she often was at three in the morning. Larry was jolted out of a murky dream by the chug of the motorbike. 'Goddamn bike,' he growled, but was soon asleep again. Ros had her light on and was reading, trying to blot out the panic that had woken her half an hour before. Sometimes she woke with her skin screaming, knowing that Martin was in the room, watching her. She took deep gulps of air until her heartbeat slowed, but she was wide awake, alert. She was glad when she heard Peter return. She felt safer. 'I wouldn't trust Larry in an emergency,' she had once said to Ruth with a laugh, 'but I feel safe with Peter around.'

They agreed about Peter, his broad shoulders, muscled arms, strong hands, and a smile that dimpled his cheek. His thick springy hair. Ros imagined Peter and Martin in the same room. She imagined Martin afraid, although that was hard. She ran her fingers over her ribs, the ribs that had been cracked, and tried to forget the mask of her bruises which followed the pain when the side of her face had hit the wall. Most of all, she tried to forget the sight of Emma in the doorway, bloodless, silent.

It was not easy, teaching a class of ten-year-olds when anything more than a shallow breath sent stabs of pain into her chest.

On the phone Ruth Montgomery had seemed brisk and capable when Ros had explained the resource centre needed an editor. She had expected a business suit and shoulder pads, not a slight, small woman in chinos and an orange polo shirt with a shapeless bag slung over her shoulder, full of typescript and notebooks. Without sitting down she had looked at the material spread across the table and said, 'You'll need to cut it by half.' Ros and her colleagues protested.

'You don't need me to tell you that you can't expect teachers to wade through that much stuff. Decide on the essential headings, then we can go through it again and make it as concise as possible.'

They gave her a mug of tea and made room for a plate of digestive biscuits.

'We have a deadline. It has to go to the printer next week, and we're all of us teaching. We have to work on it after school.'

'That's okay. Make your preliminary selection now, this afternoon. Then we can get together at the weekend to finish it off – that is, if you don't mind giving up time then. You can come out to my place if the resource centre is closed.'

So it was arranged that Ros would come to Netherburn, but when she arrived she had a child with her and was apologetic. Her husband had had to go out, it was lucky he didn't need the car. 'This is Emma, my daughter. She's brought colouring books and things.' Ruth smiled. 'Hi Emma. Why don't you take the dog and explore outside.'

'Will she be alright?' Ros asked anxiously.

'Of course. She can stay in if she prefers but it's a lovely afternoon.' And it was, a warm, hazy late September day.

Emma had loved it all, the house, the dog, the cats, the old swing, the musty stables, the space, the trees. When Ruth and Ros had finished they found her sitting on the gate into the back field with Dixie at her feet.

'Mum, can I have a dog?'

They picked a bagful of apples to take home.

'Do you live alone here?' Ros had asked.

'Not quite. There's a flat that I let out, and an artist in the attic,' Ruth said with a smile, but offered no further explanation.

Emma hadn't wanted to leave. 'Come again,' Ruth had said. And they did, Ros and Emma, they came and took Dixie for walks and raked the leaves. Ros and Ruth talked in the kitchen over mugs of tea, the large, cluttered kitchen, pots and pans, and magazines and letters, recipe books, boots drying by the Aga, animals. Emma knelt on a chair and reached into the biscuit jar and ran outside again into the damp autumn air. And Ros pushed up her sleeve to show Ruth the bruises on her arm, and began to cry. But it was January before they came, she and Emma with two suitcases and a rucksack, in a taxi from town.

'Of course you can stay,' Ruth said.

'Just until I get something sorted out.'

In the morning Ruth drove Emma to school and Ros to accident and emergency. She had given them the bedrooms at the end of the house, with the boys' posters still on the walls and the drawers still full of old T-shirts and odd socks. The hospital confirmed the cracked ribs and said nothing in response to Ros's account of falling down the stairs. Ruth had a deadline. She sat on a plastic chair in the hospital waiting room correcting proofs, while the man next to her, with a bloody arm, talked to himself in a low drone. That night Emma gave her a picture, a white house, a green field, trees, two smiling women, two smiling men, a dog, a sign in capital letters, correctly spelt, NETHERBURN.

Ros was told to take a week off work, and every day Ruth drove Emma to school in town, and collected her at three. She felt bad because she could not sit with Ros in the kitchen and talk. She had to get on. Whenever Ros tried to thank her she began to cry. Ruth assured her that she liked having women in the house, as for most of her life she had shared her space with men and boys. She had two older brothers and no sisters. She had three sons, but she didn't, yet, mention a daughter. She talked of her mother, Dr Fay Cameron, an archaeologist, often absent, and her father, who wrote a gardening column for *The Scotsman* – the name Andrew Cameron was once well known to people who read gardening columns. He provided childcare, of a kind. In the evenings he made a meal for Ruth and her brothers before opening the whisky bottle.

It was her father's house. 'The place was a wreck when I bought it,' he'd tell the children as they ate their supper of macaroni cheese or sausages and beans. 'You won't remember what it was like.'

'Yes we do, dad,' said Michael, bored, leaning his chin on one hand while with the other he made his fork squeak on the plate.

His father paid no attention. 'The roof leaked, the garden was all to buggery. It took years to get it right.'

Andrew Cameron was happy, remembering, but of course the house, which he had bought with the proceeds of a best-selling gardening book, was never right. He was haunted by that first success, burdened by it, and had never written another book. Ruth had been three years old when they moved in, her brothers older, and their father had found jobs for them all in the vast neglected garden. She had lived in the house, with one seven-year gap, ever since. Wherever she went now – if she ever were to leave – the microbes, the smells, the sensations of the house were in her lungs, in her veins.

They all had to do their bit. Even as a three-year-old Ruth was sure she had been weeding, tugging out small handfuls of groundsel. Her brothers painted their own rooms. 'Happy as sand boys,' their father said. 'Happy as sand boys.' They all had their allocated chores. By nine or so in the evening her father would often be slumped on the sofa, placidly drunk, unless her mother was home. Sometimes her father would read Beatrix Potter to her, later the *Just So Stories* and *Alice in Wonderland*. Michael and Alex played cricket on the grass that once had been a tennis court, and her own sons did the same. She had a clear but timeless memory of boys' voices and the sound of bat meeting ball and bursts of argument. Sometimes she would join in, half-heartedly, knowing her brothers barely tolerated her, although she had a good eye. She played with her sons too, all-purpose fielder with the three of them in a line, bowler, batsman, wicket-keeper, Sam growing tall like his father, with his father's light straight hair, James with his mother's eyes, and Ewan behind the wicket, invariably missing the ball.

She was sent out to dig potatoes for supper. There was a light, sweet-smelling summer rain. She came back with her gingham school dress damp and her hands coated in mud. Her mother was at home, in an apron, arranging rolled fish fillets in a dish. Ruth emptied her flower pot of earthy potatoes into the sink. Her mother smiled. 'Just give them a good scrub, love,' she said. Her father was in the living room, watching the six o'clock news with a glass of whisky. The children never questioned his dual routine. Two or three drinks before dinner when Fay was at home, half a bottle after supper when she was away. In her damp dress Ruth scrubbed the potatoes, letting the cold water wash the dirt from her hands. 'Nip out for some mint, love,' her mother said.

Michael had gone to Oxford and had never come back, except for occasional visits, once with his wife, later with his daughter, then with a different wife. He was unaccountably tall and big-boned, and it was perhaps that awkward height, apparent by the time he was ten or eleven, that made him feel out of place beside his slight, delicate-fingered siblings. Fay said that Michael favoured her father, whom the children remembered as a stooped, shambling man not quite in control of his long limbs.

Alex had, more quietly than Michael, removed himself, though the distance was less. He and his wife ran a second-hand bookshop in Inverness. They had no children. Michael's were – how old? Lucy was a little older than Sam, but the others, the second family? Ruth had lost track. Perhaps grown up and gone, like hers. That's what families do, she often reflected, when she found herself dwelling on the absence of her sons. They disperse. The young depart. You couldn't expect anything else. She had departed too, but circumstances had brought her back. She thought it unlikely that circumstances would bring her sons back.

She enjoyed having Emma in the house, but that, too, would have to come to an end. 'Just until I get myself sorted out,' Ros had said. They would go, but for now they were settled, even if Emma often could not sleep. Ros was less weepy now, and looking out for a job that was easier to get to. Emma had transferred to the local school and had made new friends. Ros might, she told Ruth, even consider giving up teaching. 'Sometimes,' Ros said, 'I can't bear the fact that I'm just carrying on as before. Something should have changed. I ought to be somewhere different.'

'You are somewhere different,' said Ruth. 'Things have changed.'

'I know, but at school it's all the same as before. I've not told anyone. I can't. It's not real, being here. I feel it's all going to start again.'

Ros came home from work on the bus. It was dark in that first month, and she wasn't used to country dark. She did not like the long walk down the dim track towards the lighted windows of the house. Occasional cars would pass on the road behind her, and she could not help listening for the sound of a gear change, the sound of a slowing engine, of tyres on a rougher surface. She would look back at the passing headlights. Then the days grew longer, and sometimes Emma and Dixie came to the gate to meet her, and it happened less often that her heart beat so fast in her throat that it made her sick. The daffodils were out, dozens of them in the ragged margins of the gravel at the front of the house. Sometimes she wished she and Emma could stay forever at Netherburn, but she knew it couldn't last.

One by one Ruth's boys had left. Ed had gone long since, soon after Ewan's second birthday. Work was the official explanation, a job in London he couldn't turn down, but everyone assumed he wouldn't be back, and they were right. How much did they know, Ruth wondered, and later discovered the answer to be, more than she did. At first he returned for occasional weekends, but spent half the time with his old journalist pals, meeting up in the Flying Scud in Market Street on Friday night, staying over in someone's flat, appearing off the bus late on the Saturday afternoon. When the boys spotted him sauntering down the track they raced to be at the gate before him, where they hung on the bars calling out as he approached. Over supper they were noisy, Ed as boisterous as his sons, Ruth making no attempt to calm things down. There was no point. The next day Ed would be on the train back to London.

After a few years he moved on, to Chicago first, then to San Francisco, where he married again and started a second family. And now Sam was there too, working on the same paper thanks to his dad, living on Green Street, having Sunday barbecues with his two little half-sisters.

One Saturday night Larry came downstairs with a bottle of red wine and stuck his head round the door of Ruth's work room. It was early October and Ruth had lit the fire. She was curled up on the big armchair with a cat on her lap and the dog on the hearth in front of her. She wore faded jeans and a baggy black sweater. The firelight intensified the bronze of her eyes.

'I thought you might like to share a bottle with me,' Larry said. Dixie thumped her tail without stirring from the hearth. 'I sold a picture today.' Without waiting for an answer, he pulled a corkscrew out of his back pocket and drew the cork. 'That's a good going fire you've got.'

'I'll get some glasses,' Ruth said, matter-of-fact.

She got up, removing the cat, and went to the battered dresser by the French window. The heavy, dark red velvet curtains were pulled. She cleared a space on a low table and set down two wine glasses. Larry poured.

'I like your working space,' he said as he handed her a full glass. There was green paint on his thumb. He looked around at the piles of papers and books, the desk at the window with a computer, phone and fax machine, a chipped mug filled with pens and pencils. He sat down on a low chair on the other side of the fire.

Ruth laughed. 'It's a mess. I should be more organised but things seem to work quite well as they are. I usually know where everything is. I read somewhere of a writer who said his desk was in a state of enlightened disarray. I like that.'

They were silent for a while. Ruth stared at the fire. Larry watched her, absorbed by her eyes, large and lucent in that thin face, still with its summer tan. On the mantelpiece were photographs of three young men. He got up again to look at them more closely. 'Your boys, I assume,' he said. 'Hmm. One of them looks like you, same shape of face, same eyes, I guess.'

'That's James, the middle one. He's just gone out to Kenya, to teach. Sam's a journalist in San Francisco, and Ewan's still at university.'

'San Francisco, eh? Neat.'

'My ex-husband's there. You're an east coaster, aren't you?'

'New York, but I bummed around California for a bit.'

He was still looking at the photographs. Ruth studied the greyish hair curling at the back of his neck.

'So,' he said, turning suddenly 'What's the story?'

The cat had returned to its position on Ruth's knee. The other cat was lying in a basket of wool beside Ruth's chair.

'Very domestic,' Larry said, without waiting for an answer. 'Woman with cats. And dog. And books and knitting and glass of wine. I could paint it.'

'There's no big story,' Ruth said.

'Oh come on. No big story? This house is crawling with stories, I bet.'

'But they're not all mine.'

'Some are.'

'Hmm.'

'Give me one, just one.'

She could not bring herself to talk of her father, not yet, or to rehearse the tale of Ed's infidelities, the tackiness of it all. She had no wish, she told herself, to protect Ed, but she felt contaminated, as if in some way she had colluded in the whole thing, as if she had knowingly allowed her marriage to fail. 'I was feeling cut out,' Ed said. 'There were you and the boys and another on the way. I wasn't part of it.' Then added, 'I know it's no excuse.'

'No,' said Ruth, but she wondered, had she cut him out? Had she, wanting always from the start to share everything, instead unconsciously excluded him?

'I know I can't expect you to forgive me.'

'No.'

'We shouldn't have come here, to Netherburn. It was all fine before we came here.'

'You can't blame the house.' But perhaps it was the house, because it was hers, and contained so much of lives that were not his.

At the kitchen table her father would say, 'Remember when we first saw the house? Remember the old fellow with the two fat Labradors showing us round, waving his stick? Lived in the house for fifty years, he said. Met his future wife on the tennis court, he said. Had horses in the stables in those days, and staff of course. Staff, eh? Could do with a staff or two, eh, Ruthie?'

Larry showed no concern at her silence. He sat down and

swallowed a mouthful of wine with an expression of exaggerated satisfaction. 'Not bad,' he said, then briskly, 'Okay, so you're going to make me work for it. Q and A. Let's see. How long have you lived in this house?'

'Oh, years and years.'

'Born here?'

'No. But I was very small when my family came here.'

'And you've lived here ever since?'

'Apart from four years at university and three years in Aberdeen when Ed worked on the *Press and Journal*. Sam was born in Aberdeen.'

'Ed's your husband?'

'Ex.'

'I assumed that, as in two months I haven't seen him around.' He was standing by the fire, one hand on the mantelpiece, the other gently swirling the wine in his glass. 'We've all got an ex.'

'Have you?'

'Sure. Name's Fran. Great girl. Took off with a Canadian guy called Terry who had a real job. Took my daughter with her. That was a long time ago.' After a pause he added, 'We were living in Toronto at the time, dodging the draft. Funny thing was, Fran didn't like Canadians...'

'Where's your daughter now?'

'New York, I think.'

'You don't know?'

'We're not exactly close.'

'What's her name?'

'Hannah. After my mother. Hannah Delia Segal. Delia was my wife's mother. Hannah Delia Segal. Kept everybody happy. Except us, of course, me and Fran. Well, I was happy enough, but Fran didn't much care for the artistic life. I don't blame her really. We were living on air most of the time. So she skedaddled. Terry was in pharmaceuticals.'

'You came to Scotland and Ed went to San Francisco.'

'There's a kind of equilibrium there.'

Larry pushed himself away from the mantelpiece and prowled around the room, peering at pictures on the wall and books on the shelves.

'Interesting,' he said.

Ruth didn't respond. Larry returned to the wine bottle and refilled their glasses. The fire hissed. He sat down opposite her.

'The logs are a wee bit damp,' Ruth said.

'I got to Scotland eventually, but it was a roundabout route. I was in Massachusetts for a bit, after the amnesty, courtesy of President Carter.' He swirled the wine in his glass thoughtfully and eyed the firelight glint. 'You know how many died? Fifty-eight thousand. And that was just Americans. Three hundred thousand South Vietnamese, twice as many North Vietnamese. "You will lose and we will win," Ho Chi Minh said. "Pay any price," Kennedy said. Plus civilians – no one really knows how many. "Bear any burden," Kennedy said, "in order to assure the survival and success of liberty." That was one burden he didn't live to bear. And do Americans bear the burden of maybe five million civilian dead? I don't think so.'

He sat back in his chair and balanced his now empty glass on his knee. Ruth was silent.

'Met a young woman in Vermont last time I was back in the States. Her brother was a survivor of Desert Storm. Only he didn't survive – killed himself. Wife and two small kids. Bitter as hell, the young woman I met, waiting tables in a café in St Johnsbury, bitter as hell.' He paused again, paying no attention to his empty glass.

'So. Massachusetts after the amnesty. Hitched up with another woman, but that didn't work out, and the little place where I was, pretty place on the coast, there were too many people there trying to paint. Seascapes. Boats. That's when I started painting buildings. That's when I started to *see* buildings, really to see. Structures, textures. But the stuff people wanted to buy, the summer visitors – waves and boats. I went to Boston for a bit, got restless, back to New York, got to know a guy who runs art trips for tourists. You know the kind of thing. You tramp round galleries, give the odd lecture, visit Constable country and the Lake District. He signed me on as a guide. I'd never been to England, let alone Constable country or the Lake District. But it was a free trip. I did some homework, busked my way through...'

Larry paused, eyed his glass, still on his knee, as if noticing it for the first time, looked up again at Ruth, curled in her chair, smiling slightly, one hand stroking the cat that was now wedged against her hip. Larry's eyes were deep blue and intense and she was aware of him watching her as he talked, as if gauging her reaction. He ran a hand over the unconvincing growth on his chin.

'So the following year we extended the trip to Scotland. Only this time I didn't go home. I jumped ship. Or jumped bus. I was bewitched – couldn't leave. I was bewitched by mountains, rivers, Highland cows, lochs, cliffs, eagles, islands, clouds, sunsets – and I don't even paint that stuff, you know. It wasn't just the scenery. Something about the air. It affects the way you look at things. Even the smell. I found that in New England. The smell of salt, seaweed, outboard diesel, they affect the way you look at the sea. Painters can't capture that, though.'

'You can't see any of that sort of scenery from here,' Ruth said quietly. 'No mountains, no cliffs, no eagles. Sunsets, yes.'

'I know. Don't matter. I know where they are. Half an hour's walk across the fields and I'm at the water's edge and there are hills on the other side of the firth. I'll paint that bridge one of these days, like thousands before me. But not yet.'

Ruth got up to put another log on the fire.

'It's nice here,' Larry said. 'I like it.'

She wasn't sure if he meant the room, the house, the countryside, Scotland.

'I can't imagine living anywhere else,' she said.

'It must be tough, keeping all this going.'

'It is,' she said. He liked that about her, her directness, no messing. 'Peter helps. That was the deal when he came. He gets the flat for a low rent and does the grass, the hedges, that sort of thing. It seems to work.' She paused and looked into the fire. 'But I do find it hard sometimes, now the boys are gone. It was hard when they were here, but harder in some ways now.' She paused again. 'I get tired. And the place is falling apart, of course.' She laughed. 'It's been falling apart as long as I can remember. When I was small my bedroom ceiling fell in. The roof was leaking. My dad was pretty hopeless at practical things, apart from gardening, and my mother was away a lot so problems could be neglected for months. We got used to broken windows covered with brown paper and sticky tape, buckets catching drips. It was a way of life.'

Michael hated it. Michael made up his mind to get as far away as he could, as soon as he could. He shut himself up in his room, the room that would become Sam's, the room now occupied by Ros, and worked his socks off to get into Oxford. He came back for Christmas after his first term, aloof, flinching at his father's slack smile and the tremor of his hands, avoiding the kitchen where his mother and sister roasted a turkey and simmered a pudding. Alex was unconcerned. Two years younger than his brother, he was still at school. He sat in the living room next to the kitchen, watching

TV and strumming his guitar at the same time. He, too, would go to university, and so would Ruth, but not so far afield.

Ruth and Larry sat on either side of the cheerful fire. The wine was finished. Larry offered to get another bottle but Ruth shook her head. Rain rattled on the window. After a long silence she said, 'This was our living room, when we were small, I and my brothers. And when Ed was here. Over the years it's evolved into my work room.' Larry glanced at her desk. Piles of typescript, dictionaries, a thesaurus, Hart's *Rules*, Fowler's *Modern English Usage*.

'Tools of the trade,' Ruth said.

'You work with words, I work with paint.'

'I work with other people's words. Your pictures are your own.'

'Well, you could argue that point I guess. I'm sure you put a lot of yourself into your editing. And most of what I paint has been made by man. It doesn't just come out of my own head. I paint what I see. Creativity's a funny business – you can't do it out of nothing. All artists are in debt.'

They smiled at each other across the fire. Dixie got up from her rug and laid her head on Ruth's lap.

'Time for her walk,' Ruth said. She got up, and Larry followed suit. 'Stay here if you want.'

'Nah, it's late. Thanks, though. Thanks for the company.'

'Next time you sell a picture the drinks are on me,' Ruth said.

'At least it means I can pay the rent.' He went out of the room with a wave of his hand, and began to sing in a low voice '*I'm goin away for to stay a little while.*' Ruth waited for a moment before she followed. The room seemed empty. He had filled the space, his long legs stretched out, his red-checked wool shirt, his gritty voice. '*But I'm comin back if I go ten thousand miles.*' He wore baseball boots. He must be in his fifties, she guessed. There were streaks of blond in his beard but his curly hair was grey, his eyes an almost violet blue. She shrugged on a jacket and opened the back door. She and Dixie went out into the rain and walked down the track and round the house as they always did.

Upstairs, Larry was at the window. It was kind of peaceful, kind of reassuring to make her out in the moonlit dark, shoulders slightly hunched, her jacket hood pulled over her head, hands in her pockets, walking slowly, the dog crossing and recrossing the track until they both disappeared beyond the dense trees. He shut his eyes so that he could still see them both.

2

THE HOUSE STOOD white and square beyond fields grazed by sheep and cattle. There were gates at either end of the track. Everyone who approached the house had to stop to open and close them. As a child Ruth would watch sometimes from her bedroom window, as a vehicle turned in from the road a quarter of a mile away, negotiated the gate, bumped down the track, stopped at the second gate. Her father might go out to open the second gate, but never in a hurry, hands in pockets, or he'd send one of the boys. She could remember times when the gate was left open and sheep got into the garden.

'Get the buggers out of my delphiniums,' her father would shout. The children would laugh as he charged them with a stick and the sheep panicked and bleated and scattered. The stable doors were rotten, the hinges broken. There was still a lingering smell of horse sweat and a couple of ancient grey straw bales languished in a corner. They used the stables as a dumping ground. Bicycles, an old pram, a rusty wheelbarrow, toys, a scooter without wheels. Cricket bats and warped tennis rackets lay in a heap. When her father died Ruth had gone into the stables, where he'd been found, and sat on the dusty straw until it grew dark. She was fifteen. Michael was away. She had come home from school, walking down the track from the road where the bus deposited her, to find her mother just returned from the hospital, sitting with her coat on at the kitchen table. She made her mother a cup of tea because that was what you did, she knew, and went out to the stables, still in her school uniform. How could dad be dead? He was only forty-six. How could he be dead when his own mum and dad still played bowls and dug their allotment in Falkirk?

Ten years later Fay Cameron came back from a dig in Jordan. She told herself that her aching limbs were a sign of age and examined herself in the mirror. Her hair was slate grey now, but she looked tanned and vigorous, as she always did when she returned from a dig. But she had lost weight, the flesh below her cheekbones had fallen away and left dull hollows. She was reluctant even to put into words that her days of sifting dry earth in relentless heat could perhaps be over, that she was slowing down. They had surely noticed, her colleagues, whom she no longer joined in the excited stampede when a find was announced, and had little appetite for spending long evenings poring over the day's haul. The pain was deep-seated, not like muscle pain, but something that could not be located. She realised, waiting in the passport queue at the end of her flight home, she had felt nothing like it before, and it seemed to shift, to bubble up in different places and scald, like lava.

The house was empty. The two young women who normally stayed in the flat at the back were away on holiday. The man she had taken on to help with the garden had not been doing much. The grass was uncut, weeds flourished among the vegetables, nettles grew tall among the currant bushes. She'd need to speak to him. There were a lot of things she needed to do, but for the first time in her life Fay Cameron felt defeated. For days her suitcase lay open on the bedroom chair, but by the time she had climbed the stairs she had no energy to empty it. Her daughter and elder son were married now, living their own lives about which she knew little. She blamed herself, but perhaps it wasn't too late to get more involved and take a proper interest in their lives. She was a grandmother now. Perhaps they would come to Netherburn, her son and her daughter with their children, bring their voices to the empty rooms. But she could hardly bear to contemplate the prospect of people in the house, small children running around, footsteps, laughter, quarrels, tears. She wanted no witness to her weakness.

Later that summer Alex drove down from Inverness and stopped at Netherburn on his way to a book sale. His mother was thin, her hands shaking slightly and her skin looked stretched and discoloured. She moved slowly through to the kitchen to make coffee. She brushed off his anxious enquiries – no, she hadn't seen a doctor. It was just tiredness, stress, she had been overdoing things, the recent dig had been particularly demanding. She spoke briskly, but her hands were clenched on her lap. That night Alex phoned his sister in Aberdeen. Ruth departed for Netherburn with her baby son, two suitcases and the boot of the car stuffed with baby gear. Fay Cameron was admitted to hospital, but after a week she was home again. She said she wanted to die in her own bed, which she did, when the rowan berries were fully red and the brambles ripening.

Ruth would remember these weeks as a strange, out-of-time period, when she occupied a world that was both deeply familiar and shockingly unreal. She knew every corner of the house, every sound that it made, every scar and scratch on its walls. August was warm and dry. The garden was bursting with peas and runner beans, lettuce and carrots, cauliflower, tomatoes in the greenhouse, raspberries, a crabapple tree: her mother could eat nothing. She sipped tea and water, with Ruth holding the cup. In the last few days she could not move from her bed without help, her frail thin limbs quite useless, yet still with an underlying anger at her helplessness. Ruth took her to the bathroom, eased her onto the toilet seat, cleaned her.

Little Sam was a year old and crawling. Each evening Ruth bathed the garden dirt from him and fed him pureed vegetables in the kitchen. She tried to persuade her mother to eat the same, but she could manage no more than a spoonful. Ruth settled Sam in his cot, the same cot that she and her brothers had slept in as infants. She sat with her mother until she, too, had fallen asleep, and then went downstairs and made herself something to eat, and took her plate outside into the lingering warmth and fading light. She made pounds and pounds of jam and wondered if anyone would ever eat it. The smell of hot fruit and hot sugar filled the house. She slept badly. She felt leaden all the time, her head heavy, unable to think beyond the task in hand.

Alex returned and each day the doctor visited, but Fay Cameron was disappearing in front of them all. They could do nothing to halt the dwindling of her limbs, the vanishing planes of her face, her fading voice and eyes. Alex returned to Inverness. 'I can be back in three hours,' he said on the doorstep, giving his sister a hug. But the days passed without Ruth being able to detect the right moment, until one morning she was up at six as usual and lifted the complaining Sam from his cot. With Sam in her arms she went to her mother's room. The door was ajar and she pushed it open. Her mother lay faded on the white sheets, her lips slightly parted. Ruth had never seen death before, but she recognised it instantly.

There were a few obituaries. Professor Fay Cameron, distinguished archaeologist, worked for many years in the Middle East, well respected, widow of Andrew Cameron whose book *The Peacetime Gardener* had been a best seller in the 1950s. Survived by sons Michael and Alexander, daughter Ruth, and grandchildren Lucy and Samuel.

Ruth had never imagined returning to Netherburn to live, but when that October Ed got a job with *The Scotsman*, there it was, empty when they needed a home. Michael had no interest in the house or its contents or the price it might fetch on the market. Alex could have done with the money but just shrugged. 'Someone needs to live in it,' he said, 'keep it all going.'

'A short-term arrangement,' said Ed. 'I really need to be nearer my work but this will do in the meantime. We can put the house on the market in the spring.'

Sam was beginning to walk and Ruth was pregnant again. She went through the house, from room to room, and opened all the windows. It was a sunny late October day and the apples had not been picked. She took Sam along the path that led up the slope where there were still ripe brambles. Her mother's books and files and papers lay as she had left them in the room that was her study. Her office at the university needed to be cleared. Ruth went into her parents' bedroom and found that her father's as well as her mother's clothes still hung in the wardrobe. Ed was soon absorbed in his new job.

It's our house now, Ruth thought, as she tried to do a little every day. She took bin bags of clothes to the Salvation Army and sorted papers and letters into boxes, arranged books and files on the shelves along one wall. She emptied the desk drawers of old diaries, used cheque books, rubber bands, rusted paperclips, theatre programmes, lecture notes, dust. She cleared the desktop and polished it.

'Terrific,' Ed said, and set up his newly purchased electric type-writer on the empty desk.

On a late November afternoon, in the dusk, Ruth lit a bonfire while Sam sat in his buggy and watched. She fed the rejected detritus of her parents' lives into the flames, old Christmas cards, photographs she could not identify, newspaper cuttings that appeared to be meaningless.

Six months later James was born. Six months after that Ruth began to do some editing work for a publisher of guidebooks. She worked at the kitchen table because it was the only room that was warm. She kept manuscripts and a selection of pens and pencils in a drawer out of reach of the children.

Ed Montgomery was tall and lean with a straight mouth and hair the colour of faded straw. He held his head back and looked down at her through narrowed eyes. It was a flat in Dundas Street, a student party. They danced to Simon and Garfunkel; Ed knew all the words. For the first time in her life Ruth felt herself moving effortlessly in synchronicity with another. He walked her home across the city, from the New Town to Bruntsfield, and kissed her in the street under a moon like a broken coin. He told her weeks later that he had fallen in love instantly with her glowing eyes.

'Charm,' said Fay Cameron, 'works well on a potential mother-in-law.' At Netherburn Ed cut the grass and sat beside Fay on the terrace with a cold beer and made her laugh. He cooked steaks on the barbecue. He opened a bottle of wine and poured generously. That night Ed walked barefoot across the hall and pushed open the door of Ruth's room. They wrapped their arms around each other in her single bed.

Ed graduated a year before Ruth and left for his first job in Aberdeen. Most weekends he came to Edinburgh. That Christmas he offered Ruth a ring out of a cracker. Of course they were going to get married, he said. My fiancée, he said to his friends with a flourish. Allow me to introduce my fiancée, and then he'd laugh with mischievous delight. The following July there was a wedding. The sun shone. All the doors and windows at Netherburn were open and people moved through the house and the garden and the old tennis court in summer dresses and linen suits. A trestle table outside was loaded with food and wine. Ruth wore a turquoise silk dress and a creamy, wide-brimmed hat. Her hair was long then, long and straight. At some point she removed her shoes and tights and walked barefoot on the grass. She ate asparagus with her fingers. All day the sun shone, and a light breeze stirred the flimsy material of frocks and lifted the corners of the sheet that served as a tablecloth.

Michael was there, opening the champagne and handing out glasses but maintaining his usual expression of aloof irony. He himself would marry a few months later, in Oxford with only a few friends present. Fay welcomed the guests, almost regal. Alex was there with a girlfriend whose hair was dyed a purplish red. He was the first to remove his jacket and tie. Ed's parents had arrived from Leeds, both of them tall like Ed, his father white-haired, his mother blonde. Ed was their only child. They had met Ruth only once and were not sure that this slight, quiet girl was what they'd had in mind for their son. But they were impressed by the house, yes, and the garden alive with roses and snapdragons and sweet william, and the smell of ripe blackcurrants. They were city people. Their terrace house had a patio and tubs of geraniums.

A few people danced on the small square of cracked paving to music floating through the French windows from the gramophone inside. As the sun was setting Ruth and Ed sat together on the low garden wall with their arms around each other, and Ruth cried with happiness. Now they were married. It wasn't just a game, after all. Now their life together would really begin.

Ruth thought of that day sometimes. She remembered her mother in the kitchen at one in the morning and the unexpectedness of her embrace, the feel of her amber necklace pressed against her. She remembered Alex, rather drunk, playing his guitar and singing 'My Love is Like a Red, Red Rose' and 'Mairi's Wedding'. And Michael, storing up an experience to be avoided when his turn came.

'No,' she said to her friend Lorna, 'no, I don't want to get married again, I really don't.'

'Love affairs, then,' said Lorna, urging her to get out more. They were in George Square in fragile sunshine, eating sandwiches. Lorna worked for the university press.

'You have to be in love to have a love affair,' Ruth said.

'What about Jack Williams? He's nice. I quite fancy him myself.'

'He's married.'

'Not any more he isn't.'

'I don't have the energy, Lorna. The boys... they drain all my love, all my capacity to care. That was the problem with Ed, I guess. He wanted a bigger piece of the cake.'

'The problem with Ed was that he was a self-absorbed philanderer who never grew up,' Lorna said sharply. 'However big a piece of cake he got, he'd be looking for something better, something he imagined to be tastier, more jam, more cream.'

Ruth laughed and shivered slightly. It was September, sunny but not very warm. 'We'd better go back in and finish the job,' she said. It was true, of course. Ed needed to be star of his own show. People do love a star, though.

'We'll do something for your birthday,' Lorna said. 'I'll get a few folk together. Get your lodgers to babysit.'

Ruth agreed, but on the bus home she regretted it.

She got off the bus in the village and met the boys out of school. They walked the half-mile home, along the road and down the pitted track. The leaves were turning. The house stood white in the autumn sunshine, and as always Ruth ran through her mind the long list of things that needed doing, the missing tiles, the blistered front door, the broken hinges on the kitchen cupboards, the worn carpets. The dog barked as they approached. There was always a dog.

Lorna phoned. It was all arranged. She'd invited a few people for a meal in Ruth's honour, so now it was too late. The two German girls who rented the flat were happy to babysit. She fed the children and read them a story, and left the three of them in a row on the sofa watching TV. She went upstairs and put on the brown velvet trousers she always wore on the rare occasions she went out, and a black top. She looked at herself in the mirror. Very sombre. She found an orange scarf and her mother's amber necklace. Make-up? Lipstick perhaps? She scrabbled in a drawer, pulled out a half-used lipstick, applied it, and stared at the unfamiliar face in the mirror. She rubbed it off, reapplied it. Would her everyday bag do, well used, scruffy even? But this was silly. Who was going to notice her bag? Oh God, shoes. Where were those ankle boots she'd bought in a sale last year?

'Ooh, mum, you look posh,' said Sam when she went downstairs. Ewan twined himself around her and had to be prised away.

'Bed at eight, you three. The minute Ursula says.'

'Yes, mum,' they choroused.

'Have a nice evening,' Anke said politely, waving her off from the back door. 'The boys will be fine.' She and Ursula were postgraduate students from Frankfurt. They had identical haircuts and helpful, reassuring smiles.

It wasn't raining but the air was damp with the sour smell of rotting vegetation. She drove through the village, past the pub and the shop and the school and the church, familiar since her childhood. There were some new houses at the far end, but otherwise little had changed. Two rows of shale-miners' cottages on either side of the street, a crescent of council housing, the manse, a farmhouse set back from the road, a petrol station. A field on the left scattered with rolled bales of straw, like giant butter pats, grey in the dusk. Another field of dark earth, newly ploughed. A few more miles and there were the bridges, headlights and tail lights crawling across one and a train like a toy on the other. The Fife shore was stippled with lights.

All too soon she was among the traffic on Queensferry Road and minutes later parking in Cumberland Street and climbing the tenement stairs to the flat of Dr and Mrs Hunter, Lorna and Neil. She paused at the door with her bottle of red wine in a supermarket carrier bag. There were party voices on the other side, laughter, music. At last she rang the bell. Just a few people, Lorna had said, but there must have been a dozen at least, shouting out 'happy birthday' with glasses in their hands. Lorna hugged her, but reproved her for being late and bringing wine to her own birthday party. Neil poured her a drink. So there she was, thirty-five years old. She looked around. Did she really have that many friends? 'Come and sit here, birthday girl,' someone called, and made room on the sofa. It was Jack Williams, smiling and friendly, and for some reason she noticed that he was wearing suede desert boots just like Ed's. She sat down and drank a mouthful of wine and closed her eyes for a moment.

At least there was something she could talk about to Jack. He had recently won a book design award and had plenty to say on the subject. On Ruth's other side was a woman she didn't know, in a long, vaguely oriental outfit. 'I'm Alison,' she said when there was a pause in the conversation. 'Just joined the university press, publicity.' She laughed. 'Don't think they've ever had anyone handling publicity before.'

'No,' said Ruth, 'I suppose not.'

'Happy birthday,' said Alison. 'Nice of Lorna to invite me. Chance to get to know a few people. Cheers.'

They talked for a bit, polite exchanges. Around them other conversations hummed. A young woman had sat on the arm of the sofa next to Jack and he had turned his attention to her. Lorna passed round a bowl of olives. Neil was talking to an author whose last book Ruth had edited. It had been hard going, and she had had to summon all her tact to persuade him to make changes. And there was Nick, manager of the university bookshop, and that must be his wife beside him, in a scarlet jacket. The author caught sight of her, and said across the room, 'Ah, the young woman who thought she could improve my deathless prose.'

'All book people, I suppose,' Alison was saying. For some reason she laughed loudly, waving her empty glass. She's a bit tipsy, Ruth thought. 'Have you ever met a book person who doesn't drink like a fish?' Alison asked.

'Well, I'm driving,' said Ruth primly.

'So the birthday girl can't drink! That's not right. Can't we send you home in a taxi?'

'Scotland has a collective alcohol problem, don't you think?' she went on without waiting for an answer. 'It's not just that people drink too much, but that we all collude. You know? Down the pub for a drink or three, fall off the bar stool, spew in the gutter, knock out the teeth of a passer-by, beat your wife. Who bothers? None of the lads, that's for sure.'

'Tradition,' said Ruth. She thought of her father. He'd never knocked out anyone's teeth, so far as she knew, or beaten his wife. His was the quiet, desperate spiral into alcohol immersion. He hardly ever raised his voice.

'Oh aye, we think it's amusing. We think getting legless is amusing.' Neil passed with a bottle in his hand and Alison held her glass out.

'My husband's a good example. Or a bad example, I should say. Out with the boys, all good fun. That's him over there.' She gestured in the direction of a stocky man with a beard and glasses who was talking to Nick. 'What do you bet,' Alison said with another loud laugh, 'they're talking about football.'

Andrew Cameron, a melancholy smile, sodden, the *Scotsman* crossword half done on his knee, his pen dropped to the floor. His son Michael in his room upstairs, the door firmly shut. His son Alexander sitting in the kitchen playing his guitar, singing fragments of Bob Dylan. His daughter Ruth, furtive at the door, not wanting to go in, yet feeling there was something she should do, and in the end joining Alex in the kitchen and doing her homework at the table. And later, 'Dad, I think you should go upstairs. It's late. I think you should go to bed.' And he smiled vaguely and looked at her with his wide dilated eyes and said, 'Yes, love,' but didn't move. 'I don't suppose your mum has phoned, has she? I thought your mum might phone. Where is she again? Some conference or other? I lose track. Has she phoned? Or is she in the middle of a desert somewhere? Beyond communication.'

Ruth shook her head. 'Dad, she's in York. And you've been here all evening and the phone is right there. It hasn't rung.'

And again he smiled, said nothing, but raised his hand indeterminately, letting the newspaper slide to the floor. Ruth went to bed, and heard him, much later, stumble up the stairs.

Ruth got up from the sofa and sought out Lorna in the kitchen, where she was arranging dishes of food. 'Can I help?' she offered.

'Absolutely not,' said Lorna. 'It's all done, anyway. Time to eat.'

And so the dozen people shifted, collected food, reassembled in different combinations with their plates and glasses. Alison was talking to Neil now, her husband was sitting on the sofa next to Nick's wife. People were clustered by a table at the window. The buzz of conversation nearly drowned out the background music – was it Miles Davis, that high, liquid trumpet? Ruth wished she had stayed in the kitchen, but these people were her friends, weren't they?

It was four years since Ed had gone.

The doorbell rang – a late arrival, with flowers and a bottle. Good grief, it was Colin Paterson. They'd been students together. He approached Ruth with a grin. 'The flowers are for you, darling,' he said. 'Many happy returns.' He kissed her cheek. Colin Paterson, with thinning hair. They'd gone out a couple of times.

'So you're back in Edinburgh,' Ruth said.

'Aye, I'm back, broke, jobless, wifeless – that's Thatcher's legacy for you. Back with my tail between my legs – at least, that's how some people see me.' He looked at Ruth, head tilted. 'Your Ed's done alright, though. Gather he's landed a job in the US of A.'

Ruth nodded, but said: 'Not my Ed any more.'

'I know. Stupid sod. Leaving you, I mean.'

'Pots and kettles, Colin.'

'Not at all. In my case the boot is on the other foot. It was Lesley who did the leaving.'

Lorna joined them. 'Ah, but why did she go, Colin, eh? Could it possibly have been because she'd had enough of your little escapades?' she said.

Colin pulled a face, laughed, rubbed the side of his head.

Lorna put a hand on his shoulder. 'Go on, get a drink, get some food.'

Lorna and Ruth watched Colin make his way to the kitchen.

It was only ten o'clock. She couldn't possibly leave her own party, not yet, but she saw herself slipping through the door, softly closing it, and no one aware until much later that the birthday girl had gone. She sat on a cushion on the floor; Colin sat beside her and ran his hand down her spine. There was a kind of inevitability about it. The following week he took her out to dinner. 'But you're broke,' Ruth had protested, which was a mistake, she realised as soon as she spoke. She should have said no, simply no. But she found herself again dressing up to go out, saying goodbye to the boys, and coming home late to walk the dog in October moonlight. It was because she knew it wouldn't last long that she let it happen. A few nights out, a few half hours of sex, Colin's long fingers almost lazy in their probing, but the abrupt surge of her response took her by surprise. When after a few weeks Colin with a rueful smile brought it to an end she felt wounded and angry with herself for allowing him into her life. It wasn't worth it, she said to Lorna, who was keen for her to try again.

3

RUTH TAUGHT EMMA to knit. They sat side by side on the sofa, Emma painstakingly looping blue wool over one needle and pulling through the new stitch, the tip of her tongue showing at the side of her mouth. Ruth rescued her dropped stitches. Ros was in the kitchen, marking jotters. The back of the kitchen door was now decorated with Emma's pictures. They had been in Netherburn for nearly four months. It was April, and Ruth had been digging the garden all afternoon. The earth lay fresh and dark, ready.

Ros finished the last exercise and came to the door of Ruth's room. She paused as Emma wordlessly held up the two inches of garter stitch she had accomplished.

'Well done, love. That's brilliant.' Ros watched as Emma slowly finished the row. 'Bedtime,' she said.

'One more row.'

'Okay, one more row, then upstairs.'

Emma didn't hurry. She completed her row without dropping a stitch, then carefully wound up the slack wool and stuck her needles into the ball as she had seen Ruth do.

'Go up and brush your teeth. I'll be up in five minutes to read you a story.'

When Emma had left the room Ros smiled at Ruth. She was still too thin, but the smile erased the wariness in her eyes. 'Did you teach your boys to knit?'

Ruth nodded. 'James was quite good at it. But he thought it would be even better if we had a machine. He knitted several football scarves. They're probably still around somewhere.' She picked up her own knitting. 'It's silly, isn't it, to assume that boys can't or won't knit and sew. I taught them to sew on buttons as well.'

Ros leant in the doorway, watching her. Ruth glanced up. 'A quintessentially female activity,' she said.

'You didn't wish you had a daughter, then.'

Ruth smoothed a dark red sleeve over her knee. 'I did have a daughter,' she said.

Ros looked perplexed, straightened up. Ruth had spoken often of her sons, but had never mentioned a daughter.

'Her name was Alice. She survived for three days.'

'Oh Ruth. I'm so sorry.'

'It's alright. It was a long time ago. She was born with a heart defect. My youngest child. She would have been seventeen now.'

'Oh Ruth,' Ros said again. 'A daughter after three boys. You must have been devastated.'

'I was. I still am. But you learn to live with it. You have to. Though I don't think Ed did. He ran away from it. I mean, not just from here, but from it. He was upstaged by real life. Poor Ed. He's got two daughters now, though. They're called Polly and Cleo. Funny, isn't it? The father of your children chooses names that you wouldn't have considered in a million years.'

'Daughters. That must be hard. For you.'

'It was at first. Not now, though. When I heard that his wife was pregnant I prayed that it wouldn't be a girl. That's dreadful, isn't it?' Ruth's knitting needles were moving rhythmically. 'But now… I have this picture of them in sunshine and pretty clothes, soft focus, but not at all real.' She came to the end of a row and started another, 'I knitted lots of stuff for the boys when they were little, and now they wouldn't be seen dead in anything hand knitted. But Alex, my brother, he's married to a woman who spins and weaves as well as knits.' For a moment or two the only sound was the clicking of needles. 'I'll knit something for Emma if you like. If she likes. She could choose a pattern.'

'That would be great. I'm hopeless at knitting. Sewing, too. Nobody taught me to sew on a button.'

'Ed couldn't stand me knitting. Some men just can't, the sound maybe, or the notion that women are always busy. Ed found that difficult. Guilt, I suppose. He was the main breadwinner but he knew that I did so much more. Men define themselves by work and money. Some of them can't deal with stuff that doesn't fit into that box.'

'Funny thing about Martin,' Ros said, still standing in the doorway. 'He's actually very good domestically. He cooked, cleaned the flat, changed nappies. Only all the time I felt he was demonstrating that he was better at these things than I was. And he *was* better – meticulous, thorough. He never started a job without finishing it. But it was always a bad sign. If he cleaned the bathroom or washed the kitchen floor I knew I was in for trouble. Sometimes he'd make a really nice meal, and we'd be sitting at the table, everything beautifully laid out, glass of wine, and he'd start criticising me, smiling, quietly, reasonably, telling me how rubbish I was. And then I wouldn't be able to eat and he'd say, "I've worked hard to put this meal on the table, and you're not eating it. Eat it, you ungrateful bitch, you useless ungrateful bitch. Eat it, damn you." And of course the more this went on – and he never raised his voice – the sicker I felt. He'd grab my face and force food into my mouth.'

Ros rubbed her hands together, staring at the floor as she remembered.

'Sometimes he'd deliberately scrape food from my plate onto the floor and then tell me to clean it up, and while I was cleaning it up he'd be sitting at the table eating his own meal and sipping his wine, totally civilised.'

Ruth watched her from the sofa. Ros had grown pale again, and stared at the wall as she spoke.

'I felt compelled to sit down until he'd finished. I couldn't walk away. It wasn't the drink. He never drank more than a glass of wine. I'd pick up his plate when he was finished and wash up, and he'd switch on the TV as if nothing had happened. Then I'd lock myself in the bathroom. Once I fell asleep on the bathroom floor and only woke up when he thumped on the door.'

Ruth said, 'He's out of your life now, Ros. It's not going to happen again.'

'In some ways that was worse, the meals I mean, than when he actually... well, he'd shake me, slammed me against the wall a couple of times. Well, you know about that. That was when I got out.'

'Ros, it's over. Try not to think about.'

'I'm sorry. It's so selfish. Compared with you losing a baby...' Ros's dark, shoulder-length hair was loose, framing her oval face and pale skin. For school she wore it neatly tied back.

'It's not selfish, not at all. You mustn't punish yourself.'

Ros smiled ruefully. 'We're good at that, aren't we? Punishing ourselves.'

'Emma will be waiting,' Ruth reminded her.

'Oh God, yes, story time,' and she slipped away and up the stairs, making almost no noise. Emma was in bed with her favourite flop-eared rabbit and several dolls. Ros read to her, but her mind wasn't on the words and halfway through the story she trailed into silence without realising it. She was thinking of the first time, when her face caught the edge of the kitchen door, and she had gone to the bathroom and washed the blood from her nose and swollen lip, and picked up Emma, who had begun to cry in her cot. The next morning there was a smear of blood on Emma's white blanket.

'Mum?' Emma's voice. Ros looked at her, startled. Her daughter was in her bed, seven years old in pink pyjamas, curly-haired, frowning.

'Sorry, love.' She began to read again. The story was one of Emma's favourites that she had read dozens of times.

'You can tell everyone you walked into a door,' Martin had said, matter-of-factly. 'That's the usual story, isn't it? And it's true – how was I to know the door was in the way? If the door had been shut, if you'd shut the door, it wouldn't have happened, would it?' He smiled.

Later Ruth went out into the dark with Dixie. Peter was at the uncurtained kitchen window of the flat. He waved as Ruth passed, but in his head he was stalling. He wouldn't stay much longer. It had been over a year. It had been fine, he liked it, he liked Ruth. He liked the way she did not question him or what he did, her calm acceptance. Why leave, he asked himself, why leave when he was happier now than he'd been for years, when he felt needed, by Ruth, by Ros? Not by Larry, but Larry was okay, all the same. Needed by Russell, too, of course, and it was Russell who was urging him, but supposing he did leave and chose not to live with Russell? How could you ever be sure?

He sometimes wondered what it might be like to have a daughter, he and Russell. They could adopt. It wasn't impossible, he knew that, difficult but not impossible. And he almost laughed, because thinking about a child created a replication of the only family life he knew, he and his sister, safe, ordinary, mother at home, father at work, affection, bickering, expectations.

Ruth looked up at Emma's dark window. At the next window the curtains were drawn but an edge of light was visible. Dixie chased a skittering nocturnal creature into the hedge and barked when an owl whooshed suddenly out of the beech tree by the gate.

Three small boys, a pile of typescript to copy edit, the house to manage, meals to cook. Sometimes on a summer Sunday Ed would cut the grass, a performance to be marvelled at. First driving to the service station for a can of petrol for the mower, then getting it started and the boys giggling at the expletives when it wouldn't. The mower up and down the old tennis court, and the formal lawn on the other side of the house. It took all afternoon. At last, the beer out of the fridge and the garden chair on the terrace with the Sunday paper. He felt good about himself then. He was doing his bit. Ruth was wonderful, of course, calm and competent, everyone thought so. She was in the kitchen, making lasagne for supper.

The boys were kicking a ball on the newly cut grass. Yes, there were times when it was fine and he knew it would be crazy to throw it all away. If he could only hold it all in balance, his wife and his affairs, his work and his children. And he turned over in his mind the possibility: Ruth was so reasonable, so accommodating, perhaps it wouldn't be impossible to find a way. After all, he did still love her, and always would. And the boys. Whatever happened, he needed to spend time with the boys, time like this watching them running on the grass, fighting over the ball, shouting. A father with his newspaper and his glass of beer satisfied that his boys were doing what boys do.

In his London flat Ed had one spare room with two narrow beds. One Easter holiday he took all the boys back with him. James and Ewan shared a bed, and squirmed and complained half the night. Ed took them to Trafalgar Square and Madame Tussaud's and the Tower of London. They travelled on London buses and the tube. He fed them on fish fingers and Chinese takeaways. He took them to the barber for haircuts. He put them on a flight home, three small boys with smart, cropped heads who were given badges and colouring books by the cabin crew.

'It's boring here,' Sam said when they got back. 'Why can't we live in London with dad?'

'Your home's here,' said Ruth, knowing her words were inadequate.

'Why?'

'It's where you were born. It's where I spent my childhood.'

'People don't have to live where they were born.'

'No.' She didn't know what else to say.

'So why do we have to live here?'

'We don't have to live here,' Ruth said. 'But I like it here, I love this house, and my work is here, and it's a good place to be, and I don't like London much.'

'You can stay here then. We can live at dad's and you can visit as often as you like.'

Ruth finished chopping onions and washed her hands at the sink. When she turned, Sam was sitting at the kitchen table pushing crumbs into a neat pile. James sat opposite him, crayoning his airline colouring book, his head on one side, concentrating fiercely.

'Is that what you want, love?' Ruth asked.

Sam shrugged, silently manoeuvred the crumbs to the edge of the table. He paused, then gave them an abrupt shove with one finger. The little heap spilled onto the floor. He looked up at his mother, gazed at her as she leant against the sink drying her hands, waited for a reprimand that didn't come.

He was silent for a moment, then, 'What's for tea?'

'Meatballs.'

'Meatballs are boring. Why can't we have spare ribs?'

'Well, I expect we could have spare ribs sometime. You could learn how to make them.'

'You don't make spare ribs, you get them from a Chinese place.'

'Somebody makes them.'

'You have to be Chinese.'

'I thought we'd have spaghetti tomorrow.'

'That's okay.'

'Do you know where spaghetti comes from?'

'Of course I know. Italy.'

'Am I Italian?'

Sam frowned and shook his head. Then slipped from his chair and stamped out of the kitchen. James had not paused in his crayoning. Without looking up he said, 'It's alright, mum. It's quite nice here.' He carefully coloured in an expanse of green. 'London's too big and dirty.' He exchanged his green crayon for a blue. 'I like meatballs.' He crayoned in sky. 'What's the biggest bird in the world?'

Calm and competent. Ruth had a routine. She walked the children to school with the dog. By nine-thirty she was at work. The study was as Ed had left it, with stacks of newspapers added to her mother's books and files. Ruth preferred to work in the kitchen, or in a corner of the living room where she set up her first computer. There was never a shortage of work. She had a reputation for reliability, for not balking at tight deadlines. She was careful, thorough, and delivered on time without reminders.

Typescripts arrived for copy-editing, proofs for correction. Scottish coalmining, Edinburgh in the Enlightenment, a World War II memoir, the biography of a suffragette. She corrected grammar and punctuation, pencilled in suggested rewrites, checked facts, politely queried dates. Sometimes the material she worked on was dull and ill-written. She tried to improve it. Sometimes it was inspired and absorbing, and she had to slow down her reading to a careful, methodical speed. Often it was far too long and her main task was cutting it down to size. They don't know the meaning of deadlines, Lorna would say, and they can't count. They. Authors. Much of Ruth's work came through Lorna.

Once a week or so she took the bus into Edinburgh and went through the amendments with publishers and authors. One historian was outraged that Ruth had drawn attention to several inaccuracies. They sat uncomfortably side by side as Ruth patiently went through the pencilled queries.

At three o'clock she and the dog went to meet the children out of school and they walked back single file along the narrow path, Sam in front holding the dog's lead, James swinging his school bag, Ewan chattering about his day. Sometimes, but not often, she would work in the evenings. Occasionally she had a night out, a meal with friends, a visit to the cinema. And two men, the interlude with Colin Paterson and, in her fortieth year, an affair – improbable from the start – with a smart, good-looking lawyer whom she met at a book launch. She never did find out what he was doing there as he didn't read much and was amused that she took books seriously.

That was Ruth Montgomery's life.

4

LARRY SEGAL REMEMBERED the smell of a hot Brooklyn sidewalk, and the Polish bakery where his Aunt Rosa worked, and getting roller skates on his seventh birthday. It was after midnight and he was in the Netherburn kitchen spreading butter and paté on a wedge of French bread. Dixie lay on her rug beside the Aga. Everyone, except perhaps Peter, had gone to bed. But the house was never silent. It seemed to shift constantly, restless, with sighs and creaks and groans. Hundreds of small creatures went about their business, under the floorboards, in the eaves, breathing, scratching, squeaking. In a house like this it was easy to believe in ghosts.

Dixie killed a rat. The cats laid dead birds and field mice at the back door.

Larry was painting a row of roofless cottages he had come upon a mile or two away. They filled the canvas. There was no space for landscape. Raw beams hung dangerously, windows gaped, gables crowstepped into nothing. 'Man's inhumanity to buildings,' he said to himself.

He added sliced tomato and lettuce to the paté. This was a good time, when he'd worked all afternoon, spent a couple of hours drinking red wine and staring at the canvas, or out of the window, or watching Ruth and Dixie on their unvaried route. He clashed with no one. In the mornings either in his bed or out with the borrowed dog and his camera. He photographed walls, doocots, service stations, dumped washing machines. At two or three in the afternoon he cooked himself a late lunch, humming in the kitchen, which he ate in his attic room. Then he'd paint, even in the winter with the light gone by four. Some days he'd be doing the rounds, agent, galleries, fellow artists. He had no car, though occasionally he borrowed Ruth's elderly Renault to deliver a picture. At irregular intervals he went to the supermarket five miles away. He had his own shelf in the fridge.

He thought about his daughter sometimes.

Ros came back from school on a rainy Friday afternoon. The house was silent. Dixie was in the kitchen snoozing on her rug, the cats in Ruth's room, but no sign of Ruth or of Emma. Ros stood at the bottom of the stairs, still with her wet jacket on, and listened. Nothing. Where was everyone? Where was Emma? Perhaps Larry was in. She climbed two flights of stairs to find Larry's door slightly open but no sound from beyond it. She paused – she'd never been in Larry's attic. She knocked.

'Yo!' She pushed the door open.

'Hi Ros.'

She didn't see Emma at first. Larry was sitting at a table where photographs were laid out among the paints and brushes. She went further into the room. There was Emma, standing at the easel, a paint-laden brush in her hand. As Ros watched she carefully smeared a trail of red across a square of paper.

'Artist at work,' Larry said.

'I wondered where everyone was.'

'Ruth had to go into town, some emergency meeting or other, so Emma came up here with me.'

'I'm doing a proper painting, mum. Larry let me. Like a proper artist.'

'That's really nice of Larry.'

Emma beamed. She was wearing an old shirt of Larry's that reached to her knees and was daubed with paint. She picked up another brush and yellow appeared. 'It's a portrait, but I'm doing the dress first.'

'Maybe you should come downstairs now,' Ros said.

'Nah, let her stay. She's having fun.'

'I have to finish it, mum. I have to do the face.'

So Emma stayed until teatime, and in the days that followed when Ros came home from work and Emma was not there to greet her, she knew where her daughter would be.

Larry took his sandwich and a glass of milk up the two flights of stairs. In his room he had his supply of wine, a kettle, coffee which he drank black. It was strange that only here had he felt some kind of freedom. There was nowhere else he wanted to be. He'd go back to New York sometime, maybe not to stay. It depended. On what, he wasn't quite ready to put into words, but of course it was all about Ruth. Could you spend your life, what was left of it, with a woman you loved but did not lust after? Not that he didn't imagine making love to her, but he was unusually content just to be in her company, to hold expectation in abeyance. Or to watch her, making soup in the kitchen, on her nightly walk with Dixie, sowing lettuce and spinach seeds in the vegetable garden. Did she know how he watched her? It wasn't that he was growing old, he told himself. From time to time, there were other women.

He'd never forget her, on the doorstep, those bronze eyes. He'd serenaded her, but she hadn't known he was doing it. Women liked his blue eyes, his curly hair, once a sandy brown. *I'll always remember those blue eyes.* Where the hell had they come from, those eyes? His mother's eyes were a lugubrious, deep brown. He'd never known his father, not even seen a photograph. The sisters, Rosa and the pregnant Hannah, had arrived in New York alone.

Lorna was on the phone to Ruth. 'I have an interesting typescript I'd like you to take a look at. Can you come into the office tomorrow?'

The next day Ruth was sitting on the only chair not stacked with papers with a mug of coffee in her hand. Lorna was at her desk. Behind her the window was open and a slight breeze dislodged occasional petals from the red geranium on the window sill.

'Does the name Millie Anderson mean anything to you?' Lorna asked.

Ruth shook her head. 'Should it?'

'I think it probably should. She was rather an extraordinary woman. And this is a biography of her.' She brandished a sheaf of typescript.

'Tell me more.'

'Born on Islay, brought up by an aunt and uncle in Glasgow. Fiancé killed in the First World War. Published one slim volume of poetry in 1921. Became a teacher. Fell in love with a married man but never married. And...' Lorna laid the typescript on her desk and smoothed both hands over it. 'And a few years ago a stash of literally hundreds of unpublished poems were discovered by the author of this, many of which are really very good. And she found notebooks with bits of diary and sketches and comments. A biographer's dream. '

'Who's the author?'

'A woman called Antonia Edie. She's been beavering away at this for years. She's some kind of relative of Millie Anderson, a cousin several times removed, something like that. She found the poems in the house in Hyndland where Millie's aunt and uncle lived. The house had stayed in the family and Antonia got involved in clearing it when another cousin died.'

Lorna picked up the thick pile of paper and handed it to Ruth.

'Read it and tell me what you think. It's a bit rough in places, but has potential. Tell me how much work you think it will need.'

Ruth glanced down at the top sheet. 'The Life and Times of Millie Anderson, 1894–1958,' she read, 'by Antonia Edie.' At the bottom of the page was an address in Glasgow, Woodlands Drive.

That night Ruth began reading. 'On the early evening of 10 October 1914 a young woman hurried home through the dusk,' it began. The story of the forgotten poet Millie Anderson unfolded. Her father was a distillery manager on Islay. Her mother died when Millie was two years old, after giving birth to a second daughter who survived only a few days. Donald Anderson did not marry again. When six years later he died in an accident, Millie was sent to her mother's sister in Glasgow. Later, she would write about sailing up the Clyde in the charge of a woman she hardly knew, overwhelmed by the blackened, flaring city that seemed to be marching towards them. On the quayside she was handed over in the dusk to her Aunt Wilma, whom she had met only once before and barely remembered. Her Aunt Wilma placed a gloved hand on either shoulder and looked down on her with a sad smile. She was seven years old.

Until then, all Millie had known was the little town of Port Ellen and the little hills that crowded the seashore. Her early poems were an attempt to recreate those early years, the smell of the sea and of burning peat and the pungent aroma of whisky mash, and walks to an ancient chapel and mysterious standing stones and stories of shipwreck, almost beyond the reach of memory.

Ruth read until after midnight. She was astonished that she had never heard of Millie Anderson. Antonia Edie's writing was uneven, clotted with dense, purple prose, then breaking loose and rushing ahead, but it was totally absorbing.

Ruth phoned Lorna the next day. 'I haven't finished it yet, but it's a great story.'

'I thought you'd like it. You'd better meet Mrs Edie.'

'It will need a lot of work.'

She continued reading. In her aunt's home Millie was treated with affection. Her uncle was in commerce and out every day, while her aunt presided over the large house. The four cousins were all older than Millie and treated her with condescending affection. One by one the boys left home, and the only daughter, Georgina, married at nineteen. Millie did well at school and went to Glasgow University, where she objected to being shunted into women-only classes but flourished nevertheless. She was going to be a teacher. She would come into a little money when she reached twenty-one, but it would be wise, her uncle said, to think of a profession. 'You have a good brain, my dear,' he'd say. 'You should use it. I approve of women using their brains.' Especially, he might have added, when they have to fend for themselves.

And then she met Archie, a medical student, and on that evening when she hurried home in the October dusk she and Archie had been drinking tea together, and had agreed that they would marry. A year later, Archie was working in a field hospital in France, and six months after that he was dead.

As Ruth sat in the comfortable lounge of the Balmoral Hotel she was thinking of twenty-year-old Millie Anderson hurrying through Glasgow's rainy streets on an October evening, elated and oblivious of the weather. Archie had taken both her hands in his. 'Millie, will you be my wife? Please say yes.' She felt a current reach to the centre of her being – that was what Millie wrote in her diary. She wrote a dozen love poems that she did not include in the 1921 volume. They were vibrant, full of sexual longing. Did she know what she was writing, Ruth wondered? Was that why she left them out? Or was it just too painful to include them? Ruth sat in a cushioned chair with a pot of tea in front of her, nursing the pile of typescript on her lap, waiting for the arrival of Antonia Edie.

The woman approaching her was long-limbed and elegant. She wore a cream-coloured skirt and a dark, belted top which outlined her bony shoulders, and carried a capacious leather bag. On her feet were heavy brown shoes. There was no sign of grey in her smooth, light brown hair, but her lined face gave away her age. Ruth got to her feet. She had said she would be wearing a red jacket and Antonia Edie had identified her at once – at three in the afternoon only a handful of people occupied the Balmoral's lounge. Antonia Edie dropped her bag onto a chair and held out her hand, without smiling.

'Nice to meet you,' said Ruth, who did smile. Antonia nodded, sat down, and as she did so caught the eye of a hovering waitress. 'Earl Grey, thank you,' she said briskly. It was Antonia who had suggested the Balmoral as a meeting place. Ruth had never set foot inside the building before, although it had been familiar to her for most of her life.

'I understand you want to publish my book,' Antonia began,

without preliminaries.

'Well…' Ruth was disconcerted. 'I'm a freelance editor working for the press. Lorna Hunter asked me to read your manuscript.'

'I understood from Mrs Hunter that they wish to publish.'

'Lorna likes the book, and so do I, but it's not quite as simple as that.'

'No? Is there a problem?'

'It needs a bit of work.'

'What kind of work? It's already had years of work. It's more than ten years since I found the poems and the diaries.'

'I realise you've put a huge amount into it – that's obvious. It's just… getting it into shape for publication. It needs to be streamlined a bit.'

'Streamlined? You mean cut. You mean you expect me to get rid of material I've laboured over. You have no idea how much effort has gone into this. Millie Anderson has been my whole life for ten years, ever since my husband died. My whole life. I don't suppose you understand what that means.' She leant forward, her pale hazel eyes narrow and hostile.

'I do understand. That's why we – Lorna and I – want the book to be as good as possible.'

Antonia's tea arrived. She removed the lid from the teapot and jiggled the tea bag. She looked at Ruth, mistrustful, her lips pressed together, deepening the fine lines around her mouth.

'I've made some suggestions,' Ruth went on. There was still no response. 'It's a wonderful story. Millie deserves to be rescued from oblivion – Lorna is thinking about publishing the poetry as well.'

'I've included many of the poems.'

'I know. But if there's an edition of the poetry you could maybe cut down a little.'

'Millie Anderson was a poet. How can I do that? She expressed her true feelings through her poetry.'

'It's just a suggestion. There are other areas…'

'Such as?'

'The war, for example. You follow Archie to France, which is fine, to give a flavour of his experience there, but you include an explication of the whole of the first part of the war. I think that could be trimmed quite a bit. You could focus on the war as it affects Millie rather than giving the whole picture.'

'How can you understand it without the whole picture?'

'Millie didn't have the whole picture.' Ruth took a breath and continued. 'And Glasgow. I think you could give a portrait of the city Millie grows up in without a whole history. And you don't need to explain all the ramifications of the Islay whisky industry.'

'So you are asking me to rewrite great swathes of the book.'

'It can be edited down – I can do it, if you prefer, or you can do it yourself.' Only select, Ruth was thinking as she spoke, only select. 'The thing is, Millie herself is in danger of getting lost in all the detail. Especially later on in her life. For thirty years she teaches in the same school – and the school becomes the story rather than Millie.' She paused, weighing her words carefully. 'We want Millie to be absolutely the centre of the book.'

'The school was very helpful. They gave me free rein to delve in their archives.'

'And there's some interesting stuff there, of course. But what is more interesting is Millie, the way her personality develops, the way her dedication as a teacher takes over. Her relationships. Here is a woman in the 1920s and '30s, whose career benefits from the dearth of male teachers in the war, who in spite of the lack of men has at least one offer of marriage which she turns down, has a long-term affair with a married man, and is documenting her life in poetry and intermittent diaries – it's terrific material. It's real hidden history brought to light. There are loads of books about the First World War, but how many books are there about the women the war affected?'

Again the pursed lips, the almost baleful suspicious stare.

'We can work together on it if you like.'

'That wouldn't be acceptable. I'll do it myself. I can't allow Millie to be hacked around by someone else.'

'The book has the potential to attract a lot of interest,' Ruth said encouragingly, though wincing at the characterisation of her work.

Antonia Edie lifted her cup of Earl Grey, sipped, set the cup carefully down on the saucer.

'I won't allow it to be compromised. It would be a failure of duty to my subject.'

'I understand.'

The waitress reappeared to ask if they needed anything more. In chorus, the two women said no thank you.

Then Antonia said, 'I have photographs.' She pulled a package out of her bag and handed it to Ruth. There were a couple of dozen photographs.

'I haven't been able to identify all of them, but in most cases I can hazard a guess.'

A blurred picture of a small child in a garden, a studio portrait of a man and a woman with four children, a young girl playing the violin, a music stand in front of her, her face turned away from the camera. Antonia remained silent as Ruth sifted through them. A young man in uniform – that must be Archie. He is handsome, smiling slightly, a narrow moustache making him look older than his twenty-two years. Then a young woman with a heart-shaped face and large serious eyes, the light catching her fair hair. She is sitting slightly forward in her chair, as if about to get to her feet, and is gazing straight at the camera. Ruth turned the photograph over. On the back, in faded ink, was written, 'Millie on her 21st birthday'. Archie was already dead.

'Is that Millie too, with the violin?'

Antonia nodded. 'Her father played the fiddle. She wanted to recreate the fiddle tunes she heard as a small child but her aunt and uncle didn't approve. They insisted that she practise classical material.'

'Perhaps that was what turned her to poetry – to words instead of music.'

Again a suspicious look from Antonia.

Near the bottom of the pile was a picture of a middle-aged man in flannels and open-necked shirt on a beach. He is grinning, a pipe between his teeth. His trousers are rolled up to the knee, his feet bare. Antonia leant over. 'I think that's Charlie Reid, the married man, probably taken in the 1930s. He and Millie went to Arran every year. It was Charlie's annual fishing holiday. His wife always stayed at home, or went to visit her sister in Dunoon.'

A later photograph of Millie, her hair tucked under a hat, in a tweed skirt and brogues, and with the same serious direct gaze.

Ruth carefully returned the photographs to their package and handed it back to Antonia, who said, 'If she had married, she would have had to give up teaching, of course.'

'You imply she made a deliberate choice.'

'Oh yes, I think she did. It's obvious from her diary that she loved teaching.'

'When she moves into her flat in Dennistoun it's as if she's decided to remain single. She's – what – thirty-five by that time. There's a decisiveness about that move. It's reflected in the poems, too. There's a sense of independence, of release – for the first time she's living her own life, not part of someone else's household. And the poetry stops looking back to the war and loss.'

Antonia nodded, her face relaxing, Ruth noticed – perhaps they were, after all, on the same wavelength.

'But she ends up back in the Hyndland house.'

When cancer was diagnosed, in 1956, Millie moved back to stay with her cousin John and his wife – she was a close friend of John's wife Marian, who cared for her until her death. It was a productive time. Not all the poems were dated, but Antonia was pretty certain that in a year and a half, knowing that she did not have long to live, Millie wrote over a hundred poems, many of them returning to her early childhood on Islay.

'Those last poems,' Ruth said, 'they are calmer, more at peace than anything she wrote earlier.'

Antonia nodded again.

'What happened to Charlie?' Ruth asked.

'He died in 1971. He visited her a few times in Hyndland.'

'Yes. Did John and Marian know, I wonder? The nature of their relationship, I mean.'

'They may have guessed. Or they may have seen him simply as a colleague. There were a few others from the school who visited.'

The two women sat silent for a while. The waitress discreetly placed the bill on the table. Ruth paid, and stowed away the receipt so she could claim a refund from the press. As they prepared to leave Ruth handed Antonia the typescript.

'I've pencilled in suggestions,' she said gently.

Antonia's mouth tightened.

'I always find,' Ruth went on, 'that once I get into the flow of things it gets easier. You'll probably find that once you start adjusting the balance it will all fall into place.'

She smiled, but Antonia did not. Ruth followed her through the foyer to the revolving door. Outside, Princes Street's pedestrian traffic swirled slowly back and forth.

OXFAM

VAT: 348 4542 38
Refugee Crisis Appeal
Thousands need shelter
and safe water
Oxfam is there, please
donate to save lives
www.oxfam.org.uk

LIZ   SALES   F5822/POS1
WEDNESDAY 7 SEPTEMBER 2016 13:37 049417
1   C1 - FICTION   £2.49

                    1 Items
        TOTAL   **£2.49**
        £5   £5.00
        CHANGE   £2.51

        Oxfam Shop: F5822
        116 Nicolson Street
        Edinburgh EH8 9EJ
           01316679150
        oxfam.org.uk/shop

LIFT LIVES FOR GOOD | OXFAM

TAKE HOME SOME NECTAR POINTS

Donate your unwanted items to Oxfam and you can collect Nectar points when they're sold.
Find out more at:

www.oxfam.org.uk/nectar

LIFT LIVES FOR GOOD | OXFAM

WARM FUZZY GLOW – TO GO

5

IT WAS JUNE, sunny and breezy, but in this corner of the garden it was sheltered. Dixie lay stretched out on the warm earth. Ruth was weeding. The peas and beans were a few inches high. The red-veined leaves of beetroot, the bright green of spinach, the paler curled leaves of lettuce were all showing. Ruth had abandoned her gardening gloves to get a better grip on buttercups and ground elder. Her fingernails were thick with dirt. She gently eased the long roots of ground elder out of the earth. If you pulled too hard half the root was left behind and the relentless creeping plant would continue its conquest.

Larry walked towards her. This was not usual. He did not spend much time in the garden, even when the sun was out. Ruth was kneeling, sleeves rolled up above her elbows. There were crumbs of earth on her thin arms. Her hair was straggly at the nape of her neck; it needed cutting. She wasn't aware of him until Dixie raised her head and he came to a halt a yard or two away.

'I'm going to paint that wall,' he said, 'but from the other side, with the nettles and blackberries and that old rusted wheelbarrow.'

'Right now?'

He gestured with his right hand, in which there was a camera.

'I'll take some pictures.'

Ruth nodded. After a short time Larry was back, and sat himself on the grass that edged the vegetable plot. This time Dixie did not move.

'You can help if you like,' Ruth said, not pausing in her weed pulling.

'I wouldn't know a weed if it jumped up and kissed me.'

'You should learn. Good for you.' She sat back on her heels. 'I like weeding. It's a very satisfying activity. What about digging? You could earth up the spuds.'

'I wouldn't trust me if I were you.'

Ruth laughed. 'That's a good way of absolving yourself from all responsibility.'

'I'm not a very responsible kind of guy. That was what my wife said, anyway. I guess she was right.'

He sat with crossed legs. He was wearing sandals, which looked oddly incompatible with his white, sockless feet.

'I'm not exactly a country boy,' he said, and then sang, '*Hear the wind blow, dear, hear the wind blow,*' as if to suggest, in contradiction, wide open spaces. 'I'm going to walk to the store and get myself some cold beer. You fancy a beer? It's a cold beer kinda day.'

Ruth wiped her hands on the knees of her jeans and nodded. Larry got to his feet.

'Back in half an hour. Make sure this plot is all done by the time I get back.' He walked away whistling.

They drank the beer on the terrace. Ros and Emma joined them. They were eating scrambled eggs for supper and brought their plates out. Peter arrived home from work on his motorbike and a few minutes later he was there too, with another couple of beers from his own fridge. The wind dropped and the terrace was washed in evening sunshine.

'Had a good day?' Ruth asked Peter.

'Not too bad. Any day I don't electrocute myself or someone else can't be all bad.' He drank from his can of Carlsberg.

'I had a good day,' said Larry.

'Well done you!' laughed Ros. Ruth looked at her, pleased that she seemed cheerful and relaxed.

'How about you, Em?' Larry asked. 'How's tricks at school?'

'Alright. There's eleven days until the holidays.'

'I think we might go to my mum's for a bit,' Ros said.

There was a comfortable silence for a few moments.

'Anyone fancy something to nibble?' Ruth asked. Without waiting for an answer she got up and soon reappeared with a plate of oatcakes and cheese. Larry was leaning back in a creaky deckchair with his eyes closed. Peter squatted on a stool. Ros and Emma sat on plastic garden chairs.

'It's like a family,' Emma said, scrambling to her feet and helping herself from the plate, which Ruth had balanced on the low terrace wall.

'Yeah,' said Larry without opening his eyes. 'More like a family than a family.'

'Maybe,' said Ruth.

'Hands up all those who had a normal family life.'

Peter put his hand up. 'That's the problem,' he said.

They all laughed, except Emma.

'Why is it a problem?' she asked.

'Because...' Peter said, hesitating. 'Because my mum and dad are normal and I'm generally considered not.'

Ros glanced at Peter with a slight frown. She hadn't put her hand up. Was her family normal? Her father had drowned at sea when she was twelve years old. Was that normal? Her older sister had got pregnant when she was sixteen and married the schoolboy father. Her mother, headteacher of the local primary school, had been devastated, hardly able to face her pupils and their parents, but her younger daughter had done well, married a decent, hard-working man, had a lovely daughter of her own, a good job.

'Why?' asked Emma.

'What's normal?' said Larry, at the same time. 'Everyone has a different normal. Riding a motorbike is not normal. Riding a motorbike is scar-ee. No one in their right mind would get on one of those death machines. I may be an ageing draft dodger, but I never had the slightest urge to hit the road on a Harley Davidson. Emma, remember, when you're grown up, never, never, never date a boy who has a motorbike.'

'That counts me out,' said Peter.

'You bet!'

'Whereas shutting yourself up in an attic all day and messing around with paint is the sign of a sane, well-adjusted individual,' said Peter.

'Sure. Why not?'

'Don't go out with an artist, Emma. Artists are crazy, unreliable, don't live in the real world, drink too much, and probably experiment with all kinds of dodgy substances.'

'What's the real world?' responded Larry.

'I might be an artist when I grow up.'

'Well, now, what does your mum say about that? Ros, tell her she'd be safer with electricity.'

'Now that's not normal,' said Larry. 'Interfering with nature, I'd say.'

'No such thing as normal,' said Ruth. Ros watched and gripped her can of beer with both hands. She had become uneasy, the skin on her face, a moment ago relaxed, had tightened. She looked at Peter, thick brown hair, deep brown eyes. How much did he know? Nothing, unless Ruth had told him. They lived in their own worlds, Peter and Larry, they probably didn't care. There was Emma, in her favourite pink denim skirt, her legs and feet bare. Ros wanted to touch her but she was out of reach, standing nearer to Larry, still reclining but with his eyes open now. They would go to her mother's. She would be pleased to see them, ask after Martin, commiserate that he couldn't get away from work. How long could Ros sustain the masquerade?

'We can all agree to that,' Larry was saying in answer to Ruth. 'All except Peter, who clearly believes he was blessed – or maybe cursed – with a normal upbringing.'

'Normality does terrible things to people,' Peter said. 'Just look at me.'

Emma looked at Ros. 'I'm normal, aren't I, mum?'

'Of course you are, love. Larry and Peter are just being silly.'

Larry reached out and ruffled Emma's hair. 'Your mom's right. We are being very silly.'

'I've had an idea,' Peter said, 'a very normal idea.'

'Go on,' said Ruth.

'Tomorrow's Saturday, right? Why don't we have a barbecue? I'll cook.'

'Oh yes, let's. Say yes, mum. Say yes, Ruth.'

Ros glanced across at Ruth, who said, 'That's a great idea, but there's a tiny problem.'

Everyone turned to her.

'I don't have a barbecue. The old one got chucked out, years ago. We've not had a barbecue since the boys left.'

'I'll build one,' said Peter.

'Lend me the car and I'll shop,' said Larry. 'We'll do proper Yankee hamburgers, none of your puny Brit efforts. And potato salad.'

Peter, a can of beer in one hand, wandered off to scour the premises for old bricks.

And there they were the next evening, reassembled on the terrace, a fire burning in the makeshift barbecue, fed from a pile of wood collected earlier by Ros and Emma. The sun still shone. Larry had shopped and made the promised potato salad. Russell arrived on the back of Peter's motorbike. Larry supervised the mixing of authentic hamburgers in the kitchen while Dixie lay expectantly at their feet. They brought a table out to the terrace and arranged a collection of garden and kitchen chairs. Ruth found an old, red-checked tablecloth.

At six everyone but Ruth was busy in the kitchen. She looked in at the door. Larry in a yellow shirt was slicing onions. Emma was counting out paper napkins while her mother mixed a salad. Ros was smiling, and turned to say something to Russell, who was beside her, drawing the cork from a bottle of wine. Her bare arms looked very pale next to his dark skin. Russell and Peter both wore black T-shirts. 'Like twins,' said Emma, which made them all laugh. 'Can you be twins if you're different colours?' Emma asked.

'Now there's a question,' said Peter.

'Why not?' said Russell. 'My sister's not the same shade as me.'

No one noticed Ruth at the door. Black, yellow, Ros in a light blue dress, Emma in a pink top, green salad, red tomatoes. Peter was putting white plates on a tray. Russell held a glass of dark red wine up to the light. Larry shook some paprika into the palm of his hand and scattered it over his potato salad.

Nice colours, Ruth thought. Nice colours. She stepped out onto the terrace. The evening sunshine was still warm. She chose the most comfortable chair and sat with her eyes closed. When she opened them Peter and Ros were putting plates and glasses on the table. She smiled. 'We seem to be having a party,' she said.

'It's normal,' Peter said, straight-faced. 'Saturday night, friends, a few drinks, nice food. Just normal.'

Ros laughed, at ease again, but Ruth knew the tension could suddenly grip her eyes without warning. It took only a chance remark, a gesture, an innocent question from Emma.

Parties. Did her parents have parties? People came sometimes to visit the garden, and sat on deckchairs drinking tea, but she couldn't remember parties. She and Ed had had a couple of parties, mostly journalists who drank a great deal. She remembered an occasion when she had gone to bed, leaving Ed and a hard core sitting in the kitchen at two in the morning. The detritus of empty bottles and glasses was still there when she and the boys came down a few hours later, and there was a shape asleep on the sofa under a blanket.

For the next few hours there they were. They ate and drank and talked. Dixie stood as close as she dared to the meat sizzling on the barbecue, her nose twitching. Someone put some music on, slightly melancholic, Joni Mitchell, John Martyn, floating out through the French windows. Peter and Russell danced. Peter and Ros danced. Larry and a giggling Emma danced. Larry clicked his fingers and wiggled his hips. Then he turned to Ruth, insistent, and pulled her to her feet. She protested, but liked the strong grip of his hand. Ros dragged a resistant Emma off to bed and came down again half an hour later to find the fire still burning and the music still playing.

'Emma was talking about families again,' Ros said quietly.

No one replied. Peter fed a few more sticks into the fire and watched as the quiescent embers licked into flames. Russell sat with his delicate brown hands hanging between his knees. Larry held up a bottle to see if there was anything left in it. 'Well, well,' he said, refilling his glass. He gestured vaguely with it. 'Happy families. Happy holidays.' Dixie, stretched on the warm stone, raised her ears.

The summer dusk was closing in.

Four days later Ruth drove Ros and Emma to the station, where they got the Inverness train. They were going to spend a week with Ros's mother in Nairn. 'She doesn't know,' Ros said while Emma was saying goodbye to the cats, 'but I'll have to tell her. I can't ask Emma to pretend.' She sat in the passenger seat twisting her hands together. On the way back from the station Ruth stopped to walk Dixie by the canal. A couple of coots scuttled across the dark, tree-edged water. Dixie made a lunge towards them, then changed her mind. A cyclist passed them, another dog-walker approached, a tractor chugged over the bridge ahead. A train rushed along the railway line a quarter of a mile away. Ruth would miss Ros and Emma, and worry about them, but at the same time she knew she would savour their absence. She'd have the kitchen to herself, almost. It was easy enough to avoid Larry.

When she got home the house was silent. Peter was at work, Larry had gone into town on an early bus. The cats slept, one on a kitchen chair, the other in the wool basket. It was a cloudy day, promising rain, but Ruth lingered in the garden, reluctant to settle in the quiet house, although there was work to be done. She checked the peas and scarlet runners, the broad beans growing almost visibly, the pale green fronds of carrots, tiny bulbs of beetroot now showing above the earth. Dixie chased off a pair of collared doves. Back in the house she listened to its emptiness, relished having possession of all its rooms. For a short time, at least, she could reclaim the whole of her space.

The house was still empty of all but Ruth and the animals when there was a knock at the front door. Few people used the front door. It opened out onto an expanse of gravel, and beyond that the field usually grazed by cattle or sheep. Ruth was in the kitchen feeding the dog and neither of them had heard a car come down the track. Dixie rushed to the door in a frenzy of barking.

On the doorstep stood a pleasant-looking young man in his

thirties, with neat light brown hair and wide grey eyes. He smiled. 'Sorry to trouble you,' he said. 'I'm not sure if I've got the right address, but I'm looking for a Mrs Connolly, Rosalind Connolly.' He reached down and patted Dixie, whose barks had subsided into warning growls. 'Lovely dog.'

'Oh, Ros, yes…'

'Is she about?'

'No… I mean…' But it was too late. It was too late even before Ruth spoke.

The man smiled again, waiting.

'She's away,' Ruth said. There was nothing else she could say.

'Do you know when she'll be back? Where I can contact her?'

Ruth shook her head. He knew. His smile became a grin.

'Not to worry,' he said jauntily. 'Tell her Martin was looking for her.'

He turned and walked away with his hands in his pockets towards the car parked a little distance from the house. Ruth watched as he drove up the track, stopping to open and then shut the two gates, his left indicator light flashing as he reached the road.

That night Ruth was in the kitchen when Larry came down for his sandwich. She watched him butter bread and cut a thick slice of cheese.

'There was a man at the door today,' she said.

'Selling encyclopaedias?'

'Looking for Ros.'

'Aha.'

'Yes.'

'What did you say?'

'Larry, I've been a complete idiot. But he took me unawares.'

'You didn't tell him where she is?'

'No. But he knows he's found her. I said she was away.'

'Ah.' Larry added a generous layer of chutney and laid a second slice of bread on top. 'Don't tell her. She'll only fret.'

'I don't know what's best.'

'It won't help to tell her. Life has to go on.'

'They could stay in Nairn.'

'Supposing he comes again, what can he do to her? If we're all here. We'll make sure she's never alone in the house. She doesn't need to know we're looking out for her.'

'I suppose not.'

'You want a sandwich?'

Ruth shook her head.

'No, I didn't think you would.'

Ruth laughed, in spite of herself.

'I told her,' Ros said, when she and Emma returned from Nairn. 'She thinks I'm overreacting. I've imagined it, it's all a mistake, Martin must have worries of his own, I'm not being supportive enough, I should have another baby, Martin's a good man, I don't know how lucky I am, being an only child isn't fair on Emma...' She stared at the kitchen table as if the dirty plates and mugs were far too complex to understand. 'She said she would never have noticed the scar on my lip if I hadn't pointed it out.'

6

IT HAD RAINED all day, not a heavy rain, but incessant. A small red car was parked near the school gate, along with half a dozen others. When the bell went the driver got out, turned the collar of his jacket up, and strolled to the gate. A couple of mothers stood there under umbrellas, one with a buggy. They were talking and scarcely glanced at him. Leaves from two beech trees in the corner of the playground were piled up against the wall. The driver of the red car watched the children emerge from the school door. A few ran towards the gate. A couple of older girls walked slowly, their heads bent towards each other. A small boy dropped his school bag in a puddle and stopped to survey the consequences. It was a two-teacher village school – it didn't take long for all the pupils to spill out onto the playground. Emma was one of the last, with her coat unbuttoned, closely followed by a taller girl with a blonde ponytail. It was a moment or two before she saw him.

'Daddy!'

'Hi, doll. How are you doing?'

'Have you come to pick me up?'

'Aye, that's right. I've got a surprise for you.'

'Caroline's mum was going to take me in her car.'

'There's been a change of plan. Run and tell her that your daddy's here instead.'

'Okay.' Emma and her friend ran to a mud-splattered Fiat. A moment later Caroline got into the car and Emma was running back. 'Are we going home?' she asked excitedly.

'First we're going shopping.'

Home, he thought, glancing into the rear view mirror to see Emma settling into the corner of the back seat. She waved at a couple of children crossing the road behind them. Where was home?

'Then you're spending the half-term holiday with me.'

'Mum never said.'

'She must have forgotten. You know your mum. She's not very organised, is she?'

They went shopping. It had been more than nine months. She'd grown. She'd had a birthday. The clothes abandoned in their haste would probably no longer fit. But they were still there, tidily folded in drawers, and the toys she'd left were still there, neatly arranged or stowed in two big plastic boxes. He'd cleaned her room, even washed the curtains. He'd thought of buying new toys, a doll perhaps, but then decided it would be more fun if she were to choose for herself. So they went shopping, first for clothes, a skirt, leggings, two tops, a warm jersey, socks and underwear. Martin had it all worked out. Emma had never had so many new clothes at one time. She carried the bags. Then for toys. Emma chose a Cindy doll, a skipping rope and two videos.

When they arrived at the flat she rushed into her old room, emptied the boxes of toys she had left behind, opened the drawers. 'Aren't you going to try on your new clothes?' Martin asked, but they lay in their bags, dumped on the bed. He went into the kitchen to make pasta for their tea. The phone rang. He picked up the receiver and replaced it, watching the door in case Emma came in. They sat together and watched *Chitty Chitty Bang Bang*. Two delightful blond children bunked off school and spoke in impeccable English accents.

'Is it real dirt on their faces?' Emma asked after the first ten minutes or so, 'Or is there make-up that looks like dirt?'

When her father didn't answer, she asked, 'Is mum coming?'

'I think she might come. In a day or two.'

Emma seemed absorbed by the film. The phone rang again and he went into the hall, again lifting the receiver and saying nothing. It rang a third time, after Emma was asleep.

In the morning Emma put on her new clothes. Martin brushed her hair and poured cereal into a bowl.

'At Netherburn we sometimes have porridge,' Emma said as she slowly spooned cereal into her mouth.

'Do you like porridge? We can have porridge.'

'Will we go back to Netherburn?'

'Sure,' said Martin. He was standing by the sink with a mug of coffee, watching his daughter carefully. 'Shall we go to the museum today, doll? Would you like that?'

'Why aren't you going to work?'

'It's Saturday, numpty, and then I'm on holiday. I have the whole week off so we can do lots of nice things together.'

'Can we go to see a film?'

'Aye, course we can.'

'Mum never takes me to see a film.'

Emma ate in silence for a few minutes. Then, 'When I go back to Netherburn, will you come too?'

'I need to stay in town, sweetheart. For my work. And you don't get the pictures in the country, or shops, or museums.'

'Netherburn's nice. Ruth's got a dog, and cats, but I like the dog best. She's called Dixie.'

'Who's Ruth?'

'She's the lady who lives there. It's her house.'

'Finish your breakfast and we'll go out.'

'Dad, when mum and I come back here to live, can we get a dog?'

They walked across the Meadows to the museum. It was a dull, breezy day. As Emma scuffed her way through trails of yellow leaves, cyclists and joggers passed them. A woman wearing a red beret sat on a bench with a can of Carlsberg Special on her lap. 'Change to spare, darlin?' she called out. Martin ignored her, Emma stared. The woman winked.

They went up the broad steps of the museum and through the revolving doors. Emma ran ahead of Martin along the marble floor of the long main hall and into the gallery where the skeleton of a blue whale was hung suspended from the roof. He followed more slowly. He couldn't remember when he had last been in the museum, maybe not since he was a kid. He'd not been with Emma before, though she seemed to know her way around. Ros must have brought her. He stopped for a moment and looked up at the vaulted glass roof. He'd come with the school, hadn't he? Come in from Bathgate on a bus. He remembered it now. They were in the Ancient Egypt gallery with sheets of questions to answer, about pharaohs and mummies and pyramids, and then free time afterwards which he'd spent in the machine hall, pressing buttons to make wheels turn. His mum was hoping he'd work in an office, not like his dad, making bits of cars on a production line. Well, he'd made her happy, at least for a bit. He'd done alright. Couldn't have more of an office job than in St Andrew's House, could you, even if it was only running the car pool? Even if you couldn't escape from cars.

Emma was standing underneath the massive grey skeleton looking up through its ribs, which echoed the curves of the roof. Then she ran up the stairs to the top floor so she could look down. When Martin caught up with her she said, 'He's very dusty.'

'So he is,' Martin agreed. 'I wouldn't like to have the job of dusting all that.'

Emma giggled. For a while he followed her lead, infected by her enthusiasm as she dashed from dolphins to kittiwakes, from barn owls to an African elephant. She came to rest in front of an Arctic fox. Martin had his hands in his jacket pockets, and did not notice that his fingers had tightened into fists. The place was beginning to oppress him, stuffed animals, dead things, lifeless information on hard-to-read labels.

'Slow down, Emma,' he said.

'It's only white in the winter, so you can't see it in the snow.'

'Emma.'

'I'd like to go to the North Pole one day, with a sledge and huskies.'

'You can't look at things properly if you charge around the whole time.'

'There's too many things.'

'Why don't we look at the butterflies?'

'Okay.'

He checked the museum plan and led the way to the insect gallery. His hands relaxed. He explained caterpillars and cocoons, back in control, remembering from his schooldays.

They had lunch in the museum café, full of mothers and children, ringing with young voices and the clash of spoons and plates. A toddler began to cry. At the table next to Martin and Emma a small boy was finger-painting with spilt orange juice. Martin clenched his fists in an effort to contain his disgust, to control the urge to walk out on the anarchy of small children, the echoing noise. An elderly woman sat alone in the corner and glared at an infant on the floor playing with a paper cup.

Ros hadn't taken her coat off. Her skin was so pale it was translucent, except for the dark cliff of her cheekbones. She held a bag of jotters clutched to her stomach.

'Mrs Baird said she was picked up by her father.'

'I don't believe it, I don't believe it.'

'I'm so sorry, Ros,' Ruth added, knowing it was useless. 'But we'll get her back. You mustn't worry.'

Ros's hands were shaking as she dropped her bags on the table and took off her coat.

'The dirty, devious bastard. I never imagined… of all the things I thought he might do. It's not as if he spent a lot of time with her. It's to punish me. He hardly ever took Emma out.'

'Sit down and have a drink.'

'I'm going to phone.'

'Have a drink first.'

'I'm going to phone now.'

She used the phone in the living room. There was no answer. She stood staring blankly at the frayed curtains as it rang and rang. She came back into the kitchen and slumped into a chair. Ruth put a whisky in front of her. Half an hour later Ros tried again. The ringing stopped and then she heard the click of the receiver. Silence. Outside, the dusk was thickening, with a yellow glow in the western sky. She heard Peter's motorbike, and there it was, its headlight on, edging slowly through the cattle that had clustered on the track. She phoned again. The split second between the click of the receiver being lifted and set down again filled her with dread.

The next day she could not eat. She phoned. I know he's there, he must be there, Emma must be there. There was no answer. She phoned again. At around five o' clock the phone was picked up. A child's voice said 'Hello'.

'Emma, darling, are you alright?'

But it wasn't Emma's voice that replied.

'I thought you'd phone,' said Martin. 'Emma is just fine, thank you. We're having a great time.'

'Bring her back.'

'Oh I don't think so.'

'Bring her back, Martin.'

'We went to the museum today. We're having shepherd's pie for tea. Tomorrow it's the pictures.'

'Martin.' She knew she must not cry. His voice, friendly, mild.

'Enjoy your time off. I'm sure you need the holiday.'

'Let me speak to her.'

'Sure.'

'Emma?'

'Hello, mum. We went to the museum today. We had lunch in the café.'

'Did you, love? Did you enjoy it?' Her voice trembled. She couldn't help it.

'It was barry.'

Ros took a deep breath. 'Did daddy say when he was bringing you home?'

'No. Shall I ask him?'

'No, it's alright, darling. Tell him... tell him... never mind, just remember school starts again a week on Monday.'

'Alright, mum.'

'And give me a wee phone, okay love? Just so I know everything's alright.'

'Okay.'

'Bye, love.'

'Bye, mum.'

Ros put the phone down. Her hand was shaking. The old help-lessness enveloped her. She was at his mercy. She had always been at his mercy, paralysed, deprived of any will of her own.

The following Sunday afternoon, in watery sunshine, Peter picked the last of the apples. The ground was matted with damp leaves and windfalls. Larry wandered out to watch and reminisce about his mother's apple strudel. Ruth was clearing the vegetable plot of withered bean stalks and the last overblown turnips. Ros was making pastry. It kept her occupied, away from the window, and they planned a special meal that night.

When Dixie barked she made herself concentrate on lifting pastry from tabletop to pie dish.

'We always go round the back,' said Emma in the car.

Peter saw the car first, from the top of the ladder. Then Ruth saw it as it swung round the old stables. Larry heard it, and strolled towards the back yard, in time to see it come to a halt. The back door opened. Dixie shot out, barking and tail wagging, and Emma shot out of the car and hugged the dog.

'I'm home, Dix, I'm home. Did you miss me? Did you?'

The driver's door slammed, and then there was a strange silence. Dixie was no longer barking. Emma saw her mother standing on the back step, flour on her hands, but Ros wasn't looking at her. Her eyes were fixed on the man leaning against the far side of the car. Larry was a few yards away with his hands in his pockets, Peter just behind him. On the other side of the yard Ruth appeared, a scarf tied gypsy fashion round her head, a trowel in her hand. Emma's eyes swivelled from her mother to her father. She knelt again and buried her face in Dixie's coat.

Ruth broke the silence. 'She's pleased to have you back.'

Ros still did not speak but took a few steps towards her daughter, who leapt up and flung her arms around her. Ros was silently crying. Martin was smiling. He reached inside the car for a small rucksack and a carrier bag and took them to the back door.

'There you are, doll,' he said, putting them down on the step.

'See you soon, eh?' He looked round at the audience of three, Larry, Peter and Ruth. Emma was trapped in her mother's arms but she twisted her head round to look at her father.

'Hi, Emma,' Peter said. 'Want to help me pick the rest of the apples?'

There was another long silence. 'Can I, mum?' Emma finally asked.

Ros nodded and her arms relaxed. Emma wriggled free and ran to Peter. 'Bye, dad,' she called as Dixie joined her with her tail wagging. Ros raised her head and stared at Martin. 'Don't ever do that again,' she said quietly. 'Don't ever do that again.'

Martin smiled pleasantly. 'Come on now, Rosalind. She's my daughter. Of course I shall do it again. There's no way you can stop me. She had a great time. Ask her.'

But Emma was fifty yards away, picking apples from a branch that Peter bent down so she could reach. Martin got into the car and wound down the window. 'I won't give you a divorce, you know, so you can forget that.' He started the car. 'No one will believe you,' he called through the window. 'In fact, I'd have a case for custody. I've already talked to my lawyer.' And the car rolled slowly forward, turned, and bumped along the track.

'He's bluffing, Ros,' said Ruth, going to her.

'Come on,' said Larry. 'We got dinner to cook. *All God's children love shortnin bread*.' He led the way into the kitchen. 'Okay, okay. What's on the menu tonight, folks? You need help with that pie, ma'am?'

Ros shook her head and reached for the rolling pin.

'Then I'll peel some spuds.'

It was the first time since the barbecue that everyone at Netherburn had had a meal together. Ruth at one end of the table, Larry at the other, Emma next to Peter, chattering about all the things she'd been doing. The museum, the cinema, shopping, meals at McDonalds. Ros was silent. What kind of place was this to bring up a child? A ramshackle house, an eccentric artist, a gay electrician, a divorcée, a dog, two cats, a sprawling garden. Custody. There would be social workers. Not exactly a model household. Look at this kitchen. Paw marks on the floor, mice in spite of the cats, rats sometimes, cobwebs, cracked windows. Compare it with life in a neat city flat with a respectable civil servant for a father. She got up to take her apple pie out of the oven.

'Hey, look at that,' said Larry.

It looked perfect, golden brown, a few bubbles of juice at the edges. Ros scattered a handful of castor sugar over the crust. Four pairs of eyes watched expectantly as she cut into the pie. Dixie got to her feet and laid her head on Emma's lap.

'Good to have you home, kid,' said Larry, raising his glass to Emma.

'Clink glasses, clink glasses,' she cried, and with her glass of juice clinked each adult glass of wine.

7

RUTH AND ED had been married for nine years when Alice was born. She came late, after several false alarms, but it wasn't a difficult birth. Ruth's hazy euphoria slid into anxiety when her baby daughter was whisked away and not brought back to her. Ed sat hunched beside her, holding her hand. She slept, and woke, and slept. Her breasts ached. When she woke again Ed was no longer there. She was in a side ward with two beds, but the other bed was empty, and as she climbed groggily out of sleep she could hear nothing, none of the usual hospital sounds, and her first thought was that she had been forgotten, that everything was happening somewhere else and no one remembered where she was. She sat up, painfully. It was the middle of the night. There was no little cot beside her bed, no sleeping baby. Ed must have gone home.

The three little boys, Sam, James and Ewan, were disappointed when it was explained that there would not, after all, be a little sister joining the family. 'Why not?' asked James. 'Where is she?' Sam was silent, sensing that something terrible had happened, wanting to ally himself with the grown-up suffering. Ewan was only three, and carried on playing with his fire engine, humming siren noises to himself. At first Ruth could not bear to touch her sons, or Ed. She felt suffocated, hardly able to speak, but Ed was back at work and she had no choice but to return to the old routine. Every morning she got Sam and James to school, and Ewan to nursery at the community centre. Every morning she performed automatically the routine tasks and if the boys misbehaved she said nothing, but stared out of the kitchen window until, puzzled by her silence, they co-operated.

They never saw Alice. She didn't come home, and the boys were not at the funeral to see the tiny coffin and the clenched faces of their mother and father. Sometimes they asked if they could have another little sister, although Ewan said he wanted a little brother. Sam said that two little brothers were quite enough, and suggested that Ruth and Ed might like a change.

Ed was away more than ever, with the paper sending him to

London, Liverpool, Berlin, Milan. Ruth got used to his absences. He was perplexed sometimes when he returned home to find life going on without him, the boys at school full of stories about people and activities which meant nothing to him, and Ruth coping. Ruth coped, of course. He knew she would. Ruth was a brick. After those first few weeks she got back into her stride. He looked at her sometimes, sitting at the kitchen table with their three sons, the chatter, the disputes, the sulks, the demands. Urging Ewan to eat his supper, restraining Sam from noisily sucking up strands of spaghetti, listening to James's convoluted tale of classroom injustice. Ed felt excluded. He was, by this time, no longer a faithful husband. He would watch his family at the same time as reliving an encounter in a Brussels hotel bedroom.

Ruth saw Ed sometimes as if on a far shore, tall, his pale hair lifted by the wind. She had not forgotten what it was like to love him, his hand holding hers in the Edinburgh streets, the birth of their first child when he lay down on the narrow hospital bed and folded his arms around mother and baby.

'Let's go for a walk,' he said one Sunday afternoon. They set off, five of them and the dog, Dixie's predecessor. They crossed the field to the burn and followed it down to the shore, the boys and dog racing ahead. Ed told Ruth he had the chance of a job in London.

'London?' she repeated, dubiously.

'I know you don't want to go to London.'

'How do you know?'

'Well, for a start you love this house, don't you? I wouldn't expect you to leave it. And the boys – they love it here, too, and they're settled at school. It wouldn't be good to move them.'

'So you're going to turn it down then?'

'I didn't say that.'

'Ah.'

'Ruth.' Ed paused. They had reached the shore. The boys were throwing sticks into the water and the dog was splashing after them. 'Ruth. Things aren't really working for us, are they?'

'Aren't they?'

But she knew he was right. In a flash she was assaulted by conflicting feelings. No, this couldn't be the end. How could it be? Their marriage, their life, their children. But also exhilaration, a breathless certainty. We can do it all without him. Of course we can. And fear. Christ, how will I manage, how can I possibly keep it all going, the kids, the house, the garden, work. What about money?

And there was Ed saying, 'The money's good, much better than I earn now. I'll be able to give you plenty. I promise you'll be okay financially.'

'You promise.'

'That's a priority.'

'You've worked it all out.'

'It'll be for the best. You'll be happier. I'll still see the boys – I'll be here every month, spend a weekend, quality time.'

'You've worked it all out,' Ruth said again.

'I…' The dog emerged from the water and shook himself all over Sam, who shrieked. 'There's something else.'

Ruth waited. She knew with conviction what he was going to say.

'Something else,' he went on, his voice dropping almost to a whisper. James had taken off his shoes and socks and had waded into the water with a stranded fish box that he was trying to launch. Ewan ran up to Ruth with a tiny plastic boot cradled in his hand. 'Look, mum, Action Man's boot. Can I keep it?'

'Action Man won't get very far without his boot.'

'Maybe I'll find another one. Help me look.' And he grabbed her hand and dragged her away from Ed, who stood with his hands in his pockets looking oddly bereft. Ruth and her youngest child moved slowly up and down the pebbled shore, fruitlessly searching for another miniature plastic boot.

That night Ed, unusually, put the boys to bed. She heard thumps and giggles coming from upstairs as she washed the supper things and tidied the kitchen, in no hurry to complete the task. Still looking for things to do, she went into the living room and picked up the scattered Sunday papers and arranged them in a neat pile. Ed insisted that all papers were kept for at least a week, but left it to Ruth to ensure they were stacked in date order in an old, blue-painted crate. Ruth moved restlessly round the room, found a stray sock and Sam's homework and a half-eaten biscuit on the mantelpiece. She had a meeting with a publisher the next day. She gathered the papers she would need and put them in the canvas shoulder bag she used for work. She heard Ed come down the stairs and go into the kitchen. A cupboard door opened, glasses chinked, and a moment later he was in the living room with two glasses and a bottle of whisky. He poured generous measures. It was late September and the day had been warm, though dusk had brought mist and a smirr of rain.

'I'll light the fire,' Ruth said, and knelt at the hearth with the matches. A corner of newspaper burned and curled, the kindling flared and a larger log slowly succumbed to the flame.

'I'm sorry, Ruth,' said Ed. He stood with a glass in each hand.

'So. You have a lady friend in London,' Ruth said without looking at him.

He nodded, but she continued to stare at the flames.

'Are you planning to live with her?'

'I don't know. Maybe.'

'How long have you known her?'

'A few months.'

'And you're ready to end your marriage?' Ruth's questions were still addressed to the fire.

'Ruth... she's not the first. I'm sorry,' he said again. The fire was now a healthy blaze. A log settled, sending a shower of sparks up the chimney.

Ruth sat back on her heels and finally looked up at Ed, who hadn't moved. He still held her glass, while his own was nearly empty. When he realised that she was not going to move from the floor, he bent to hand the glass to her, and then sat down in the armchair closest to the hearth. He leant back and closed his eyes. A lock of his pale hair lay diagonally across his forehead. He hasn't changed much in ten years, Ruth was thinking, still tall and lean, the geometry of his features clearly defined, his mouth spare and narrow. But he looked tired, and she felt weary beyond measure, without the strength to raise herself from the floor. She shifted slightly, crossed her legs and drank from her glass.

'Well,' she said. 'I guess you'd better tell me everything.'

Ed opened his eyes. 'You don't want to know everything,' he said flatly.

'Oh I think I do.'

He refilled his glass. He told her about Sarah, who had welcomed him into her bed two days after Alice's funeral, when he was, he said, distraught with grief. He told her about Maria, whom he had met on an assignment in Milan. And about Jan, a sub-editor on the paper. And now there was Alison, a TV critic, who wanted him to move in with her, in her flat near King's Cross, very convenient, but he wasn't sure. He was thinking of the boys – they would always come first. His voice was dull, earnest.

And when he'd finished Ruth put another log on the fire and watched the crackle of flames for a moment before finally getting to her feet. She said, looking down at him, 'Are you expecting me to give you advice?' He shook his head.

Ruth felt a strange void encircle her, cold, silent and paralysing. Ed sat motionless, looking beyond her. He began to talk again, but now she was hardly able to take in what he said. His plans, the job, where he might live if he didn't move in with Alison, a spare bedroom for the kids, back in Scotland every other weekend, he now said as if that concession would change everything, arrangements, money: it was as if he were speaking from a great distance. She was aware of him filling his glass, leaning forward in his chair, gesturing with his left arm. She was aware of herself moving to the opposite armchair, picking up the cat and resettling him on her knee, stroking his fur as Ed's words spun into the air. Then suddenly she heard, 'You'll always be my best friend,' and her husband came into focus again, lean and handsome, telling her that he was about to leave, but discussing his future as if it were something they shared, something they were planning together.

She had nothing to say. She leant back in the chair and stroked the cat, staring at the shabby curtains drawn against the dark and thinking, as she had often done before, that she must replace them. A snagging list permanently occupied a corner of her mind. Her hand moved unconsciously, rhythmically, over the cat's fur. She knew that Ed was grasping for a response, but she could not provide it. She knew he wanted her support. She knew he wanted her to tell him it was okay, she would be fine, the kids would be fine, he was doing the right thing for everyone. But she couldn't, although she had no wish to stop him going. She had no wish to hang on to a husband who considered her a best friend, who wanted her to listen and approve. She tried to recall the exhilaration of their early love and yes, she could remember, her body remembered, but at the same time now recoiled from even imagining his touch. There was no way she could attempt to entice him back. Whatever her head and heart might urge, her body said no.

She comforted herself with the cat's warmth and his rhythmic purring. Was Ed hoping that she would persuade him to stay, seduce him back into the matrimonial bed?

'You look tired,' he said kindly. He reached a hand vaguely in her direction.

The word running in her head could not be spoken, at least not by her. Don't bloody feel sorry for me. And don't expect me to come to the rescue. I won't, I bloody won't, I fucking won't. It's your move, your fucking move. Literally, metaphorically, every way.

Ed smiled faintly, boyish but sad. 'I wish you'd say something, Ruthie. Anything. Tell me I'm a bastard. I know I've treated you really badly, and I'm so sorry, but we've got to try to do the best with the way things are, for the kids. I know you understand.'

The way things are. Was it ever possible for two people to have the same perception of the way things are? Ed got suddenly to his feet. He'd tried to handle it all carefully, patiently, but she could be so damned stubborn. 'I'll take the dog out,' he said abruptly, and left the room. He never took the dog out.

8

SOMETIMES WHEN RUTH was in the fields around the house, picking brambles perhaps, or just walking with Dixie, she would think she had caught the unforgettable smell of the shale mines. The mines had filtered through their childhood lives, the smell, the ponies brought to the surface for their annual holiday, men on the street in their pit boots, school playground comments about 'the Irish'. You couldn't see the shale bings from the house, but their steep red slopes were only a couple of miles away, and sometimes the smell lay like an oily mist over all the neighbouring fields. Ruth remembered when the mines and oil works closed down. She remembered the fathers of classmates being out of work. She climbed the nearest bing sometimes, she and Dixie crossing the main road, the railway and the canal. From the top of the bing, in the winter when there were no leaves on the trees, she could just see the house. Now, apart from the bings where trees and whins had sprouted, and the miners' rows in a few villages, there was nothing left of an industry that had flourished for over a century.

Andrew Cameron, a whisky in his hand, brooding. 'You wouldn't think now,' he'd say to Ruth, the only one of his children to pay much attention, 'that respectable Edinburgh was an island in the midst of coal mines and shale mines and refineries and glass works and potteries.' And he'd smile wryly at his glass, not expecting Ruth to reply, and add, 'And distilleries.'

He did not often go to the city. It made him nervous. He hated to walk amongst the crowds on Princes Street and did not believe that traffic would stop at red lights. He flinched at the sound of heavy vehicles.

Ruth was in the kitchen ironing when Ros came in from school. She was pale, her eyes sunken and shadowed and her hair dull. Her clothes seemed uneasily attached to her body, as if they belonged to someone else. She let her heavy bag slide to the floor and sat down wordlessly, her coat still on. Ruth switched off the iron and filled the kettle.

'Emma's next door,' she said. 'She's fine. No ill effects that I can see.'

Ros nodded. 'I couldn't sleep last night. School was hell.' Her face sunk onto her hands. 'How can I go on like this?'

'Ros, Emma is fine.'

'But I'm not fine. You don't understand, Ruth. He's a monster, Emma doesn't realise... He'll do it again. He'll do it at the least likely time, and there's no way I can stop him.' She spoke tonelessly, her words slightly muffled as her hand still covered her face. When she let it drop the scar on her upper lip was starkly visible.

'He's not a monster to her.'

'You're going to tell me I should let her be with him. But I can't, I can't.' She dropped her hands and her voice became shrill. 'He's not doing it for her, he's doing it to get at me. He doesn't really care about her.'

'She cares about him.'

'We'll have to go away.'

'You can't hide from him.' Ruth made tea and put a mug in front of Ros. 'If he really wants to, he'll find you wherever you go. Unless you decamp for Australia or somewhere, but that wouldn't be fair to Emma. He is her dad. Maybe you'll need to work out something with Martin, regular access so he has no excuse to be unpredictable.'

Ros stared at Ruth, hostile and miserable. 'He doesn't need an excuse.'

Ruth went on, 'You can stay here as long as you like. I like having you here. It's lovely having a child in the house. There are people here – I think you need that. People who care about you, both of you.'

Ros ignored the tea that stood cooling in front of her, got to her feet and shook off her coat. She went to the window and looked out onto the yard where Martin had brought his car to a halt and Emma had jumped out, all smiles in her new clothes. Her arms were folded tightly across her chest. She looked gaunt and awkward. Ruth returned to her ironing, and then realised from her trembling shoulders that Ros was crying.

'While I've got the iron on I'll do Emma's school things, if you fetch them down.'

Ros turned slowly and gave Ruth a bewildered, angry look, before leaving the kitchen. Ruth could hear the sound of the television next door and pictured Emma, sitting on the sofa probably with a cat on her knee, absorbed by the screen, and giving no thought to either of her parents.

That night Ruth was woken by the wind buffeting the roof and shrilling through the trees. As she lay wide awake it got stronger and louder. Ros got out of bed and knelt down beside her sleeping daughter, who breathed softly and evenly. She laid her cheek on the pillow and breathed in her warmth and the smell of her curly hair, listening to the crescendo of wind. In Larry's attic the wind was even louder. He opened a window and leant out into the gale. Peter came to suddenly and wondered if he should investigate the reverberating thud that had woken him, but fell asleep again before he had made up his mind.

Ros went to work the next morning without a word to Ruth, who as usual walked Emma to the road to be picked up by the school bus. It didn't seem so long ago that she had walked the boys to school, but now there was a bus, and each morning Emma joined the clamouring gang already on board.

Branches torn off by the wind were scattered everywhere, and a tree was down in the far corner of the field. The wind was still roaring in from the northeast, with lulls from time to time followed by angry gusts. As they waited for the bus Ruth held on to Emma and the gatepost, fearful that they might be hurled into the road. Dixie pressed herself against Ruth's leg, her ears flattened. She did not like the wind. The bus was late. Half a mile back, the driver shouted, a fallen tree was partly blocking the road. The clamour among the children was more excited than usual as Emma climbed aboard.

Bent against the wind, Ruth walked back to the house with Dixie following closely, and then circled it. She picked up three dislodged slates. She always worried about the chimneys because she knew they were in need of repair. They looked intact, but a shooglie stretch of garden wall had lost some stones. Peter came out of the back door of the flat fastening the strap of his helmet. Ruth shouted across to him to take care. 'It's still blowing hard.' Peter replied with a wave, threw his leg across the bike and started it. He edged slowly down the track and round the corner behind the trees. Ruth listened for the pause when he stopped to open the lower gate and the roar as he started off again and picked up speed. On the doorstep she looked up at the sky where to the east a heavy curtain of cloud was approaching, fringed by sunlight, and she watched as above her screaming gulls fought the sweep of the wind. Inside the house the whine and rattle of the gale filled every corner.

If you don't do something about those chimneys, hen, the roofer had said, one of these days they'll be through the roof. Money. Five thousand? Six? he had ventured speculatively, in answer to the question she hadn't asked. No use approaching Ed, with a growing American family. Or Alex, who was always skint. Michael perhaps, though, like Ed, he had married for the second time and now had an infant son. She'd got the house, he would probably say, and the responsibility. It was nothing to do with him. Michael did not visit, and Ruth had never met the new wife or the new son.

Michael, preparing to go up to Oxford, mocking what he was about to leave behind. 'How can anyone take Scotland seriously? It's a joke. This country run itself? Per-lease.' His mother laughing, tolerant of her clever eldest child, the only one who showed any signs of achieving anything, going anywhere. She looked around the table at the three of them. Alex, sixteen, long-haired, his chair tipped back, gazing at the ceiling. Ruth, thirteen but looked younger, quiet as usual, her narrow chin propped on one hand, her glowing eyes wide. And Andrew, her husband, sitting at the head of the table, looking faintly surprised to find himself there, married to a distinguished archaeologist, father of three teenaged children.

'That's because,' Alex said slowly, still looking at the ceiling, 'the talent all leaves.'

'Are you surprised?'

'Well, I don't intend to leave.'

Michael let out a sharp, barking laugh. 'My point exactly. We're talking about talent, Alex. What is there for anyone with half a brain to do in Scotland?'

Ruth, her chin still cupped in her hand and frowning at her brother, said, 'Mum hasn't left – she's got more than half a brain. I'm never going to leave. And anyway, Scottish schools are much better than English schools.'

'Don't you believe it, Ruthie,' Michael said in a voice of condescending kindness. 'That's propaganda. That's what we say to try and convince ourselves that Scotland still has a shred of independence. And mum spends more time abroad than she does here, in case you hadn't noticed.'

There was no visible tremor to disturb Fay Cameron's benign regard of her son. Andrew turned his head from Michael to Ruth and smiled gently, unaware of any intended insult, to himself or to his wife, or simply unaffected. The collar of his shirt was frayed, and shreds of leaf clung to his gardening jersey. His hands were not very clean. At one time Fay would have nagged him to wash his hands and comb his hair, but not now. She stood up and briskly cleared the plates without looking at him. But he watched her as she placed on the table a bowl containing the last of the garden's late raspberries. He liked to be among his family, although when Fay was at home, when she presided at mealtimes, he felt like an intruder, or perhaps like a phantom, because sometimes he felt invisible. He could not always believe that the hands holding a knife and fork were his own.

Andrew Cameron often thought of the years immediately after the war. They were good years. They slid through his head like a quiet burn easing its way gently through a meadow. He'd written his book in their damp rented cottage and looked after the children while Fay completed her degree. For a while he was profoundly happy, relishing every moment of domestic life, the garden, the hens in the run at the back, the first Border collie pup from the farm along the road, the stray cat that took up residence. This is what he had dreamt of in North Africa, his skin gritty with sand and greasy with sweat and engine oil, thinking of home, Fay and the baby son he had not set eyes on in her parents' Bruntsfield flat. This was what he had dreamt of in Italy while the bombs and shells pounded around him and his head shrieked for silence. This is what he held on to when the three men with him in the cellar on the road to Rome were torn to shreds and he mechanically gathered the body parts, determined to match them correctly and astonished that none of the blood he slipped on was his own. That night he sat half inside a makeshift tent, mesmerised by the fireflies. It often returned to him, that night, the fireflies dancing like sparks, untouched by the wreckage of war. Sometimes he deliberately dropped a log onto the fire in his own hearth to release a shower of sparks, to make sure he didn't forget, the fireflies and Reggie's hand and unblemished wrist with the watch still intact.

He could smell the raspberries. His elder son was still orating about pusillanimous Scots and his younger son was still looking bored. It was odd, but he could hardly remember that brief week of leave, it must have been early 1944, when his wife and his eighteen-month-old son had seemed like strangers, and how foreign he must have appeared to Fay, lean and tanned and certainly better fed than she had been in recent months. In his uniform he had seemed to fill the flat. They had tentatively made love in the small, cramped

Bruntsfield bedroom, trying not to wake the baby, trying to keep the sound of their activity from seeping through to Fay's parents in the next room. Trapped by the awkward closeness forced by a single bed, her smooth, slim body seemed unfamiliar, unresponsive. He remembered the disappointment that what he had anticipated for so long was reduced to a stifled, perfunctory release. He remembered whispering an apology at the same time as he was thinking, I deserve better than this. How extraordinary that Alex was born as a consequence of those blurred and uncomfortable few days. And how extraordinary that now his eldest child was about to leave home.

Voices were raised. Alex had been provoked and was shouting. Ruth, dear little Ruth, had a tight arc of frown above her nose. Fay looked simultaneously irritated and amused, typical Fay, he thought, and then she put down her spoon and said, 'Enough!' There was silence for a few moments and then Michael said, 'I can't wait to get away from all this,' and Alex, pushing back his chair, responded with, 'And I can't wait for you to go,' and left the room. There was silence. They all knew what to expect and were not disappointed. The sound of guitar chords drifted from next door.

'There's a worm in my raspberries,' Ruth said.

Andrew leant across with his spoon and gently lifted a tiny creature from her plate and rinsed it down the sink.

It was the spring of 1946 before he came home. All he wanted to do was to get Fay and his two sons out of her parents' flat and to grow things. The damp and derelict cottage had half an acre filled with brambles and ground elder. Near the canal, at the end of a rutted track, no one had dug for victory there. He had borrowed a car to take them, Fay in a green summer dress and a knitted cardigan, Michael four, Alex a toddler. Fay ran her hand over the rotting windowsills and flaking paint, but said nothing. Ruth was born a year later.

It took five years to put the house and garden to rights, another year to finish the book. By that time Fay had become the first woman to be appointed as lecturer in the university's department of archaeology. She was beautiful and clever, and he was proud of her. He said that to anyone who was inclined to listen, apparently unconcerned that there were those who considered it odd, and even reprehensible, that Fay Cameron so often left her family to dig amongst foreign ruins. Poor Andrew Cameron. Poor chap, after all he's been through, you'd think the least his wife could do would be to stay at home and support him.

'We're the perfect couple,' Andrew would say, with his appealing, distracted smile. 'We both get our hands dirty.'

At the corner of the house the wind grabbed Ruth and nearly knocked her off her feet. She picked her way through fragments of trees, found another slate and some broken glass. A window in the old stable was shattered. Struggling against the wind she swept up the glass, and stacked the fallen slates at the back door.

Larry was in the kitchen cooking eggs. 'Phone's dead,' he said. 'Line must be down somewhere. Want a coffee?'

Ruth nodded.

'Upstairs it feels like the roof is going to blow off.'

'One of these days it probably will.'

By lunchtime the rain had started, lashing against the French windows as Ruth tried to work. Larry stayed in the kitchen, drinking coffee, scribbling in a notebook, his feet on the table. Ruth and Dixie struggled up the track again to meet Emma off the bus, the rain finding its way down the back of her neck. By the time they got back to the house Emma was drenched. Ruth sent her upstairs to change and lit the fire. Larry reported a leak in the corner of the attic and took a plastic bucket upstairs to catch the water.

The roar of wind and rain meant that Ruth did not hear a vehicle bumping down the track and pulling up at the front door, so she was startled at the knock. Dixie leapt to her feet with a volley of barks and rushed to the door, with Ruth following. It was John Guthrie from the village. Two cottages had been badly damaged. A young couple and Lisa Somerville who ran the local farm shop were having to move out. Did Ruth have any room?

She responded instantly. 'There's one rather musty bedroom. It's full of junk but we could clear it out. Or put a folding bed in the dining room, which is never used.'

'That might do for Lisa, just for a day or two. Half her roof's gone, but it should be possible to rig up something temporary.'

Ruth nodded. 'She can stay as long as she needs to.' But she thought, why do I do this? Another refugee. Another package of problems.

'They're all in the manse at the moment, drinking the minister's Glenlivet. I'll help Lisa rescue some of her stuff and load her car. She'll be over later.'

Ruth nodded again. 'I'll dig out the folding bed. It might take a while to make the bedroom habitable.'

It was reflex. She couldn't turn Larry away when he arrived on her doorstep, or Ros when she phoned in tears. Peter was different, a bona fide tenant. They had always had tenants in the flat. Ruth stood in the hall after John Guthrie had driven off in his elderly Land Rover. A low bookcase against the wall was filled with a motley collection of outdated travel guides, disintegrating children's books, dog-eared paperbacks. They had always been there, or at least a similar random jumble. The pictures, the chipped ornamental mirror on the wall, the rickety coat stand, the worn rug with a turned-up corner that one day someone was bound to trip on. She looked around. People came to the front door so rarely that she wasn't often in this space, and when she was she didn't really look at it.

When they moved into the house it had seemed palatial. The children ran from room to empty room, shouting, swinging their arms, twirling round. They'd have a bedroom each. They raced up the stairs to choose. Their meagre furniture hardly impinged on what appeared to be infinite space. And now this, more than forty years of accumulated stuff, much of it already second-hand when it came into the house, or brought back by Fay from Turkey or Iraq, brass coffee pots, rugs already faded by the sun.

She opened the dining room door. There was a handsome oak table and eight chairs, and a dresser with silver candlesticks and several jugs and decanters. Ruth remembered when her grandparents' Bruntsfield flat was sold up and a van-load of its contents arrived, to be swallowed up by capacious Netherburn. Family photographs were ranged on the mantelpiece. Parents, grandparents, Ruth and her brothers, various dogs and cats. The dust was thick on every surface.

Emma appeared in the doorway in dry clothes and asked if she could make toast.

'Come on then. We'll make some toast and then you can help me dust in here.'

It was dark when Lisa Somerville arrived in her Mini, with a suitcase and a rucksack and several carrier bags. She also came to the front door. She stood in the hall with her things stacked around her, a tall blonde woman in her forties, wearing jeans and a Barbour jacket, her eyes and mouth heavy with make-up, her fingers stained with nicotine.

'You're a star, taking me in.'

'I hope you don't mind camping in the dining room. Maybe

tomorrow we can sort out the spare room upstairs.'

'Just put me wherever, I'm really not fussy. Do you mind?' She fished out a cigarette packet from a large, brown, leather handbag. 'It's been quite a day and I didn't dare light up at the manse.' She scrabbled for a lighter. 'Did John tell you? There's a bloody big hole in my roof. We've rigged up fertiliser bags to keep the rain out but I'm not convinced they'll do the business. Still, the wind's dropped a bit. Worst is over, with any luck.' She closed her eyes as she blew out a mouthful of smoke. 'Jesus. I'll be glad to get my head down.'

Ruth showed her the dining room, the table pushed to one side and the folding bed made up. She went to the window and pulled the curtains, but could feel the draught seeping through. The room was cold.

'Come into the kitchen when you're ready. There's a pot of lentil soup on the go if you're hungry.'

Lisa shook her head. 'No thanks, love. Mrs Walker sat us all down for lamb hotpot. Wartime spirit, you know. Very generous, considering I've never set foot inside the church. Maybe they're hoping for a convert.' She pulled at her cigarette again, and coughed.

They had all gathered in the kitchen, a sense of emergency bringing them together, although there was nothing for them to do. The Aga was draped with wet clothes. Larry, unsettled by the wind and the drip of water which, he said, had made it impossible for him to work, moved restlessly round the room. Peter consumed two bowls of soup and told them about his journey home, negotiating floods and fallen trees. Ros had come in soaked and flushed from her walk down the track, and now sat at the table without eating, her hair still wet. That was where Lisa found them, when she made her way along the passage towards the sounds and the warmth. They all looked at her as she came through the door.

'Come and sit down,' said Ruth. The only vacant chair was at the head of the table and Lisa sat on it. She knew everyone by sight; they had all been in the farm shop at some time or other, so she aimed a smile round the table and said in a rather loud voice, 'Hello all. I'm Lisa.'

Only Larry responded. 'Hi. Larry.' Her eyes widened, then shifted to Peter, whose slight frown did nothing to dissipate the magnetism of his dark eyes and long lashes.

'How long are you staying?' Emma asked.

'Emma!' Ros's protest was half-hearted. Lisa laughed, an abrupt eruption which was overcome by a grating cough.

'Dunno, love. Depends how long Ruth will have me and how long it takes to get my roof fixed.' She pulled out her cigarettes again, then, catching Ros's expression, put them away. 'At least the shop's in one piece, so it'll be business as usual tomorrow. So... quite a storm, eh folks? Almost as bad as '87. Not that I was here then, but it was pretty scary down in Suffolk. Me and my ex were still together then, had a smallholding, pick-your-own strawberries, and a shop. A lot of damage, trees down, windows blown in. But we were okay, pretty much. Neighbour's car got crunched, though. Beech tree.'

The kettle was simmering on the Aga. Ruth got up to make tea and assemble mugs. Peter declined and said he had things to do. Larry said he'd prefer coffee. Ros said nothing. She liked to do her marking at the kitchen table and could not get beyond a sense of helplessness in the face of a disrupted routine. Lisa abruptly came to an end of her account of the storm of '87, accepted tea and added two spoonfuls of sugar. Ruth rummaged in a cupboard for a packet of digestive biscuits. Peter gave a wave as he left the room, with raised eyebrows and a shake of the head directed at Ruth. There was silence. Larry made himself instant coffee and continued his prowling with a mug in one hand and a biscuit in the other. Emma ate two biscuits without Ros noticing. Ruth sat down again and wished that someone would say something, and it was of course Emma who obliged.

'Ruth, what will we do if our roof blows off?'

'Maybe we could camp in the stable.'

'It's not very nice there. There's a funny smell.'

'Mouldy straw,' said Larry.

'Would we have to sleep on it?'

'Yeah, but it'd be quite comfy. We'd have sleeping bags, and a camping stove to heat up soup.'

'Do you have a camping stove, Ruth?'

'I think I do, somewhere, but there's probably no fuel for it.'

'Dixie and the cats would have to come with us,' said Emma.

'Of course.'

'The roof's not going to blow off, honey,' Larry said. 'Listen. The wind's died right down.'

They all listened, and it was true, the windows were no longer rattling and the rain had eased.

'A tree might fall on Ruth's car.'

At that moment, the lights went out.

'Oh for God's sake,' someone said.

'Don't panic. We've got candles.'

Lisa flicked on her cigarette lighter. Ruth fumbled her way to a drawer and found candles, and within seconds they were burning in a pair of glass candlesticks and two empty wine bottles.

'Maybe you'll need to find that camping stove.'

Larry stopped his prowling and watched Ruth in the candlelight, which smoothed her skin and eliminated the grey in her hair. She could be Emma's older sister, he was thinking. But out of that thought of Ruth as a child came something very different, to do with the exigencies of storm and darkness and the need for comfort. If they had been alone, perhaps. But not now, with Ros withdrawn and hostile, and this woman Lisa, with her bottle-blonde hair and deep red lipstick which had now imprinted her mug, an alien presence who didn't have a clue about the house and the people in it. And Ruth, worried because she would be feeling the resentment and wanting everyone to be friends. But Ruth, you can't do it, you can't make everything alright for Ros, you can't make us all love each other, you can't bring amiable Peter back into the kitchen to be friendly to Lisa. And who the hell is Lisa anyway? What is she doing here?

How long are you staying, Lisa?

It was quieter that night, but Ruth lay awake for a long time thinking about her charges, and about the fact that that was how she saw them. Peter in the flat, his own separate space, without Russell but nevertheless probably content. Larry in his attic, breathing in the fumes of paint and linseed oil. Ros, possibly wakeful like herself, still angry, still fearful. Emma, sleeping soundly – or was she also awake, still not able to settle, perhaps more disturbed since her week with her father? And now Lisa, on a folding bed, not very comfortable, dust still drifting in the stale air in the dining room, her suitcase half-unpacked, clothes strewn on the backs of chairs. The woman from whom Ruth bought carrots and potatoes when her own supplies dried up, whose darkly outlined eyes and red lips contrasted with her stained fingers and earthy boots. 'Loud Lisa,' as Larry had described her the first time he bought eggs from her. 'That woman has a laugh like a shell exploding.'

Another member of the family? Ruth thought she heard the sound of someone moving about downstairs. It was nearly two. It was probably Lisa. In five hours the whole house would be stirring.

By seven-thirty Ruth would be in the kitchen, and Ros and Emma would be having their breakfast, although Ros would probably not sit down to drink her half mug of tea and would eat nothing. She'd be the first to leave the house, then Ruth, Emma and Dixie walking up to the road, then Peter on his motorbike. Larry might come down to cook himself a late breakfast, or might not be seen all day. Ruth would be at her desk by nine, except tomorrow, or today as it now was, she'd have to sort out the spare room. Or perhaps she could just leave Lisa in the dining room, perhaps that would be better, it might discourage her from becoming too settled.

In the early hours Ruth contemplated the possibilities of the day. It was a habit she had not been able to expunge. All of the life within the house occupied her mind. Even when she was a child it was like that, as she shadowed her father and tried to make up for her mother's absence. She worried that Alex's football kit would not get washed, or that her father would forget that Michael had important exams coming up. She made sure everyone's birthday was marked on the calendar that hung in the kitchen.

Sometimes she longed to know what it would be like to feel no responsibility whatever for the individuals who had found a place under her roof. Perhaps like floating in space, suspended without gravity.

9

THREE WEEKS LATER Lisa Somerville was still in occupation. After a week, she moved upstairs to the spare room. Ruth had emptied it of boxes of papers and photographs, and had removed the old clothes from the wardrobe and the drawers. She found a bin bag full of children's soft toys, a shelf of jigsaw puzzles, and under the bed a dress box filled with her old school jotters. She removed a broken chair, and took the rug from her own bedroom to cover the stained carpet. She assembled the collection in the hall downstairs. Some of the clothes belonged to her mother. Why hadn't she got rid of them twenty years ago? Even now she found it difficult to deliver them to the charity shop. In a drawer she found the navy fisherman's guernsey her father had been wearing when he was found and it still had the faintest smell of leaf mould. It was a shock to find it there, folded into a polythene bag from Jenners. Fay must have kept it.

Around the house the wreckage of the storm was still in evidence. Ruth and Peter had cleared the broken branches from the track and Peter had spent a Sunday afternoon with an axe reducing them to kindling and small logs for the fire. The roofer had been, shaken his head at the leak in the attic, confirmed the need to replace slates, eyed the chimneys speculatively, said that he had a list of urgent jobs as long as his arm but would be back as soon as he could manage. The dislodged slates remained neatly stacked at the back door. The tree that had come down in the field still lay where it had fallen. Peter said he would borrow a chain saw.

They saw little of Lisa. Most mornings, including weekends, she was away in her Mini before the others were up, and twice a week she was off at five to go to the market in town for supplies that the local growers could not provide. She brought bags of potatoes and onions to Netherburn, but most nights she made a detour on her way home to pick up a fish supper or a Chinese takeaway. She brought the electric kettle and television set from her cottage and installed them in her room. Yet although they did not see her, they felt her presence. Ros in the kitchen would hear the back door open and know that Lisa was standing on the step with a cigarette. The sound of *Coronation Street* would leak from her room.

'We never watch *Coronation Street*,' Emma said to her when they met in the passage. 'We like *EastEnders*.'

Lisa was smoking on the doorstep late on her first Sunday afternoon – the shop shut early on a Sunday – when Ruth and Dixie came back from a walk. It was the end of October now and dusk was closing in.

'Why don't you join us for supper tonight,' Ruth suggested. 'I've got a stew on the go – there's plenty. We often all get together on a Sunday night.'

'Okay. Thanks.'

'Around seven. Don't know who'll be there. Ros and Emma, and I think Larry's around.'

Lisa nodded and ground her cigarette into the gravel. 'So Larry's an artist,' she said.

'Rather a good one. I think, anyway. From New York.'

'Must be interesting, having an artist in the house,' said Lisa, following Ruth into the kitchen.

'I suppose it is,' Ruth laughed. 'Not boring, at least. People in the village think he's a bit mad, but whether it's because he's American or because he's an artist, I'm not sure.'

'I like a touch of madness in a man myself.'

A little later Ruth heard the Mini leave, and return after half an hour. When Lisa appeared at seven she had a bottle of wine in her hand. She had changed into a close-fitting black sweater and had hung a heavy gold chain around her neck. Her lipstick was freshly applied. Emma was setting the table, Ruth draining potatoes in a cloud of steam. Ros and Larry appeared together, also with bottles. Lisa watched as Larry took the potato masher out of Ruth's hand and got to work. Ros, Ruth, neither of them exactly sexy, Ruth older, duller apart from those eyes, but Ros too thin, her face haggard as if she hadn't slept in weeks, and that little crooked scar above her lip. Lisa's antennae were usually pretty good at picking up vibrations, but she couldn't figure out what was going on there. And dishy Peter. He'd been seen in the village with a black man, but that didn't necessarily mean anything.

As if on cue came the sound of a motorbike. 'Peter,' said Ruth, looking out of the window. 'And Russell.'

'Shall I tell them to come?' Emma volunteered.

'You can *invite* them, Emma. Go and ask them if they would care to join us for dinner.'

Emma paused at the kitchen door and turned to Lisa. 'I like Peter. He's nice. And Russell comes from Africa. He's nice too.' Then she ran out into the yard and shouted, 'Ruth says would you care to join us for dinner?'

Larry moved familiarly around the kitchen. He knew where the corkscrew was kept and opened the wine. He offered some to Lisa, poured glasses for Ros and Ruth as if he knew exactly what they wanted. Ros stood with her back to the sink, holding her glass in both hands. Her hair was pulled tightly off her face, which accentuated her sharp cheekbones and hollow eyes. Her grey jersey made her skin look grey. A bit of friendly advice on make-up wouldn't go amiss, Lisa thought. Ruth, too. Why do women not look after themselves? She fingered the gold chain round her neck and took a deep swallow from her glass.

Emma returned with Peter and Russell in tow. A pity, thought Lisa, two good-looking boys. Not much doubt really. What a waste. Peter gave her the briefest of nods and introduced Russell, who shook her hand. Lisa couldn't remember if she had ever before held a brown hand in hers. Probably not. Peter went to Ros and put an arm around her without saying anything, and Ros responded with a brief and tentative smile.

'Sit down everyone,' commanded Ruth. She put a dish of mashed potatoes and a large pot of stew on the table. Larry poured more wine.

'Here's to the passing of the storm,' he said, raising his glass, and then asked Lisa, 'How's business?'

'Not great. The weather's played havoc with supplies and people have other things on their minds than veg. And my baker has flu. It's difficult at the best of times, a bit hand to mouth, you know.'

Ros had asked Ruth if Lisa was paying rent. 'In kind,' was Ruth's reply. Now she said, 'We're eating farm shop spuds,' as if she knew what was in everyone's mind.

Lisa had contrived to sit next to Larry. 'Mashed by a master,' she said with something like a giggle.

'Years of practice. I'm not much of a cook, but I always got to mash the potatoes, back in the old days when I had a domestic life, of a kind.'

'I was never up for the domestic life,' said Lisa. 'Maybe that's why my husband left me.' She laughed her explosive, croaky laugh. There was a silence, until Larry came to the rescue.

'Maybe it's why my wife left me, but I don't think so.'

Lisa and Larry exchanged a complicit look, the shared experience of errant partners drawing them together. Ruth noticed. Ros stared at her half-empty glass while beside her Emma concentrated on identifying pieces of turnip in the stew and pushing them to the side of her plate. Larry looked at Ruth sitting opposite and raised his eyebrows. Peter reached across with his fork and stabbed Emma's pieces of turnip. 'I love turnip,' he said. Emma squealed. 'That's rude.' Russell got up to open another bottle of wine, and paused before he placed it on the table, observing the odd assortment of people who had become part of his life. If Peter left, if he and Peter found a place of their own, would they still come to Netherburn? He would miss it. He would miss coming down the rutted track on the back of Peter's motorbike towards the house, white and ramshackle, and knowing that from Ruth he would get a quiet smile and a matter-of-fact welcome. Dixie's barking would subside into eager tail wagging.

And Ruth was thinking, there is nothing to connect any of these people to this house, it is accident that has brought them here, and they will all leave, just as everyone who has been connected has left. Ewan had not been home during the summer vacation, vaguely explaining that he had a job in an art gallery in Brighton. Sam and James were in distant continents. They'll all of them go their own way. I'm the only one who is tied here. Ros got up to clear the plates, first removing her own, which was still half filled.

They ate apple crumble and Ruth watched Lisa flirt with Larry and wasn't sure if it mattered. They finished a third bottle of wine. Larry began to sing, '*I'm a poor lonesome cowboy, I'm a poor lonesome cowboy.*'

'Are you going back?' asked Lisa.

'Maybe. Who knows? *No tengo padre, no tengo madre.*'

'Don't believe a word he says, or sings,' said Ruth. 'He's no cowboy and he definitely has a mother. And I bet he's never ridden the range.'

'I was in Wyoming once. Got off the Greyhound bus in Cheyenne. *I got to Cheyenne, no gold could I find.*'

'Where's Cheyenne?' asked Emma.

'Wyoming, kiddo, Wyoming. Cowboy country.'

'I've never been to America,' Lisa said.

'None of us have,' said Ruth, looking round the table. 'Unless you have, Russell.' Russell shook his head. 'But that doesn't mean we can be taken advantage of.'

'My friend went to Florida,' said Emma, and turning to her mother added, inevitably, 'Can we go?'

'Maybe. Sometime. When you're a bit bigger.'

'It's something to dream about, honey,' said Larry. 'Everybody dreams about going west. If you get as far as the Pacific Ocean you stand on the shore with a strange feeling of disappointment because there's nowhere else to go. Except, of course, there is. But for most Americans, that's it, that's where the dream ends. Maybe that's why so many people jump off the Golden Gate Bridge, a last desperate attempt to keep going west. *Come back before it's too late, you're drifting too far from the shore.* That's where your Sam is, Ruth, isn't he, San Francisco?'

'Yes, but I don't like to think he may be contemplating jumping off the Golden Gate Bridge.'

'Why go all that way to jump off a bridge when there's a perfectly good one in his own back yard?'

They all laughed although Ruth, Larry noticed, looked a little uncomfortable. He may have thought she was thinking of Sam, but in fact she was picturing unknown individuals who leapt into the grey firth and were pulled out dead by the rescue boat. Lisa went to the back door for a smoke. What a rum lot. She couldn't figure them out. While she smoked the phone rang and Ruth went to answer it. The voice at the other end surprised her: it was Ed.

'I'm in London,' he said. 'I thought I might come up to see you. Sam sends his love.'

'When were you planning to come?'

'Well, tomorrow. I'm booked on a ten o'clock flight. I've got people to see, but why don't I take you out to dinner?'

'Tomorrow?'

'Or I'll come out to Netherburn. I'd like to see the place again.'

'Ed, why didn't you let me know?'

'It was all very last minute. The paper sent me. I only had a couple of days to get organised. Look, is that nice place near Uphall still going? Why don't I take you there, if you'd rather not come into town?'

'It's such short notice.'

'I know. I'm sorry. Look, I'll see you around six tomorrow. Book a table.'

Ruth returned to the warm kitchen where Lisa was back at the table and even Ros was joining in the conversation. She said nothing about the phone call, and no one asked her.

Ed was on expenses. He arrived in a taxi from Edinburgh, which deposited him at the front door. 'Book a table.' But Ruth hadn't booked a table at the place near Uphall – she did not relish the prospect of being taken out to dinner by her ex-husband. Instead she had set off in the car to buy salmon steaks and white wine. At five o'clock she was in her bedroom looking at herself in the mirror. It was nearly seven years since she had last seen Ed. There had been no grey in her hair. She was determined to be as she had always been, but could not decide what to wear. She wasn't going to dress up, but her everyday jeans and sweater wouldn't do either. Black velvet trousers? A cord skirt? She settled on the skirt and a sweater in stripes of cream and beige, but found the image in the mirror slightly unreal, as if it belonged in another time or another place. Or was that just the effect of Ed materialising, demolishing the years? She hung a swirly glass pendant round her neck that the boys had once given her for her birthday. A touch of lipstick perhaps? She shook her head at the face in the glass.

Ed stood on the steps with flowers in his hand. Whatever Ruth might have found to say would have been drowned by Dixie's barking.

'Different dog,' were Ed's first words. He saw in front of him a small, slight woman of indeterminate age but looking almost schoolgirlish in a knee-length skirt and pale jumper, thick black tights, Scholl sandals, no make-up. Her hair, threaded with grey, was cropped in a style that had not changed in more than twenty years. And her eyes. They hadn't changed either, those burnished eyes that had electrified him on their first meeting. He handed Ruth the flowers with an odd formality, and with equal formality she thanked him. He looked older. His fair hair had faded and thinned, the lines at his eyes grown more pronounced, but he was still handsome, and Ruth felt a tremor of recognition, not of Ed standing at the door but of the man she had once loved, the man she had met at a student party, who had walked her home and held her hand and kissed her in an Edinburgh street. She bent to hush Dixie, the flowers in her arms.

'I thought we'd just eat in,' she said, straightening.

'Oh… right then. If you're sure. I'd have been happy to take you out.'

And Ruth knew at once she had made the right decision, as a hint of being patronised hung between them.

'I'll put these in water.'

Ed followed her along the passage to the kitchen. Sitting at the table was a thin, dark woman with stringy hair and eyes the colour of day-old bruises, a pile of papers in front of her. Ruth introduced them, and Ed leant across the table to shake her hand. The dog settled beside the Aga. Ros started to clear up her papers.

'It's okay, Ros, you don't need to move. We're going to eat next door,' Ruth said. She took a bottle of white wine from the fridge and offered Ros some before pouring a glass for Ed. Ros shook her head and continued to gather her things together. Ruth busied herself with food and Ed propped himself against the Aga and looked around.

'It's not changed.'

'Nope. Not likely to either.'

'Could do with a lick of paint.'

'Netherburn could do with a great many things which it's not going to get,' Ruth said sharply. 'The roof is leaking – again – and one of these days the chimneys are going to fall down.'

They all heard a motorbike sputter into the yard.

'You've got a visitor,' Ed said.

'Peter,' responded Ruth, without further explanation. She gestured for Ed to move so she could put the salmon steaks in the oven. Moments later there was the sound of a tenor voice singing. This time Ed said nothing but just looked a question.

'Larry,' said Ruth. The singing stopped and they heard a male and female voice in conversation. 'Talking to Lisa. Come on, let's go next door.'

On the other side of the kitchen door a tall, blonde woman with a packet of cigarettes in her hand was talking to a dishevelled looking bearded man in his fifties who smelled of paint. This time Ruth made no introductions, and they both moved away, Lisa to the back door, Larry towards the stair, with a wave. Ed followed Ruth into the living room, where the fire was lit and the table set and television on. At first he didn't notice a small figure curled up on the sofa.

'Bedtime, Emma,' Ruth said. The figure, in pink pyjamas and a pale blue dressing gown and clutching a floppy-eared woolly rabbit wearing red trousers with braces, slowly uncoiled herself.

'Can I have a story?'

'Not tonight, love, I have a visitor.'

Emma slid wordlessly off the sofa and left the room. Ed stood with his back to the fire. 'Who are all these people?'

'Friends. They live here.'

'Well, well. I didn't know you were running a boarding house.'

'I'm not, really. They're just people who needed somewhere to stay. Peter, with the motorbike, rents the flat, the others are in the house. It works out just fine.'

'Do they pay their way?'

'One way or another. But it's no concern of yours.'

'So long as you don't ask me for money.'

Ruth shook her head but frowned. 'Ed, I wouldn't dream of asking you for money, although there's no reason why I shouldn't. I know the boys have all left home, but James and Ewan still get support from me, and I have to maintain this house single-handed.'

'You don't have to. Why don't you sell it? It doesn't make sense for you to stay here on your own.'

'I'm not on my own, as you can see.'

Seven years ago they had had the same conversation. Ed had urged her to sell the house and look for somewhere smaller. Sam would soon be going to university. It would be crazy to struggle with this big house with the boys gone. Ed himself had just bought a hilltop house in San Francisco, and his new wife was expecting their first child. Ruth deduced that he felt bad. Things had worked out well for him, but here was Ruth, bringing up three sons on her own in a ramshackle house, not to mention a garden, that she couldn't possibly look after.

And going further back, Ed's parents, on a cloudy summer afternoon. They had written to say they would be passing through Edinburgh and would like to visit, see their grandchildren. Of course, Ruth had replied, and invited them for lunch. The day before they were expected the phone rang while she was in the garden. James, running through the living room towards the French windows, diverted to answer it.

'Hello,' he said.

'Hello,' said the voice at the other end. 'Is that Sam?'

'No.'

'It must be James, then. Hello James, it's granny. Is your mother there?'

'No.'

'She can't be far away – can you call her to the phone?'

'She's in the garden. She's busy.'

'Well, can you give her a message for me? Tell her there's been a change of plan. We can't manage lunch tomorrow after all, but will come this afternoon, if that's alright. We have to be in Dundee tomorrow. Can you tell her that?'

'Alright.'

'You run and tell her right away, there's a good boy. And we'll see you very soon.'

'Alright.' James put the phone down and continued on his way. Sam and Ewan were waiting for him in the den they had made among the trees in the corner of the barley field.

Half an hour later the boys saw a white car coming down the track.

'Oh, I forgot,' said James, and raced off without explanation. He got to Ruth just as she heard the car. 'It's granny and grandad,' panted James. 'They phoned.'

She was bending over foot-high runner beans. She slowly straightened up and wiped her hands on her faded jeans. She frowned at James.

'When did they phone?'

'Oh… just… not very long ago,' he said.

She looked at him. He was wearing patched, grass-stained trousers. His hair needed cutting and his hands were filthy. His T-shirt had a row of tiny holes near the hem. She heard the dog barking and then the slam of a car door. There was no escape.

When Ruth and James came round the corner of the stables, John and Virginia Montgomery were standing side by side in the yard, the sleek white Audi behind them incongruously parked next to Ruth's mud-spattered Renault. They were in their sixties, tall, John Montgomery white-haired, Virginia silvery-blonde. He was wearing a light-grey suit, she a beige linen dress with a loosely knotted yellow silk scarf and a white handbag hanging from her arm. As Ruth and James approached, Sam and Ewan appeared from the far side of the house. Ewan was wearing shorts and a checked shirt that was missing a button, his feet in rubber flip-flops. Sam was in jeans that appeared to be intact, but his T-shirt was smeared with what looked like earth, and there was another smear on his face.

John and Virginia smiled but did not move. Ruth hesitated. She felt they should be exchanging kisses and looked for a sign that that was what was expected.

Ewan ran up to them. 'It's tomorrow. You're coming tomorrow.'

'Hello, young man,' said his grandad, bending slightly. 'So we were, but there's been a change of plan, so we've come today instead.' He put his hand out and didn't flinch at the grubby paw offered in return. Sam and James hung back.

'I'm sorry,' said Ruth. 'We've been gardening. I'm afraid we're all rather filthy. Come inside and sit down while we get cleaned up.

I'll make some tea.'

They trooped in. Ruth washed her hands at the kitchen sink, while they all watched silently, clustered by the door. She sent the boys upstairs to get washed. 'Sam, make sure you all get properly clean, and change your shirt.' And ushered Ed's parents into the living room, where she removed knitting and a pile of typescript to make space on the two good chairs.

'How are you, Ruth?' Virginia asked.

'I'm fine.'

'Are you coping?'

'Of course.' Ruth glanced around the room, opened her mouth to say more, but thought better of it.

'The boys look well.'

'Yes. They're fine.' And she could not refrain from adding, with a defensive laugh, 'I know they look scruffy but they're pretty healthy underneath the dirt.'

'Doing alright at school, are they?' John asked. Neither of them had sat down.

'They're doing fine,' said Ruth. 'Do sit down. I'll put the kettle on and they can tell you themselves what they've been up to.'

The boys reappeared, looking slightly cleaner. They had combed their hair and Sam had put on his best blue shirt.

'Well, young man,' said John to Sam, 'tell me how you're getting on at school.'

'Alright.'

'What's your favourite subject?'

'Don't have one really.'

Ewan, desperate to be asked, couldn't keep quiet. 'I like making things, with glue and stuff.'

His brothers looked at him with irritated condescension.

'Making things,' said their grandmother brightly. 'That's nice. What do you make?'

'It's just baby stuff,' said James. 'I like reading and writing and sums and history. We did the Vikings.'

Sam drifted away into the kitchen where Ruth was assembling rarely used cups and saucers on a tray. She removed one that had a crack and gave Sam a plate of biscuits to carry through. James was still talking.

'Well, he's a bright one,' said John Montgomery as Ruth set the tray down.

'Show off,' muttered Sam.

Ruth straightened and looked at Ed's parents, side by side and beaming at James. It occurred to her that her children now looked rather more presentable than she did, still in her gardening clothes. She poured tea. John and Virginia at last sat down, one at each end of the sofa, smoothing the fabric of grey trousers and beige dress over their knees. James abruptly tired of being the centre of attention and wandered out through the French windows. The sky had darkened.

Once the biscuits had been consumed Sam and Ewan also melted away. They left a silence broken only by the clink of a teaspoon as Virginia compulsively stirred her tea. She must have stirred her tea at least a dozen times, Ruth was thinking, placing the teaspoon in the saucer, picking it up again seconds later. John cleared his throat.

'We were wondering... we know Edward is contributing, but is it enough? Are you managing?'

Ruth was startled, embarrassed. 'We're fine.'

'We can help out. We want our grandchildren... we don't want the children to do without.'

'They're fine,' Ruth said, more sharply than she intended. 'They're healthy, they're happy. We're all fine.'

'They must miss their father,' said Virginia.

'They've adapted. They like to spend time with him, but when he's not around they just get on with things.'

'Boys need a man, a role model.' There was a pause. 'I expect their teachers are all women.'

Ruth took a deep breath, telling herself not to allow her irritation to show. 'They have football on Saturday mornings with a couple of the dads.'

'We're not suggesting you're not doing a good job,' her mother-in-law persisted. 'But it's a lot to expect. On your own, this big house, three lively boys.' She reached to set down her cup on a pile of copies of *The Bookseller*.

'Have you thought...' John began. Ruth knew what was coming. 'Have you thought of selling the house? You'd get a good price. You could get somewhere more convenient, easier to manage, and have plenty left over.'

Ruth said nothing, but slowly shook her head. They were looking at her, the two of them at either corner of the sofa, Virginia's smile deepening the lines at her eyes and mouth, John with an expression of serious concern. They were waiting.

Finally Ruth felt compelled to say, very quietly, 'No, no. I'm not going to sell the house.'

'Think about it,' said Ed's father.

'We can help with the practicalities, the move and so on.' Ed's mother leant forward, still smiling. 'I imagine you'd need to dispose of quite a lot. We can help you get a good price.'

Ruth got briskly to her feet and smiled in return. 'I do appreciate your offer,' she said, 'and your concern. But we're just fine here. The boys love it, I love it. It's my family home.'

'Oh we do understand, how attached you must be to the house… we're thinking of your welfare, and the boys…'

Ruth gathered up the teacups. Through the open French window she could hear the boys' voices. A drop of rain slid down the glass, then another. John and Virginia stood up in tandem. Ewan came racing in, his feet bare, holding something in cupped hands. He came to a halt in front of his grandparents and wordlessly opened his hands, to reveal a ladybird. They exclaimed, patted his head, instructed him to take it back outside, which he did. In the rain, he knelt down on the terrace and with a lilac leaf carefully removed the ladybird from his hand and onto a rose bush.

John and Virginia Montgomery paused at the back door and among the wellington boots and dog leads each kissed their daughter-in-law good bye. Their grandsons were nowhere to be seen. John stepped out into the now steady rain, walked briskly to the car and held the door open for his wife, who followed him across the yard and gracefully slid into the seat. She placed her handbag on her lap. They both lifted a hand as the car turned out of the yard. Standing at the back door, Ruth slowly raised her hand in return, before going back to the living room and watching through the window as the Audi stopped at the lower gate and her father-in-law got out in the rain to open it. She should have sent Sam to do it for them. She continued to watch as the car made its way up to the top gate and John got out again.

Ed settled himself in an armchair and stretched out his long legs. 'It's nice to be back,' he said. 'I'm fond of the old place. But I still think you should sell it.'

Ruth thought, and are you hoping to get your hands on some of the proceeds? Is that why you've come tonight? But she said nothing. Ed went on. 'I thought you might have got yourself hitched again by now. You haven't changed, you know. You're looking great.'

Ruth laughed. 'That *would* be a change, if I were looking great.

But no, getting hitched again is not on the agenda.'

'I'm sure there've been offers.'

'Ed, you know nothing about it, and don't be patronising.'

'Sorry, sorry.' He drained his glass.

Ruth remained standing, arms folded, looking wary. Ed stared at the fire, played with his empty glass. 'Sam sends his love,' he said after long moments of silence. 'He's doing well.'

Ruth nodded. She took a breath, and asked after Ed's daughters. His face brightened. 'They're just fine.' And he fished in his back pocket for his wallet and pulled out a photograph of two fair-haired little girls in sundresses. Ruth looked at it and smiled, and handed the photograph back to him. 'They're lovely,' she said. He replaced the photograph carefully without looking at her.

'What about James and Ewan?' Ed asked. 'They don't communicate much.'

'They're okay.'

'Ewan doing alright?'

'Seems to be. He wants to get into publishing. Though I may be out of date, he may have moved on to something else now.'

'I'm worried about James. He can't spend his life doing good in Africa.'

'It's only for a couple of years. And why not, anyway? Why not spend his life doing good in Africa?'

'Because it's a waste of time. Do you really think he can achieve anything, that he'll make a difference?'

'Yes, actually, I do.'

'You always were a romantic.'

'Maybe. I do believe you have to keep trying.'

'Why waste time and effort on a hopeless case? You need to be realistic. You need to accept that there are causes that will stay lost forever.'

'I agree. But I don't agree that James teaching in Kenya is a waste of effort, nor that Africa is a basket case, nor that Europe should give up on its responsibilities.' She paused, then went on. 'I'm glad that James is doing what he's doing. It makes me feel better. That, of course, is not a good reason for him to be in Africa, but it's an acceptable side effect.'

She left the room before Ed could reply, and came back with a tray of food. If Ed had intended to prolong the conversation he thought better of it, and sat meekly down at the table opposite Ruth. For a few minutes they ate in silence, then Ed began to talk about San Francisco and his work on the paper and how well Sam had fitted in – a natural, Ed said. He had a Chinese girlfriend, who made documentary films. Ruth filled their glasses with the last of the wine, pushed away her empty plate, and cupped her chin in her hand. Ed leant back in his chair. He had a way of smiling, thin-lipped, just the corners of his mouth turned up, which made him look amused but in control.

'I can't believe you're still living here, just as you were twenty years ago.'

Ruth shook her head. 'No, not just as I was. A lot has changed. The boys have grown up and gone, for a start. They don't see this as their home now. I'm not even sure if they see Scotland as their home. Will Sam come back? Or James? If he doesn't stay in Africa, he'll be off somewhere else. Ewan loves London, though how he can afford to live there beats me. I don't suppose he'll be looking for a publishing job in Scotland.' She didn't add, 'And I don't have a husband.' It didn't seem relevant.

'You seem to have successfully replaced them.'

'Replaced them? How can you replace your children?'

'Well, filled the space, then.'

Ruth shook her head again, and was silent for some moments, before saying, 'You haven't a clue, Ed, have you?'

He sat forward suddenly and picked up the empty bottle. 'Do you have another bottle of this stuff?'

'In the fridge.'

He got abruptly to his feet and left the room, returning with the wine and a corkscrew. When he had refilled their glasses he sat down again and took a deep drink.

'I know you're wondering why I came.'

Ruth smiled. 'You've only ever come here to see the boys. So there must be a reason.'

'You don't believe I could have come just to see you?'

Still smiling Ruth said, 'Of course I don't.'

He drank again, set down his glass, put his hands to his face. Letting them fall he said, 'I came to tell you something.'

'Go on.'

'I wanted to tell you... that I don't feel guilty anymore.'

'Did you ever feel guilty?'

'Oh God yes. Of course I did. I'm not a total bastard.'

'But it didn't stop you from doing what you did, having affairs, leaving.'

'That's the thing about guilt, isn't it? If it stopped you, the world would be a very different place.'

'You never really believed in marriage, did you?' Ruth looked at him, her head slightly tilted, speculative. 'I hope you do now.'

'I'm not going to discuss my marriage, Ruth.'

'Thank God for that.'

He flushed.

'I mean,' Ruth went on, 'that I believed we would live together into old age, I really did. I projected us forty, fifty years into the future, an elderly, companionable couple being kindly to each other, visited by our grandchildren, celebrating our golden wedding anniversary. Maybe you're right, maybe I have always been a romantic. You didn't share that picture of the future, did you? You never thought that you might live out your days at Netherburn.'

'I guess not.' Then, resentfully, 'Why should I have done? Netherburn was nothing to do with me.'

They were silent for a while. Ruth had almost said more, had almost spoken of how, whatever might happen now, hitched or not, it was too late to grow old with a man she had fallen in love with in her twenties, with the father of her children. That possibility was lost forever. Ed stared at his glass, pushed it with his forefinger, lifted it.

'I'm sorry if I messed things up for you,' he said, 'but I always reckoned you got on perfectly well without me. I found that difficult, you know. You were so bloody capable. Still are, obviously. You didn't really need me, did you?'

'Didn't I?'

'Be honest, Ruth. You ran the house and garden, looked after the kids, did your editing work, never complained. Like your mother. I was intimidated by your mother, you know. I'd never met a full-blooded career woman before, but I thought then that you were not at all like her.'

'Have you changed your mind?'

'Maybe.'

'I'm hardly a full-blooded career woman, not in my mother's league anyway. I just potter along.'

Ed emptied his glass and looked at her. 'Now that I no longer feel guilty, there's no need to ask you to forgive me.'

'Was there ever a need?'

'It might have made me feel better.'

'If you had asked me, I'm not sure what I would have done. I'm not sure I know what "forgive" means.'

'You're the professional word person, Ruth. Look it up in the dictionary.'

'Forgive us our trespasses. It must mean more than simply "pardon". "Forgive" seems to imply that the trespass no longer matters. But it does matter. It certainly mattered then, and it matters now, because of the consequences, because... it was an end to continuity, to the possibility of sharing an adult lifetime.' Perhaps even that was saying too much. He was looking at her – she thought perhaps there was mockery in his eyes. 'Forgive them, they know not what they do,' she went on. 'Does that mean if they do know, you don't forgive, that ignorance redeems and knowledge condemns? You knew what you were doing. After such knowledge, what forgiveness. Was that a question? I can't remember. Was there an answer?'

'Alright, alright.'

'I wonder if it's easier if you're a Christian.'

Ed got up from the table, went to the mantelpiece and stared at the pictures of his sons, turned to face his former wife.

'What changed, Ruth? The direction of your life didn't change. You're doing now what you were doing then.'

'Who knows what I would have been doing if we had stayed together?' she said lightly, trying to divert Ed from any serious intent. 'I might now be living in San Francisco.'

'I doubt it. I doubt if I could have persuaded you to leave this place.' Then after a pause, 'Do you forgive no one? What about your father?'

'What about my father?'

'He wasn't much of a father, was he? I know he had a bad war, but even so, you have to get on with life. You can't take it out on your wife and children, blight their lives.'

'He didn't.'

'I doubt if Michael would agree with that.'

'Probably not.'

'Do you forgive your father?'

'What was there to forgive?'

'He let you down.' Ed returned to the table and sat down.

'It didn't seem like that to me. I felt let down when he died, but I could hardly blame him for that.'

'He drank himself to death.'

'How do you know?'

'It's pretty obvious.'

'Maybe you're right. But if I'm called upon to forgive him, as I'm not sure I know what forgiveness means how can I do it?'

'There's a poem by Kipling, about machines, not being able to love or pity or forgive.'

'I know what love means, I think, and pity. I loved my father. I understood why he did what he did. Even when I was very small I understood. He talked to me once, just once when he'd had a few drinks, when mum wasn't around, about the friend who had saved his life on the beach at Salerno, saved him twice, in fact. Well, he wasn't really talking to me, just talking, and I was the only one there. I was often the only one there. His friend pulled him out of the water when he lost his footing and couldn't move because of all the equipment he was carrying. They were being shelled from the cliffs. And then later he was trapped by an anti-tank gun. It was chaos, no one knew what was happening. And his friend came back for him, got him out. He never talked about it again, not to me at least, but I've never forgotten it. It was a year or two before he died, in this room. And then his friend was blown up. Dad kept his watch. He went and fetched it from the study and came back with it strapped to his wrist alongside his own watch. He said he wanted it to be buried with him.' Ruth stared at the fire for a few moments. 'It was the only time I ever heard him talk about the war.'

Ed had filled his glass and was watching her through narrowed eyes. 'To understand is to forgive,' he said.

'Is it? It seems too easy, somehow.' Ruth wasn't looking at Ed, but somewhere beyond him. 'I was only thirteen, fourteen when my dad told me that story, but I think even then I realised that forgiveness didn't come into it. Something happened to him that was completely out of his control and affected him forever. But you knew what you were doing.' She looked straight at Ed now. 'It's too easy,' she said again. 'You say you're sorry, I say that's okay, I understand, no problem, I forgive you.'

'Why make things difficult?'

'Don't you think there are some situations where forgiveness is just not right?'

Ed shrugged. His glass was empty again. 'On a scale of one to ten my bad behaviour doesn't get much beyond two, I'd guess. Nobody died as a consequence of my transgressions.'

'I found Reggie's watch when I was sorting out the desk in the study. Do you remember? You took it over when we moved here. I found the watch in the desk drawer – I still have it upstairs.' Ruth stood up and gathered the plates. 'So it didn't go into the grave with dad, or rather into the fire. I don't suppose mum knew that was what he wanted, and I forgot. Or maybe I wanted the watch for myself, a memento... not so much of dad as of what happened to him. I'll make some coffee.'

The kitchen was empty and silent. There were no sounds from other parts of the house, and when she turned on the tap the noise of water filled the room. She waited for the kettle to boil, wondering how Ed was going to get back to Edinburgh, wishing that he would go, that he had never come. She put cups and the coffee pot on a tray. When she carried it through Ed had left the table again and was standing with his back to the fire. Dixie lay with her head on her front paws, watching him.

'You'll need a taxi to get back,' Ruth said.

'Or I could stay here, get an early bus in the morning. I have a breakfast meeting.'

'We've a full house, Ed. I'm sorry.'

He shrugged again. 'Not to worry. I'll get a taxi.'

He drank his coffee standing up. Ruth heard Larry come down the stairs and go into the kitchen. He was whistling but she couldn't catch the tune. Ed was absorbed in the photographs again. He picked up one of them, a recent picture of James, taken by the banks of a muddy river and a sign saying 'Beware of Crocodiles'. He was grinning. He was deeply tanned, with a green bandana tied round his thick light brown hair. 'Good looking boy, our James,' Ed said.

'There's a photo of my father somewhere, grinning just like that, standing beside a tank somewhere in the North African desert. Michael has the same look, but he doesn't grin much.'

'Doesn't fit with the academic life,' Ed said. 'Professors don't grin.' He sat down on the sofa and settled comfortably, stretching out his legs. He gave every sign of not intending to go anywhere.

Ed didn't leave until the next morning. He slept on the folding bed in the dining room. He appeared in the kitchen soon after Ruth, looking surprisingly fresh, and accepted coffee. Emma stared curiously, Ros scarcely looked at him, but they left together to catch the bus into town. Ruth watched them walk up the track, imagining Ed's efforts at conversation. Ruth had not slept well. At some point while she was lying awake she realised that her teeth were tightly clamped together.

IT WAS EARLY on a Friday evening. Ruth had gone up to her bedroom with a pile of clean clothes to put away. The house was quiet. Emma and Ros were downstairs in front of the TV. Peter was out. Ruth hadn't seen Larry all day, but as she was sorting underwear she heard voices coming from the attic. It was so unusual to hear anything other than music from Larry's record player or his own singing that she stopped to listen. Two voices, Larry's and a female voice. It was Lisa. Larry and Lisa. She sat down on the bed. She heard Lisa's laugh and smelt cigarette smoke and imagined Lisa's perfume.

It took her by surprise, the feeling of anger, of dismay, of something else that she couldn't quite put her finger on, disappointment perhaps. She wasn't sure how long she sat motionless on the bed, and then became aware of footsteps on the attic stair, not Larry's sneakered feet she thought. The footsteps carried on along the passage, Lisa going to her own room. Ruth listened for more sounds from the attic but there was silence. Then a door opened downstairs, leaking the BBC's six o'clock news. It would be Ros going into the kitchen to make tea for herself and Emma, scrambled eggs or fish fingers, which Ros would eat less of than Emma. Every day Ruth fought down the urge to make them chicken soup or macaroni cheese, favourites that her father used to make. Doors were closed again, and the life within the house was muffled. Silence in the attic, silence along the passage, only the faintest hints of sound from the kitchen.

Ruth sat for a long time. Her bedroom was the only space in the house where she was totally private. No one sought her out there. Even Emma, who went everywhere and never hesitated to run in and out of Ruth's work room, seemed to understand that the bedroom was out of bounds.

It was dark outside, the window black, the curtains open. She should go downstairs, into the kitchen where Ros and Emma would be eating, or clearing up by this time. She should try to escape the gnawing disturbance lodged in the pit of her stomach. The repairs to Lisa's roof should have been finished that week. It should be watertight at least, but Lisa showed no sign of moving out.

Ruth had heard nothing from Ed since his visit, and nothing from any of her sons for probably a month. Sam's last email was brief, and made no mention of his father's visit to Scotland. She had phoned Ewan a couple of times but got no reply. She struggled to write a letter to James that wasn't prosaic and predictable. She had long since taught herself not to worry if she heard nothing from the boys, but a thin current of anxiety was with her always. She had said to Lorna once, I never stop thinking about my children. They are there lurking in some cranny of my consciousness all the time. Lorna had expressed surprise. She claimed she went for days without allowing her children into her head at all. She'd done the mothering thing, she said. They were away south, out of her life, her teacher daughter married in Sunderland, her son working for an electronics company in London. I don't know much about their lives, she said to Ruth. And Ruth had agreed that she, too, was unable to picture the way her sons lived, what occupied their minds, but it didn't mean that she did not think about them.

It was unlikely, Ruth readily conceded, that she and her brothers had colonised her own mother's mind in the same way. As a child she had not questioned her mother's absences, and found it odd that often the mothers of her school friends were at home all day. But she did not spend much time in the homes of friends. None of them lived close enough for them to be visited without complicated arrangements, and she knew instinctively that her father could not be relied on. She also knew that her home was different. By the time she was twelve or thirteen that difference mattered. She did not want her friends to see her father in his filthy corduroys and earthy fingernails, unshaven, without the words to communicate with pubescent girls. Drunk or sober, he was a difficult proposition.

Saturday afternoon, early December, and unusually warm under a pale sun. Larry worked on a picture, a burnt-out car in an old quarry, its back seat torn out and a split bag of empty bottles nearby. Pinned on a board beside him was a series of photographs from which he took what he required. He brought the back seat into the foreground and moved the yellow whins closer together. 'Still slapping paint on canvas?' an acquaintance had asked a few days before. 'Not tempted to be a bit more adventurous? Not much money in paint on canvas.'

No, he wasn't going to give up paint, that quickening of the pulse when he moved colour across a flat surface.

It was chance that took him to the window. He hadn't heard the car coming down the track, but when he saw it, it seemed familiar. When the car stopped at the gate, the figure that got out to open it seemed familiar too. The car came through, the figure got out again and closed the gate. Now Larry recognised him.

Ruth was outside, clearing the end of season detritus from the vegetable garden. The wheelbarrow was filled with wizened bean stalks and the lanky remnants of bolted spinach. Peter was tinkering with his motorbike, and Emma sat on the back step of the flat, watching him. The three of them heard the car follow the track round the back of the house. It was too early for Lisa. Peter looked up when a red car appeared and parked in the yard. For a few seconds Emma stared curiously, then jumped to her feet. 'It's daddy!' Martin emerged with a smile.

'Hello, doll. I thought I'd give you a surprise.' He swung her off her feet. Peter straightened up, a wrench in one hand. Ruth tipped the contents of the wheelbarrow into the compost, and reluctantly decided she should find out who had arrived. When she rounded the corner of the stables she stopped. Father and daughter were standing side by side and hand in hand, while Peter remained by his bike, gently rubbing his palm over the wrench. The back door opened. It was Larry. There was no sign of Ros.

Martin nodded to Ruth and turned back to Emma. 'Where's your mother?' he asked.

'She's making my costume. I'm a shepherd.'

'A girl shepherd, eh? Good for you, sweetheart.'

'Are you coming to see me, at the school, in the Christmas play? We sing as well.'

'Of course I'll come, doll. Just tell me when and I'll be there. And then you can come and spend Christmas with me and your nana and grandad.'

'Can mum come too?'

'Let's go and find her, eh?'

They moved towards the back door of the house, where Larry was propping himself up. Ruth also moved.

'I'll find her,' she said quietly. She was surprised at the fierceness of her repugnance at the thought of Martin entering the house. And she could not allow him to take Ros by surprise. Emma looked puzzled. She was still holding her father's hand.

'It's alright, love,' Ruth said. 'I won't be a minute. You stay out here with your dad.'

Larry moved aside to let Ruth pass, then resumed his casual position, saying nothing. Peter turned his attention to the bike again.

'Nana and grandad are very excited about you coming for Christmas. They're getting the biggest Christmas tree,' Martin was saying to his daughter.

'We're going to have a big one here, too,' Emma said. 'And a party. Ruth has a brother called Alex who can play the guitar, and he's coming, and his wife who's called Sheena and can spin on a spinning wheel. She does it with wool from her own special sheep.'

Inside, Ruth found Ros in the dining room at the sewing machine, which had drowned the sound of the approaching car. The table was covered in fabric and the contents of a sewing box. She was totally absorbed, head bent, but she looked up when Ruth came into the room and smiled. 'I'm not very good at this,' she said, 'but I quite enjoy it.' Ruth almost turned on her heel, to go back to Martin and order him to go, to leave them all alone. Ros was looking so much better. But now her smile was fading and she looked puzzled. 'What's the problem?' she asked.

'Ros. I'm sorry. It's Martin.'

'What about him?' Ros asked abruptly.

'He's here.'

'Oh God.'

'It's alright, I'm not going to let him in the house. Larry and Peter are in the yard. But Ros, he wants Emma to spend Christmas with him.'

'She can't. She mustn't. He can't do that. She's so much looking forward to Christmas here, you know that.'

'Yes, I do know. But Ros, if she wants to be with her dad you shouldn't stop her. It will only make things worse.'

'How can I have Christmas without her? Don't ask me to do that, Ruth. I couldn't, I just couldn't.'

'Maybe we can figure out a compromise.'

'What do you mean?'

'Well, we could decorate the tree and have a present-opening before Emma goes, do something special.'

'I don't trust him. He'd find a way of spoiling it.'

'He doesn't need to know. We'll just do it, make sure Emma has a good time.'

'He wants to hurt me. It wouldn't hurt enough if I just agree to what he wants. He needs to see me suffer.'

'Don't give him that satisfaction.'

'He'll find another way, something worse, something that might be worse for Emma.'

Ros's face, a moment before smiling and relaxed, was drained of colour. She bit her lip.

'Come on,' said Ruth.

Ros stood up woodenly and automatically brushed shreds of fabric from her skirt. She followed Ruth out of the room, but Ruth then stepped aside to let her take the lead. Larry vacated his position at the door. Ros saw Martin first, leaning against the car with his hands in his pockets, and was aware of Peter squatting beside his bike. It was a moment before she realised Emma was sitting in the car's driving seat. Her stomach turned over. Martin smiled but made no move. Ros stopped in the doorway, her hands pressed against her thighs.

'Christmas,' Martin called out. 'Emma wants to spend it with me.'

Ros looked at the shadowy form of her daughter in the car. 'How do you know?' she said, but in a thin voice that didn't carry.

'What?'

'How do you know?' More loudly this time. Larry was whistling under his breath.

'She told me. Didn't you, doll?' The car window was rolled down. 'She wants to spend Christmas with me and her nana and grandad.' From inside the car Emma said something no one could hear. Ros could see her daughter's hands on the steering wheel. She forced herself to walk towards the car, putting one foot in front of the other with great difficulty, while Martin looked on, his arms folded, smiling. Ros stopped within a few feet of Martin, visibly shrinking. Larry was still whistling. Peter was now sitting sideways on his bike, polishing a piece of engine with a cloth, but watching.

'Em,' Ros said, but either Emma couldn't hear or was pretending not to hear. 'Em, can you get out of the car a minute?' There was no response. Without moving and still smiling Martin said, 'Get out of the car, sweetheart.' He opened the car door and Emma jumped out. 'I know what to do,' she said brightly to her mother, 'I know how to start the car, dad showed me.' She stood between her parents, looking from one to the other, her father relaxed, casual, her mother pale and knotted.

Before Ros found her voice again Martin said, 'I'll pick her up on Christmas Eve, take her to Bathgate.'

'Is that what you want?' Ros finally managed to get out. 'Do you want to spend Christmas with your father?'

'We're going to stay with nana and grandad. It'll be brill.'

'You don't mind missing Christmas at Netherburn?'

'Well, I do… But I can't be in two places at once, can I, mum?' Emma said briskly. 'I could help decorate the tree and things, couldn't I, before I go? When we come back from Bathgate dad's going to take me to the pantomime. Aren't you, dad?'

Martin nodded. 'I've already got the tickets.'

Ros looked at him sharply, wondering if he was telling the truth. She tugged nervously at her hair. 'You'll miss Christmas dinner with everyone here, and opening presents…' Her voice tailed off.

'But we'll have presents and turkey and mince pies and everything, won't we, dad? Just like here. And grandad and nana would like me to be with them. I am their only grandchild, you know, and I don't see them very often, do I, dad?'

'Not often enough, doll. We'll have a great Christmas, we'll have whatever you want.'

Peter pushed himself off the motorbike and said, 'We'll drink a toast to you, Em, on Christmas Day. A toast to absent friends.'

Emma looked puzzled for a moment, then smiled. 'Is that when you say cheers?'

'Absolutely. Cheers, *slàinte*, *salut*.'

'*Lechaim*,' added Larry. 'We can call you on the phone. And I'll draw you a picture, and you can draw us a picture.'

Emma beamed from one to the other. Ros wanted to scream at them, don't make it easy for her, make it hard, make her think about choosing her father and not me. She looked close to tears. She folded her arms tight across her chest as if to hold herself together and backed away from Martin's car, defeated. Martin jiggled his car keys.

'Right then,' he said. 'That's sorted.' He reached out to Emma and put his arm around her. 'See you soon, doll.'

They all watched as he got into the car and drove out of the yard, and listened to the sound of the engine making its way to the gate and stop, continue, stop, continue again. Only when the sound faded did anyone move, Peter turning back to his bike, Ros, head down, back into the house followed by Larry, Ruth to finish her task in the vegetable garden. Emma hovered beside Peter, who lifted her onto the bike.

The press was having a Christmas party, and Lorna phoned to make sure Ruth was coming. She dug out a paisley-pattern skirt in an effort to dress for the festive season, and arrived late to find a room filled with conversation and smoke. It was while she hesitated at the edge, casting around for a familiar face or at least the source of the glasses they all held in their hands, when she felt a tap on her shoulder. She turned. A bland face loomed above her, smiling with unparted lips.

'My favourite editor!'

'Oh hello, Bill. How are you?' Ruth responded automatically.

'All the better for seeing you, my dear.'

She should have known that Bill Preston would be there.

'But you haven't got a drink. Come, let me steer you in the right direction and you can tell me all about what you're working on now.' He put his hand on her arm and guided her through the crowd, nodding to people as they went, his smile unwavering. He poured Ruth a glass of wine.

'Now then,' he said, 'that's better, isn't it? I'm in the mood for celebration. I've just finished my edition of short stories – *A Century of Scottish Stories*. Will the press's most empathetic editor be looking at it, I wonder? I tell everyone, Ruth Montgomery has the magic touch.' He paused, looked down at Ruth with his head on one side, his pale eyes neutral. 'Pretty busy, I imagine?'

Ruth nodded.

'I'm just back from Boston, lecturing in New England, *very* interesting time, the Americans certainly know how to treat their guests. Splendid audiences, bright students. There's a real appetite for Scottish literature there, you know, lapped it up, especially the contemporary stuff, Eddie Morgan, Irving Welsh. Ever been to the States? No? I'm surprised. I must have been, oh, at least a dozen times. They seem to like me there.'

'My son's in San Francisco. He likes it.'

'Ah yes, California, very different of course. I was there a couple of years ago, at Santa Barbara. Travelled around quite a bit. The San Francisco St Andrew's Society invited me to speak on Stevenson, full house. They meet in an old firehouse, wonderful building. Turned up in their kilts. You should go, my dear.'

'Perhaps I will.'

'So what are you working on now? Anything good coming up? I'm doing a second volume of the short stories of course, there was just too much material for a single volume. Such good stuff I've found, and neglected for so long. We need to soldier on you know, make it available. The students these days, so keen, we get the very best. Of course, the department's very strong. The new Regius Professor, have you met him, very impressive, from Oxford. He's here somewhere I think, I'll introduce you.'

Ruth was hoping for an opportunity to slip away, but she had never learnt the art of extricating herself from Bill Preston.

'He should meet Edinburgh's most thorough editor,' he continued, looking around the crowded room as he spoke. 'Don't see him, another time perhaps. We must have lunch.'

He leaned towards her. He was older than she was, but his complacently amiable face was unlined, his smooth hair faded but hardly grey. 'I'll send you an email. Do you have email? Yes, of course you do. Have to keep up to date don't we? Nothing like the young to keep one up to date – one of the rewards of teaching.'

Ruth backed away, she could not help herself.

'You don't feel isolated sometimes, out there in the sticks? I'm so fortunate, where I am, five minutes walk from the university. Ah, now there's Tim Sinclair, have you met him, very bright, one of my postgraduates, got him a research fellowship.' This time he smiled with his lips slightly parted. 'I need to have a word...'

'There are a couple of people I must say hello to,' Ruth said hastily, but Bill Preston was already moving away in the direction of a tall young man who waved at his approach. She found Lorna.

'I've just had the full works from Bill Preston,' she hissed.

'Patronised you, did he?' Lorna laughed.

'He's been patronising me for twenty years. He wants to have lunch. After all this time he wants to have lunch.'

'I take it you'd rather not take on *A Century of Scottish Stories*.'

'Spare me.'

The two women edged into a corner and talked shop until Lorna was dragged away by her boss, and Ruth made for the door, trying to avoid catching the eye of anyone she knew. Out in the street the air was thick with a chill damp. For a moment she couldn't remember where she'd parked the car and stood confused on the wet pavement. It was only now that she thought, I could have asked Larry to come with me, that would have given them something to talk about. She found the car, and drove down the Mound, past the tall lit Christmas tree and the floodlit castle. Although it was late there were still plenty of people in Princes Street.

Back home half an hour later, she leant against the warm Aga and listened to the night sounds of the house, the walls breathing, a slight scuffling, a creak of floor boards.

Larry drew a picture of them sitting at the table in paper hats with their glasses raised, and coloured it with crayons. Peter wore a purple shirt. Russell's hat was blue to match his sweater. Lisa was there in black with large reindeer earrings. Larry coloured Ruth's eyes with a gold pen. Ros was wearing a red dress, with her dark hair pulled back under a yellow crown. Larry made her smile. And Larry himself in a white sweatshirt and a red Santa hat that he had bought specially in Poundstretcher. On a green tablecloth was a turkey, dishes of green and orange and yellow vegetables, a huge Christmas pudding, bottles of red wine. The bookshelves behind were festooned in multi-coloured paper chains which Emma, Ros and Larry had made at the kitchen table the day they decorated a tree set up in the front hall. Peter lifted Emma up so she could place a silver tinsel bird on the top of the tree. 'No angels in this house,' Larry had said.

On Christmas Eve she waited at the window for Martin to collect her, her bag packed and her flop-eared rabbit and new Cindy doll sitting on top of it. Cindy was wearing a hat and scarf knitted by Ruth. When Emma saw the red car coming down the track she ran to the back door, but then hesitated. Ros and Ruth were in the kitchen making mince pies. The radio was on, and they were singing along to Christmas carols. Half the table was covered in pastry, the other half with a pile of red-berried holly and strands of ivy Larry had brought in. There was a rich, warm smell of spices. Dixie hadn't heard the car, and was lying inert alongside the Aga. Emma turned away from the back door and walked slowly into the kitchen.

'Dad's here,' she said.

Ros put down the pastry cutter and wiped her hands. She slowly raised her head and looked at her daughter. She made herself smile.

'Are you all set then?'

Emma nodded, but didn't move. 'Mum?'

'Yes, love.'

'I wish I could spend Christmas with you *and* with dad.'

'Isn't that what you are doing?' Ros said brightly. 'We had presents yesterday, and a special tea.'

'But you're going to have another special day tomorrow.'

'And you are, too.'

'I know...'

'More presents, a lovely Christmas lunch.'

There was a thump on the back door. Dixie was instantly on her feet and barking. No one else moved. It was Ruth who, after what seemed like many minutes, at last went to the door and with one hand gripping Dixie's collar told Martin that Emma was just coming. Ros zipped her daughter into her jacket and gave her a kiss but didn't leave the kitchen. It was Ruth who stood waving at the back door as the red car departed. When she returned to the kitchen Ros was sitting with her hands over her face. Out of the radio came *ding dong merrily on high*.

Ruth and Dixie were making their way along the edge of the burn, the light fading and the sky in the west a blur of orange and pink, when headlights appeared through the trees and another car came bumping down the track. A blackbird sang defiantly against the approaching dark. Ruth knew it was Alex and Sheena in their battered jeep, and turned to cross the back field towards the house. The kitchen light was on. She had left the scene of continuing preparation, Larry peeling potatoes, Lisa, who had closed the farm shop early, making stuffing. Ros's mince pies were stacked beside the Aga.

By the time Ruth reached the house Larry was helping Alex and Sheena unload bags and parcels and Alex's guitar. Ruth hugged Alex and then Sheena. Dixie jumped up and placed dirty paws on Alex's chest. From inside came the sound of Lisa's laugh, and soon they were all in the kitchen's warmth, Peter and Ros as well, milling around, filling the kettle, exchanging introductions. Space was cleared on the kitchen table for mugs and milk and sugar, tea was made, Alex and Sheena relieved of their coats and made to sit down. Ruth also sat. Alex always brought with him a reassurance, a reminder that she was not alone, that although Michael and Ed had deserted her and her sons were far away he was not so distant. He was opposite her, smiling, his curling hair the same colour as hers and greying in the same way as hers. With the passing of years brother and sister looked increasingly alike, and Alex was growing more like his father, slender, not very tall, the horizontal lines of his face deepening, the same open, almost innocent smile. Their eyes met. Alex raised his eyebrows with a look that enquired how things were and Ruth gave a nod in response.

Sheena's long, fading, reddish hair was tied back with a velvet ribbon. She wore large gold hoops in her ears and a black crochet sweater over an emerald green silk shirt. Her skirt was long and black and scalloped at the hem, and the toes of her black boots were scuffed and spotted with mud. Her green eyes were fretted with thin lines at either corner. The presents they had unloaded and heaped in the hall would all be the products of Sheena's spinning and weaving, or books from the shop, old guide books, out-of-print memoirs, abandoned histories. They were not labelled. They would be handed out at random, and afterwards swapped or shared.

It was a moment Ruth cherished, this blend of bustle and comfort that came after a welcome arrival, and the entry of something faintly exotic, that brought with it a heightening of the atmosphere. Peter leant against the Aga eating a mince pie. He was young enough to be her son. He glanced at his watch. Shortly he would walk up to the road to meet Russell off the bus. Lisa, her sleeves pushed above her elbows, shoved handfuls of stuffing into the turkey as she explained to Sheena the origins of the bird, free-range from a local farm. Larry rejected tea for instant coffee and sat down beside Ruth, whistling under his breath. Even Ros was smiling, at something Alex was saying. The absence of a child was briefly forgotten in the room filled with adult exchange. Tears came to Ruth's eyes as she looked around her, knowing that she could not capture and preserve this coming together, missing her boys, yet knowing also that over the next few days the people assembled in her kitchen would be the source of great pleasure.

And then it passed. Peter went out into the dark with a torch, and Ruth took Alex and Sheena upstairs to their room – her room, which she had vacated, to allow them the double bed. She would sleep in the study, which she had spent two days resurrecting from its moribund and overcrowded state, uncovering the sofa bed, which was buried under boxes of gardening notes and papers from conferences her mother had attended. It was odd the way the space had been reclaimed, after Ed's departure, like a neglected garden going back to nature.

Everything was now neatly stacked at the far end of the room, a rampart in front of the shelves that still contained Fay's books. For the second time in a couple of months Ruth had cleaned and dusted to liberate another room from its past. But she could not free herself. It was tidy, organised after a fashion, and that made her feel good, but she could not get rid of the results of excavation. They were part of the house, part of her life.

For the first time in years every room in the house was occupied. Anyone looking from the road would see lights burning in every window, the Christmas tree bright through the hall window, and as Peter and Russell came down the track they would smell the wood smoke rising through the chimney. That night, eight of them would sit down round the kitchen table and eat pasta and drink red wine, and perhaps afterwards Alex would get out his guitar and sing 'Henry Martin' or 'The Gallowa Hills', and then accompany Larry singing 'Muleskinner Blues' or 'Midnight Special'.

And that indeed was what happened. Ruth sat on the floor and fed the fire with logs and when she knew the words sang them softly. Dixie was stretched against her. If Alex could not play and sing, she thought, everything would be different. Only the fire and half a dozen candles provided light. It drew them together, the music making and the shadows. When midnight came Peter and Russell quietly got up and went to the door. 'Thank you, everyone,' said Russell. 'Good night.' Peter put one hand on Russell's shoulder, and with the other blew a kiss to the half-lit figures near the fire. They closed the door gently behind them.

For a few moments there was only the hiss of the fire to infiltrate the silence. It was burning low. Ruth made no move to add another log. Then Alex picked up his guitar again and he and Sheena began to sing 'Huntingtower'. Alex's reverberant tenor replied to Sheena's clear but reedy voice. *Blair in Athol's mine, Jeannie...* Larry had got to his feet and was standing with one hand on the mantelpiece. He looked down at Ruth. *St Johnston's Bower and Huntingtower, and all that's mine is thine, lassie.* All that's mine. But I don't have a goddamned thing, except for a few paintings. The boot's on the other foot – she's the one with the house and land. Larry's struck gold, the sodding world would say. Ruth, still sitting on the floor although the chair she leant against was empty, had shut her eyes, which the firelight had burnished to a glowing amber. A year and a half of muted yearning lurched his pulse into his throat. He didn't just want to look after her, damn it, he wanted to get into her bed. Lisa, on the sofa, saw that look. She blew softly through slightly pursed lips, although she had no cigarette.

Ros was sitting in the big armchair, sharing it with the cats, her arms braided around her drawn-up knees. Ruth opened her eyes and caught Larry's look, part illuminated by the dying fire. He raised his eyebrows, ran a hand over his stubbly beard. She felt the rise and fall of Dixie's breathing. What about Lisa, she was thinking, what was going on there, and does it matter? *All that's mine is thine, lassie.* Alex played a final chord. 'Right folks,' he said, laying down his guitar, 'bedtime.'

Slowly everyone unwound themselves. Larry reached out to help Ruth to her feet, feeling the warmth of her hand and the tug of her slight body as he pulled her up, and reluctant to let her go. Dixie got up as if attached by strings to Ruth, who removed her hand and fondled the dog's ears, but wondered at the same time if it had been noticed, that brief connection of hands. Sheena stretched her slim, heavily bangled arms and turned to Ruth, whom she embraced. 'A wonderful night,' she said. 'Perfect.' There were murmurs of agreement. 'Night all,' said Lisa, rather loudly, and left the room. Ruth could not help herself, but glanced at Larry and noted that he did not seem aware of Lisa's departure. She put the fireguard in front of the embers. Dixie wagged her tail.

11

ANDREW CAMERON CROUCHED in the April sunshine beside the two parallel rows he had drawn in the earth. His ten-year-old daughter was beside him. From a paper packet, he shook out parsnip seeds into her open palm and then into his own. 'Like this,' he said, and moved forward, still crouching, every few inches dropping a seed into the row. She kept pace, poking the seeds with her finger to keep them in a straight line, frowning in concentration. When they reached the end of the rows, they turned and covered the seeds with earth. Andrew followed the rows again and gently tamped the earth down with his foot.

'There!' said Ruth, brushing earth from her hands.

Andrew bent to pull a stray weed, straightened, and smiled at her. 'The worse thing about war,' he said, 'is all the growing things that get destroyed.' He took his pipe from the breast pocket of his checked shirt and spent several minutes getting it alight. Ruth said nothing. 'Imagine tanks and armoured cars crossing fields, churning up all the young plants, wheat ready for harvest, vines. Hundreds of men tramping. It broke my heart.'

He looked around the rectangle of ground he and Ruth had planted and puffed his pipe. 'If we can't bring an end to war, we're done for.' He stooped for another stray weed. 'Done for.' He turned to his daughter and smiled. 'Come on. Let's see what's doing in the greenhouse.' She followed him. As if talking to himself, he said, 'Too late for me of course. Doesn't matter how much I plant and cultivate, I'll never get death and destruction out of my head. Don't let your brothers go for soldiers,' he said, as they went into the greenhouse and breathed in the smell of infant tomato plants, 'or your sons if you have them. Whatever happens. They may not be killed, but they'll certainly be destroyed.'

In a few years they would study it at school, THE WAR, and the class would exchange stories of their fathers, uncles, grandfathers. They brought in medals, an air-raid warden's helmet, a ration book. Some mothers had driven ambulances, worked as land girls, a few had been in the forces. They mentioned the dead, but not the ruined living. Ruth said nothing of the whisky bottle on the sideboard, of the way her father would sometimes hug her painfully and unsteadily, and envelop her in a cloud of whisky breath. She never replied to her older brother's scornful dismissal. 'They were all in the war, but they don't all drink.'

After the birth of her third child, Fay Cameron turned her back on her husband. Ruth did not know that, of course, but years later began to understand that it was not just work that took her mother away so often. Michael, on a rare visit home from Oxford, was blunt. 'It was the only way she could put up with him. She had to escape. Too bad about us kids. Don't know why she had us, really. Why bother, if you're not going to be around?'

Alex and Ruth were uncomfortable, but made no attempt to defend their parents against the onslaught of the firstborn. They were relieved when Michael went away again, removing his determination not to belong. Ruth wondered sometimes, after the passing of many years, if she should try to bring the family together again, persuade Michael to visit, but she flinched at the prospect. She could not bring herself to make the first move. Now, on the day after Christmas, she and Alex walked with Dixie under a damp grey sky. They crossed the burn on the rotting planks that served as a bridge and climbed the slope beyond. From the top they could see down across the steely firth where a single tanker was heading out to sea.

'What about Michael?' Ruth asked.

'What about him?'

'I hate it that he's cut himself off.'

'It's his choice,' Alex said, his eyes focused on the distant hills beyond the water.

'I've never been to see him in Oxford, not met his second wife and family.'

'Me neither.'

'He's our brother.'

'Sure. And I'm his brother and you're his sister. Look, Ruth, don't feel you have a responsibility here. As I say, it's his choice.'

'I send presents, I always send presents. I get a card sometimes, in her handwriting.'

'He doesn't need us. And speaking for myself, I don't need him. He didn't think about us when he buggered off. We had to deal with it all.'

Ruth realised it still mattered to Alex, after more than thirty years.

'He's not been in Scotland since mum's funeral.'

'He was once. He was at a conference in Edinburgh and he came out here on a Sunday afternoon. Before Ed left. When he and Caroline were still together. That's the last time I saw him.'

They were silent for a while as they walked along the ridge, the water to the north, a view across fields to Netherburn to the south. They were exposed to a thin, northeast wind. Alex pulled up his collar and rubbed his hands together. He had come out without gloves.

'But you're alright, Ruth?' Alex said at last. 'Managing, I mean? Money... and things.'

'Of course I'm alright. The house is falling down, but apart from that everything's fine. I wish the boys weren't so far away, but I'm not going to tell them that. Ewan's in Paris this Christmas, seems to have found himself a French girlfriend. I have plenty of company, too much sometimes, if I'm honest. As long as publishers want to employ me I can earn a reasonable living, and I like the work. Yes, I'm just fine.'

'I'll come down again in the spring and give you a hand with things around the house.'

'What about you? How's business?'

'Not great, but we get by – though we wouldn't if we relied on selling old books. Sheena's craft classes are crucial, but you know our aspirations are modest and we like our life.'

'Chalk and cheese,' laughed Ruth.

'What do you mean?'

'You and Michael. When he was here last he was describing in great detail the big house he and Caroline had bought. He'd just been made a reader at some ridiculously young age, and Caroline had a new job, some kind of marketing, and they had an au pair for Lucy. He wanted me to know all that, while we were racketing around with a leaking roof and the boys in third-hand clothes.'

'I reckon that if he was a happy bunny he'd not have a problem about coming here.'

'Maybe.'

They began to walk back down the sloping path. There was a glimmer of pale winter sunshine and some shelter from the wind.

'You've done well, you and Sheena, still together, living a life you've chosen.'

'No kids, though.'

'Do you regret that?'

'Sometimes, a little. But, you know, Sheena had a crap childhood, and I... They were such a disappointment, mum and dad. I couldn't bear the thought of having kids who would be disappointed. Look at us now, bumbling along, ageing hippies, breathing the dust of second-hand books and growing our own jumpers. Losers, any self-respecting kid would have thought. Happy losers, but losers all the same. Why does Michael never come to Netherburn, let alone to Inverness? Because he despises us. Imagine having a child who despised you.'

'But you didn't despise mum and dad – I'm not even sure Michael did.'

'No, I didn't, but I felt let down, in a way I couldn't put into words. I suppose I just wanted to be noticed more. And Michael – he despised dad alright, he said so, and he felt that it was mum's fault, that she should have stayed at home and sorted him out instead of buggering off to indulge her passion for ancient stuff.'

'You're looking more and more like dad,' Ruth said.

'Am I? You're probably the only one to know – Sheena never met him. No one in Inverness knows anything about him, though a copy of his book came into the shop once. It's probably still there.' He negotiated a muddy patch on the path. 'I may look like him, but I'm not *like* him.'

'I think you are, in a way.'

'I'm not umbilically linked to a whisky bottle, for a start.'

'No... but maybe, without the war, he would have been like you.'

'You mean thoughtful, caring, reliable...'

'He was all those things, Alex. Well, perhaps not reliable, but it was only the drink that got in the way of that.'

'Only the drink.'

'Come on, Alex. We all drink. Look at last night. Did you count the empties this morning? I've seen you put away a fair amount without the excuse of Christmas. Not to mention dabbling in other substances.'

'There's drinking and drinking.'

'He was a good father, all the same. Or goodish.'

'You're very forgiving.'

'Forgiving?'

They had reached the bridge. Alex stood aside to let Ruth cross first – she was practised at avoiding the weak spots. He then walked by her side as they crossed the field to the gate at the back of Netherburn.

'Forgiving?' Ruth questioned again. 'I don't think so.'

'And mum. What about mum?'

'Do you think she needs to be forgiven too?'

'I suppose I do. If she'd stuck around more, maybe...'

'Don't say that.'

'I can't help thinking it, Ruth.'

They had reached the gate. Alex released the catch and swung it back for his sister and her dog to go through. He was thinking he was glad they'd had a chance to talk, and when they got to the back door he put his arm around Ruth's shoulder and gave her a quick hug. 'You're doing alright, lass,' he said, 'and don't mind me. Whatever it sounds like, I'm not hung up on the past. I'm amazingly content, really.' He laughed, and gave his sister's shoulder another squeeze. 'I'm fifty-one. I'm not going to waste time nursing old hurts and resentments.'

Alex and Sheena left the next day, and shortly afterwards Martin's red car again descended the track and deposited Emma at the back door, wearing a new jacket with a fake fur trim. Out of the back of the car came a gleaming bicycle. Ros took all this in from the kitchen window, rooted to the floor, unable to move to greet her daughter. It was Ruth who opened the door and Dixie who ran up, tail wagging, to welcome Emma home. Emma hugged the dog. Martin again stood beside the car with his slight, mocking smile, his arms folded.

Emma was strangely quiet when Martin had gone. With Ruth's help, she wheeled the bike into the shed where they moved a broken tricycle, an old pram and several garden chairs to make space.

'I can ride it,' Emma said, without elaboration, and Ruth was remembering her own childhood efforts at riding a bike on the rutted track and the gravel, and the grazed knees that resulted from spills. She carried Emma's little suitcase and a carrier bag full of presents into the house. Ros was there, waiting. Her 'Hello, love' sounded loud and strained. Emma grabbed her hand. 'Come and see my bike, mum.'

'Why don't we have some lunch first?'

'Just for a minute. It's brilliant. It's much better than my old baby's bike. I'll show you.'

So Ros allowed her daughter to pull her out of the house and to the shed where the bike had just been stowed away, and stood with her arms folded against the wind as Emma wheeled the bike out again and hefted herself onto the saddle to ride across the yard and precariously down the bumpy track. Halfway back she wobbled to a halt and had to get off and push the bike up the slight rise.

'It was for my Christmas,' she said unnecessarily. 'When we went back to dad's flat we went to the Meadows so I could ride it. It's brand new. Dad took my old bike to the dump. He said it wasn't much good for anything.'

'It's a beautiful bike,' Ros forced herself to say. 'But let's go in now. It's cold. You put it away for now.'

Ros had learnt to ride her older sister's bike, bought second-hand and repainted a dark blue by her grandfather. Emma's bike gleamed turquoise and silver.

'We went to the pantomime, mum. *Aladdin*. It was barry. I liked the songs. And the dancing. Dad said I could have dancing lessons.'

'Don't forget we're going to grandma's for New Year,' Ros said, not wanting to comment on dancing lessons.

'Aw mum, do we have to? I want to stay here and ride my bike.'

'Of course we have to. What would grandma think if we didn't see her?'

'You could go and I could stay here with Ruth.'

'Emma, we'll only be away for a few days. And Ruth's got better things to do than look after you.'

'I'll take the bike with me then.'

'Don't be silly.'

'It's not silly. Bikes can go on trains, I've seen them.'

Mother and daughter were in the kitchen, Emma still in her coat and woolly hat, truculence spreading across her face, but it was Ros who looked close to tears. Emma stamped out of the room and up the stairs. Her suitcase and bag of presents were still in the back hall, where Ruth had set them down. Without taking off her coat and hat, Emma went straight up to Larry's attic, where he was working at his easel.

'Hello, gorgeous,' he said, without seeming to look at her. 'Where's my picture?'

Emma looked stricken. 'I forgot.'

'It's not too late. You can do it right here.'

'Have you done one?'

'Sure thing. It's over there.' And it was, pinned to a drawing board propped on a shelf.

Emma took a couple of steps towards the picture. 'I got a bike for my Christmas.'

'You did? Some people have all the luck.'

'From my dad.'

'Good for him. That's what dads are for, to provide bikes for daughters. I never got a bike for my daughter, so I guess I failed in that department.'

'Do you have a daughter?'

'Yep.'

'What's her name?'

'Hannah.'

'There's a girl called Hannah in my class. I don't like her. She shows off.'

'Well, I guess we all show off sometimes.'

'I don't. My mum doesn't.'

'You're right there. Your mom is not a show off.'

'She won't let me take my bike to Nairn, to my grandma's.'

'It'd be kinda difficult, wouldn't it?' Larry put his paintbrush down, looked at his picture with his finger to his mouth, looked at Emma. 'Are you going to do that picture for me?'

'Do you want to see my bike?'

'Sure.'

'I'll show you my bike first, and then I'll do a picture. After I've had my lunch.' She pulled her woolly hat slowly from her head.

'Tell you what,' Larry said. 'You go and have your lunch. I'll come down in half an hour and you can show me your bike. Then you come back up here and you can do your picture.'

'Can I bring my own crayons and paints? Ruth gave me new paints.'

'Sure you can. Or you can borrow mine. Okay, Em? Off you go then, and I'll see you in half an hour.'

That evening Lisa stamped into the kitchen in a cloud of cold air and dumped a bag of potatoes and parsnips on the table. Ros was standing at the Aga lethargically stirring baked beans in a pan. She had been crying. Tears had glued a strand of hair to her cheek. Ruth was sitting with a kitchen knife in her hand. A tomato and half a cucumber sat on the chopping board in front of her. There was a heavy silence. Ros drew the back of her hand across her mouth, removed the pan from the heat and left the room. The bag, precariously balanced, slowly toppled over and rolled three or four potatoes across the tabletop. Ruth automatically reached out and prevented them from falling to the floor.

'Jesus,' said Lisa. 'That girl needs to get a grip.'

Ros had got no further than the other side of the kitchen door, which she had not fully closed, and heard her. She stood frozen, another cataract of silent tears flooding her face. She could not move. Her feet felt like lead. She could not bend a knee or raise her hand to wipe her face. Minutes passed. They seemed like hours. She heard Ruth say, 'She's been having a hard time,' and Lisa reply, 'Some people are born to be victims. I'm not surprised her husband hits her.' She heard the sound of Ruth's protest but couldn't make out the words because there was a noise in her head like a high wind or a waterfall.

Two days later Ruth took Ros and Emma to the station where they caught the train north. Ros had made an effort. She wore her smart coat and a jaunty cap over her smoothed hair. She was steeling herself to be told again by her mother that she should return to Martin. Ruth drove back from the station through sleety rain, and although it was still early in the afternoon, the light was already going. Lisa left in her car the same day, to visit friends in Yorkshire. The house felt empty. Tomorrow, Hogmanay, it would be emptier. Peter would be off partying somewhere with Russell. Ruth had scarcely seen Larry since Christmas and had no idea what he might be doing to see in the New Year. Lorna had phoned to ask Ruth to a party with her and Neil – 'Just a few friends, you'll know everyone' – but Ruth had declined, saying she had people staying. It wasn't quite a lie.

The house was cold and she put a match to the fire and settled into her ample chair with a minimal shifting of cats. The thought of artificial conviviality depressed her, and it made no difference if she knew everyone or no one, if her hosts were old friends or casual acquaintances. The pleasure of Christmas had felt organic, uncontrived, however accidental the circumstances that had brought them all together and whatever unhappiness lay beneath the surface. They had none of them forgotten broken marriages, destroyed families, damaged homes, but had included them all in the occasion – or so Ruth was thinking, curled up with her cats as the flames took hold and the biggest of the logs began to burn.

She was tired. She was relieved that Ros had gone, that she had a few days of respite from her needy presence, from all the time feeling that she should do something to help. This was, of course, something to keep to herself – she would admit it to no one. And that itself was a burden from which she could not free herself, the burden of responsibility without complaint that somehow she had inherited. She shut her eyes and thought about putting some music on, Schubert perhaps, but didn't want to erase the silence. The windows had darkened. Dixie was stretched flat on the hearth.

12

AT AROUND NOON on the last day of the year the telephone rang. Ruth was working at her desk, sorting illustrations for a book on Highland customs and checking captions. She reached for the phone, thinking it might be one of her sons. It was a female voice, asking for Larry. She climbed one flight of stairs and called his name at the bottom of the second. She wasn't sure if he was in. Larry had a way of moving silently around the house and beyond it. He might have gone out with his camera, although it wasn't a good day for taking pictures. But a voice answered. 'Yeah?'

'Phone for you.'

She went back down to her desk and when she heard Larry's voice on the extension replaced the receiver. Almost certainly an invitation for the evening, one of his girlfriends. It was what she might have expected. She continued numbering the illustrations and sliding them into transparent wallets. She would have the job finished before the day was over. She would end the year with a tidied desk, ready for whatever came next, but with that anxiety, never far from the surface, that one day the work would cease to come.

Later, she set off with Dixie to walk the mile and a half to the shore. The sky was ominously heavy with cloud and there was a smell of snow. On the shore, at the mouth of the burn, the sea birds were restless. The gulls' screams seemed more than usually harsh, the oyster catchers' cries more edgy. Ruth stood at the stony margin of the water, her hands shoved into her pockets, her knitted hat pulled down over her ears. Dixie dashed into the water at a pair of eiders and quickly retreated. On the far shore, lights were on already in Rosyth and Limekilns.

It was too cold to stay motionless for long. 'I think it's going to snow, Dix,' Ruth said, as she turned away and crunched over pebbles to the path. The dog trotted in front. Ruth had seen the start of more than forty new years in Netherburn. Ed was right. She didn't have much sense of adventure. A couple of Mediterranean holidays. In Yugoslavia when the children were small and it was still

Yugoslavia, because it was cheap. There were snapshots somewhere of the boys in Dubrovnik, and on the old bridge at Mostar, which she had watched on television being destroyed. She had never been beyond Europe. 'A new year, a new continent?' Ruth speculated out loud to the dog as she trudged along the path through the trees. Should she make that her resolution for 1997? To Kenya to see James, or to San Francisco? Travel needed money of course, that was the snag. Money, and time not working, not earning.

From the top of the ridge she looked down on Netherburn. There were lights on in the attic and in the kitchen. So Larry hadn't yet gone out. As she scrambled down the slope the first snowflakes began to fall and by the time she reached the house her shoulders were white.

Larry was in the kitchen making coffee and a bacon sandwich.

'Looks like a white Hogmanay,' he commented as she hung her damp hat and gloves on the Aga rail.

Ruth nodded.

'Partying tonight?'

She shook her head.

'Me neither. So how about we keep each other company? I'll make dinner, if I can borrow the car and get to the shops before it's too late.'

'You don't have to.'

'What do you mean, I don't have to? Of course I don't have to. There's no coercion involved, there's no gun to my head. I'd like to. Want some coffee? There's plenty in the pot.'

Without waiting for an answer he poured her a mug of coffee. Was he staying in through some notion that she should not be alone on the last day of the year? Instead of taking his sandwich and coffee upstairs he sat down at the table and ate silently, watching her. She leant against the Aga, drawing in its heat, her hands cradling the warm coffee mug.

After several minutes Ruth said, 'I meant, you don't have to go to the shops. I have food in the house.'

'Yeah, but is it the right food? I'll get us some steak, and a bottle of something decent. I've finished a picture and I'd like you to see it.' He took a bite of his sandwich and chewed for a few moments before adding, 'How about cocktails in the attic at seven?'

Ruth laughed. 'Cocktails already! It sounds like a seduction gambit.'

Larry's dark blue eyes regarded her steadily as he continued to chew. He swallowed, took a gulp of coffee, sucked in a slow breath, tipped his chair back. 'Yeah,' he said. 'Could be.'

Ruth blushed. 'It's nearly four o'clock. You'd better get moving if you want to buy steak before the snow gets serious.'

Ten minutes later she was back at her desk and Larry was in her car turning onto the road in a flurry of snow. She began sorting papers and tidying files. In half an hour the files had been stowed and the books stacked on the floor had been returned to their shelves. The book on Highland customs, text and pictures, was ready to go as soon as the holiday was over. She drifted round the room with a duster and rearranged the Christmas cards on the mantelpiece. She drew the curtains against the dark and the swirling snow and checked the supply of firewood. She went upstairs and changed out of her dog-walking clothes. She put on a white jersey and a red enamel necklace that Sam had sent from San Francisco. Larry should be back any time.

An hour later he had not returned. The appointed time for 'cocktails' came and went. Ruth went to the back door and looked out at the snow, still falling heavily. She lit the fire and sat with a whisky and a book on her lap, but not able to concentrate. She closed the book, got to her feet, hesitated, sat down again. She was reluctant to put on music or the television, and gave up any pretence that she was not listening for the car. But when, at nearly eight o'clock, she heard the back door open and a slumbering Dixie was startled awake it took her by surprise.

Larry was on the doorstep stamping the snow from his shoes and brushing it from his jacket and hair. A scarf was wrapped round the lower half of his face.

'What happened? Where have you been?' Ruth heard her voice rise. Then, looking beyond him into the empty yard, she added, 'Where's the car?'

Larry continued shaking off the snow before stepping into the house and taking off his sodden shoes. He padded into the kitchen leaving a trail of wet footprints, and dumped a bag of shopping on the table. He carefully unpacked the contents.

'Sirloin steak,' he said, 'two bottles South African pinot noir, Stilton, mushrooms. And the secret ingredient.' He flourished a small jar.

'Larry...'

'That should do it.'

'You need dry clothes, a hot bath.'

He looked at her, head tilted, water dripping from his wet hair.

'Almost as bad as New York.'

'Hot bath.'

'Sure. Give me half an hour... Sorry about the cocktails.'

'Larry. The car.'

He'd reached the door but he paused. 'The car... is approximately five miles away, it's nose in a snow drift, near a field gate with a double strand of barbed wire across the top and some very dejected sheep on the other side. I think I'll be able to find it again. But it's a long walk in the snow.'

'Did you...'

'Half an hour.'

She didn't hear him come into the room, where she knelt in front of the fire, lost in the flames, one hand absently pulling at Dixie's ear. He noted that she had changed but as usual was wearing no make-up. As he watched she ran her hands through her hair, and left it ruffled and irregular, the nape of her neck exposed. In a year and a half they had only once before spent an evening alone together, that time he had sold his picture of the old distillery and they had shared a bottle of wine. He would always associate her with the smell of wood smoke. The white of Ruth's jersey and the pale skin of her neck shimmered in the light of the fire and candles burning on the mantelpiece. Light from a single low table lamp just reached the hand that lay absently on the sleeping dog. She could be a child sending her letter to Santa Claus up the chimney. Emma's paper chains hung across one wall and a tinsel reindeer on the dresser glittered. He did not want to intrude. She occupied her own space, self-contained, without expectations, it seemed to him, although she had got herself ready for something.

Ruth suddenly became aware of his presence and turned her head. Straight out of the bath, in clean clothes, his hair plastered flat, he looked neat and wholesome in spite of the scruffy beard. She smiled, and gestured towards the bottle and two glasses on the table. So there is a welcome here, Larry thought, I am after all allowed into her world.

He said, again, 'Sorry about the cocktails.'

'Were you really planning on cocktails?'

He shook his head. 'Of course not. But it sounded good. Cocktails in the attic. Maybe I'll paint it instead – "cocktails in the attic". Painting makes up for all kinds of deficiencies. I used to mix a mean mint julep but that's not quite right for Scotland in winter.'

Ruth waved again towards the bottle on the table. 'Malt whisky is much more appropriate.'

She reached across and poured two drinks. Larry still hadn't moved from the door. He was reluctant to narrow the distance between himself and the woman in the firelight, whose face as she turned it from fire to candle to lamp exposed different planes and edges of illumination. Those eyes, opaque then suddenly burnished, her skin shadowed then like rosy satin. She pushed up the sleeves of her sweater. Her thin wrists were almost coppery in the firelight.

'I'm going to cook that steak,' he said.

'I'll help.'

'No, don't...'

But she was on her feet and had picked up the two glasses and was coming towards him, breaking the spell.

In the kitchen she watched him slice mushrooms and use his fingers to smear the steaks with olive oil. As he was making a sauce with the contents of the little jar, he said, 'I don't do people, but I've just finished a picture with nine of them. It was fun. I might do more.'

'When do I get to see the picture?'

'We'll eat first.'

Ruth sat absorbed by his busyness, doing nothing to help. She had forgotten her anxiety as she relished the experience of freedom from caring for others. Larry made no call on her sympathy and did not ask for support. An hour ago he was trudging through snow in sodden trainers, the sleeves of his jacket pulled down over his gloveless hands, hardly able to follow the whitened road. Now he was grilling steaks.

They took their food next door and moved the little table by the curtained window nearer the fire. They sat in an island of warmth.

'So what happened, Larry?' Ruth asked at last, picking up her fork.

'I was rounding the bend by the old mill and these two headlights were coming straight at me, and then there was this truck, looming out of the snow, and I had to dodge it. Ended up off the road and there was no way I could get moving again. The truck didn't stop. Don't blame the guy, really – if he'd stopped he wouldn't have got moving again either. So I started walking. Two cars and a van passed me, then half a mile from home I got picked up by a Range Rover, a woman with three kids in the back.'

Larry sat back in his chair with his glass of wine in his hand. 'A little adventure, Ruth. Nothing to write home about. Not that I ever write home.'

'People die in circumstances like that. You read about them, dying of exposure, hypothermia.'

'Sorry about the car.'

'The car doesn't matter.'

'I'll retrieve it, tomorrow or whenever the road's clear.'

'Don't count on a snow plough being out tomorrow.'

'It was beautiful. The moon out, almost as light as day. But you couldn't see the edge of the road any more, so I fell into a ditch a couple of times and after an hour or so I forgot where my feet were. When the Range Rover pulled up at the Netherburn gate I could hardly move to get out. Coming down the track was worst of all. You know, you read about guys who expire within sight of their destination. I thought that might be me. I'd have been calling for help and you'd be snug inside in front of the fire, not hearing anything except the wind. And then Dixie would suddenly raise her head and prick up her ears and that would be the very moment when I took my last breath.'

'And we'd find you the next morning frozen stiff, yards from the back door. We'd have a great funeral, full of bluegrass and country and western, and we'd drink all your wine – assuming you've still got some up there – and organise a retrospective exhibition and sell your pictures for thousands of pounds, as everyone knows that an artist is worth more dead than alive.'

'And the glitterati of Edinburgh would be vying with each other to have a Larry Segal on their walls... but hey, Ruth, there's one Larry Segal which I'm leaving to you. Not that I have a will, but when I'm gone it's yours.'

'Which one is that?'

'The one I've just finished, the one that's on the easel right now and which I'm going to show you as soon as I've had some of that Stilton.'

Ruth climbed the stairs in front of Larry, who had picked up the second bottle of wine, but he wouldn't let her go first into his attic space. It was full of moonlight and thick with the smell of paint. He stood in front of the easel with his arms outspread, a glass in one hand, the bottle in the other.

'Okay,' he said, 'you can turn on the light.'

She did so, and he stepped back from the canvas to stand by her side. It was the picture that Emma had shown her, an A4 sketch in crayon translated into a blaze of paint and colour. There they all were, seated at the big table laden with plates and glasses and food and candles and a bowl of holly in the centre, nine people ranged in a row in nine different attitudes. At one end of the table Larry, turned away from the assembled company, staring straight out of the picture, a ruby-red glass in his hand. Then Ros looking slightly to her left, as if towards the door, and Emma beside her, a red ribbon in her mop of hair, holding aloft the two halves of a Christmas cracker. Next to her was Peter, smiling at Sheena on his other side, then Russell looking up to the ceiling with one brown hand raised as if asking a blessing. Lisa came next, her mouth wide in laughter, and Ruth, unsmiling but with glowing eyes, and at the far end Alex playing his guitar.

'It's stunning,' Ruth said, 'but you've made it up.'

'Of course I have,'

'Emma wasn't there. That was the point of the picture.'

'The point of the picture is that you can paint what you damn well please.'

'If she'd been there you wouldn't have painted it.'

'That's why I put her in.'

'You should give the picture to Emma.'

'She's got the sketch. I did this one for you.'

Ruth stared at the picture for several minutes, saying nothing, then, 'Thank you.'

'There's a message in it.'

'There is?'

'I mean, a message for you.'

'Ah,' Ruth said uncertainly.

'You said that Emma's absence was the point of the picture. That's not true. *You* are the point of the picture. It couldn't exist without you.'

'Larry, do you realise it's after midnight?'

'Good grief, you're right, we've missed the bells. Happy New Year.' He put his arm around her shoulder and kissed her cheek.

'Happy New Year,' Ruth replied, still looking at the picture. Larry didn't move his arm. She was tense, wary, as if she were holding her breath.

'How about,' he said, 'we return to real life?'

'Real life? What's that?'

'The here and now. You and me. Flesh and blood. Not approximations in oil paint.' He put his other arm around her and pulled her close. 'I didn't do justice to your eyes,' he said. 'It's all a game, really. I do it because it's fun.'

What was all a game? Ruth's face was buried against his chest and she couldn't speak. From a great distance came the sound of a phone ringing. She felt locked in by the muscles of his arms, but protected, for a moment safe. Then she pushed herself back. The phone stopped.

Larry didn't release her, his hands gripped together at the small of her back. 'They'll leave a message,' he said.

'It will be one of the boys.'

'Do you need to go down and check?'

Ruth nodded. He slid his hands apart but before she could step away took her by the shoulders and kissed her.

'Go on then.'

To check the answering machine, she had to go down two flights to the living room. It was Ewan, with voices and music in the background. 'Hi mum, happy New Year. Hope you're out enjoying yourself. Speak to you soon.' She sat in the restless light from the fire's embers, with Dixie still stretched out on the hearth, the cats on the chair. She went to the window and pulled the curtain back. The snow had stopped, and suddenly that was where she wanted to be, outside in the clean bright silence. She heard Larry coming down the stairs.

'Do you remember the night of the storm, when Lisa arrived and we were all sitting in the kitchen?'

'Hmm.' She remained staring through the dark window.

'That was the night I fell in love with you.' It wasn't quite true, but would she have believed him if he'd said, 'The first time I set eyes on you...' It was true enough. He hummed *My Dixie darling, my Dixie belle*. She still had her back to him. The fire's embers glowed faintly.

'I'm going out,' she said.

'I'll come.'

They pulled on boots and coats and scarves and with Dixie walked into the untouched field of white at the back of the house. Larry took Ruth's gloved hand.

13

A WEEK INTO the new year. Lisa came in on a Friday evening awkwardly carrying a box of vegetables, a cabbage perched precariously on the top. The kitchen was empty. She was ready to announce her departure, but there was no one to listen. The door into Ruth's room was open, but it too was oddly silent. The kitchen was unusually tidy, no dirty dishes in the sink, no pots on the Aga, no nests of dog hair in the corners. No dog. She lit a cigarette and sat down. It was the first time she had smoked a cigarette in the kitchen.

She had been putting off the return to her cottage in the village. She could have moved back in before Christmas, the roof was done, the attic bedroom habitable, but it wasn't a good time to get used to being alone again. She shouldn't have come to Netherburn, grown accustomed to the movement and sound of people, the ripple of radios in other rooms, the banging of doors. She'd turned forty-six on the third of January, the day after she got back from Yorkshire, driving through the snow-clad Borders with abandoned trucks still at the roadside. She'd not mentioned her birthday. She couldn't face another party, another jolly evening with Ruth as improbable earth mother and Larry's snatches of country and western. She couldn't face the misery of Ros or the chatter of Emma or the indifference of Peter.

So she said nothing, but in the car coming back decided, as she had to, that it was time to leave. The sun came out and the Border hills were dazzling, hill farms, naked trees and stone walls etched darkly against the white, a few cattle and sheep disconsolate in the snow. A tractor laboured slowly across a field pulling a trailer loaded with neaps. She drove through Jedburgh, most of the shops still closed and the town's gutters clotted with grey slush.

Lisa didn't regret her decision to come to Scotland, but there were times when she was overwhelmed with gloom. Ros's misery. She recognised it very well, which was why she couldn't stand being close to it. It was no use looking to Larry to lift the gloom, or to anyone else. With a low hiss she blew cigarette smoke into the clean kitchen. Her dreary constant companion was not going to be shamed into submission by a bottle of wine or a meal cooked by Ruth.

She'd already packed most of her stuff. She had thought that when she told them all she was going they would have suggested a farewell meal together, a last supper. But then, she didn't want that, did she? She put out her cigarette and bit at her nicotine-stained forefinger. She liked Larry, she had to admit. She'd not met anyone else she liked so much, not in a long time. But then, what was the point? He wasn't going to be around for ever. And then she allowed herself to imagine, a flight to New York, the Manhattan skyline, a yellow cab, and some undefined connection with the artist Larry Segal as he revisited old haunts. (And spent time with his ageing mother and aunt in Brooklyn, but that she could not picture.) She leapt ahead. Larry Segal's pictures selling for tens of thousands of dollars, Lisa on his arm in an evening dress, cameras clicking. She laughed. 'Get real, girl,' she said aloud.

Where was everyone? They can't have all gone out and left the door unlocked. She went to the bottom of the stair and listened, but there was no sound. She stood on the back doorstep. It was a clear night, the sky crowded with stars. And then she heard a dog bark and the sound of laughter coming from somewhere at the back of the house, and then she saw lights, and there was Dixie running ahead, and Ros and Peter tossing snowballs at each other, the torch Peter carried swinging wildly, and Larry pulling Emma on a sledge, and Ruth bringing up the rear with another torch.

'We've been sledging in the dark,' shouted a delighted Emma when she saw Lisa at the door.

Peter lobbed a snowball towards Lisa, which landed on the toe of her shoe. Emma followed suit and another snowball, chased by Dixie, landed just inside the open door.

'Okay, Emma, that's enough,' warned her mother. But they were all laughing, all stamping the snow from their boots and shaking it from their woolly hats. Lisa stood aside as they trooped in through the door and pulled off wet jackets and gloves. She followed them into the kitchen.

'Hot soup,' said Ruth.

'I'm off,' Lisa said.

No one responded. Ruth was guddling in the fridge, Peter filling the kettle, Ros arranging wet gloves on the Aga rail.

'I'm off,' Lisa said again.

'Look out for black ice if you're driving,' said Larry.

'Only to the village.'

Now Ruth was chopping onions. She looked up, caught by the unusual quietness of Lisa's voice.

'There'll be soup on the go if you want some later.'

Lisa shook her head. 'I won't be here later.'

This time everyone heard and looked at her. 'I'm off,' she said for the third time. 'This is me away. House is done. I'm moving back.'

'You didn't say you were going,' said Ruth, and 'Kinda sudden,' from Larry at the same time.

'Didn't know until today that it was all done,' Lisa lied. 'And you know, I really can't wait to get back.'

'Have a meal with us first.'

'Thanks, but no. I'm keen to be back in my own home. I'll just go and finish packing.'

When she came downstairs again half an hour later she found them all still in the kitchen, a large pot on the Aga, a bottle of wine open, Larry drawing a picture of reindeer with Emma's crayons. He looked up at Lisa as she stood in the doorway.

'I'll help you with your stuff,' he said, getting to his feet.

'No need, I can manage.'

'Anything else to come down?'

She nodded. Without a word he went upstairs to her room, heaved a rucksack onto his back and picked up a box. He found Lisa out at the car.

'Why the rush?' he asked.

'It's time to go. And anyway, I feel I may have outstayed my welcome.'

'Nah, course you haven't. It's liberty hall here, you know.'

'I've said my goodbyes. I'll have a party at my place sometime, a house re-warming.'

'Sure.'

Larry closed the car boot and they stood side by side. He glanced towards the brightly lit kitchen window and put his hand on Lisa's shoulder.

'So long, then,' he said, 'take care.'

Without a word she turned away and got into the car. He stood and watched the tail lights disappear round the corner. Back inside, everyone was quiet. Emma was colouring in the picture he had drawn. The others sat around the table with glasses of wine in front of them. But Ruth looked up and their eyes met. All he could think of doing was to give a slight shake of his head, but she had no idea what he was trying to convey, and she never asked him. She tried to tell herself that Lisa's departure was no big deal, but remained unconvinced.

The snow melted and by the end of the month the snowdrops were out. Around the back door there lingered a smell of muddy boots and wet dog. Ros started going out on Friday evenings, an end of the week drink with colleagues, she said, and talked of looking for another job, moving away. Ruth insisted that there was no rush, Emma was well settled in school, but she welcomed Ros's change of mood.

'It's been a year, we can't stay here for ever,' Ros said. Ruth thought she was looking better, perhaps even putting on weight.

No one mentioned Martin, or the Easter holiday.

A Sunday in March. Peter found Ruth spreading compost on the vegetable garden, and offered to give her a hand. 'You can fill up the barrow with another load,' she said. She looked round the neglected fringes of the garden, the straggly growth that needed cutting back and the withered stems that deadened the new green shoots. There were daffodils out at the front of the house, and the first daisies open in the grass. Above her, roofing her in, was a heavy grey sky. Dixie lay in the grass under a forsythia that was beginning to show yellow.

Peter returned with a barrow load of dark compost and began shovelling it out. After a few moments he paused.

'I really came out to tell you I've finally made up my mind,' he said.

'Good,' said Ruth, evening out a layer of compost. 'What about?'

'About my future.' Peter laughed. 'Our future. Me and Russell. We're going to look for a place together. We reckon we can afford to buy somewhere.'

Ruth pulled off a gardening glove and pushed her hair out of her eyes. 'That's great, Peter. I'm pleased for you.'

'I won't be leaving straight away. I just wanted you to know.'

Ruth nodded.

'I thought maybe Ros and Emma would like to have the flat.'

'That's an idea.'

'Shall I get another load?'

Ruth nodded again. 'One more should do it.'

When he returned, she asked, 'What have you told your parents?'

'I haven't.'

'They'll need to know, won't they?'

'I guess so.'

'You don't think they'll have worked it out for themselves?'

Peter looked pained and shook his head. 'I'm sure it's not occurred to them. Why should it? I'm a bloke-ish kind of guy, with a motorbike. And I've tried my best not to allow them to know. The last time I saw them I mentioned Ros, on purpose, so they'd think I was keen on her. Better a married woman with a child... They're decent people. They just... don't have the experience, the imagination.'

He crouched down and broke up a clod of earth with his hand. 'They'd blame themselves, they'd think they'd made mistakes.' He stayed close to the ground, looking at the earth on his fingers.'

'What about Russell? His parents, I mean.'

'His sister knows. She's okay. His parents are in Johannesburg and, well, they're not going to be around. They've only ever been once to the UK and don't have plans to come again. Russell reckons they don't need to know. They're teachers, they teach kids who are HIV positive, orphans a lot of them. Russell reckons that they wouldn't just be knocked sideways, but scared.'

Ruth stamped earth from her boots. 'It makes me uncomfortable,' she said. 'I know my own sons have lives about which I know very little, but to be ignorant of something so radical to their existence, to be their mother and unaware... but perhaps I'm not aware and they're like Russell, thinking, mum·doesn't need to know. Maybe not even putting it into words, but just allowing it not to be communicated. That's the way so much misunderstanding happens, isn't it? Things don't get said that should be said.'

'And things get said that shouldn't be. Heat of the moment stuff.'

'We're not very good at it, are we? Communicating, I mean.'

Peter stood up and wiped his hands on his jeans. 'I think you are, Ruth.'

She jabbed her spade firmly into the ground. 'My job is to advise people on ways of conveying the meaning they intend. Doesn't mean I can do it myself. My track record isn't great.'

'You get my vote.'

'Thanks, Peter.' She paused and contemplated the dark rectangle of ground. 'I'm going to miss you. I'll miss having your help.'

'Get Larry to help, the lazy sod.'

Ruth laughed.

'And Russell and I can still come out, give you a hand. We'd like to do that.'

Ruth smiled. She said nothing, but she knew it wouldn't be like that. The focus of their lives would change and gradually Ruth and Netherburn would slip into the margins and then, probably, beyond the margins.

'So what have you got in mind?' she asked. 'Have you started looking?'

So Peter began to tell her, flats, prices, areas, streets. It was getting cold and she was only half listening. She pulled the last of the leeks and parsnips as he was talking, and then they walked together towards the back door, round the corner of the stables, trailed by Dixie. The cloud had thinned to reveal the sun, low and dull.

A few days later a red car came down the track, but there was no one in the house to see it. The driver knew his way round the back. He parked in the yard, got out, stretched. There was no sign of life. He went to the back door and knocked. When there was no response, he banged harder. He stepped away from the door and peered in through the kitchen window, then walked round to the front door, where he knocked again. Still nothing, and no dog barking. He returned round the side of the house, and spotted the French windows. There were a couple of tubs on the terrace with daffodils nearly out. Through the glass he could see a large, rather untidy room, a table piled with books, a computer. He put his hand on the door, breathed on the glass which wasn't very clean, wiped the blur away. He touched the handle, pressed it down, pushed the door. It opened. He saw that the key had been left in the lock and shook his head. Stupid cow.

Once inside the room he could smell wood smoke but there was no fire in the hearth. He walked slowly, quietly through the room. The sofa was piled with shabby cushions where a sleeping grey tabby cat twitched its ear. A large armchair held another cat and some knitting and a pile of papers on its broad arm. Beside the computer were more papers, a cracked mug stuffed with pens and pencils, a stapler, a packet of envelopes, files. Photographs on the mantelpiece. A vase of daffodils on a side table. On the wall opposite the fireplace were bookshelves crammed with books. He went up to them and pulled a book out at random. *Annals of the Parish*, it said, by John Galt. He'd never heard of it. He looked around, then placed the book on the swivel chair drawn up to the computer desk. He smiled, went back to the bookshelf, pulled out another book which he dropped on the floor.

At the door out to the passage he stopped and listened. Not a sound. He went into the kitchen, still moving slowly and silently. There were food smells in the kitchen that he couldn't identify. There was a pan on the Aga with cooked potatoes in it. Half a loaf of bread, a bread knife, a tub of margarine, a jar of peanut butter. At one end of the kitchen table was a pile of mail – envelopes, bills, circulars, a postcard. Two dirty mugs beside the sink, and clean plates and mugs in the dish rack. On a shelf, glass jars filled with rice and beans and lentils. Beneath them sticky-looking bottles of cooking oil, olive oil, wine vinegar. He looked out through the kitchen window into the yard, where his red car was parked in the same place he had parked before. The sun was shining.

He turned away from the window and gazed thoughtfully round the room. A green jacket hung over a chair. His eye fell on a large biscuit tin. He removed the lid, stuck his hand in and grabbed as many biscuits as he could hold and crushed them in his fist and dropped them back into the tin. He shook the crumbs from his hand onto the floor.

He followed the passage to the wide hall at the front of the house. More bookshelves, a hat stand, two chairs. A few crumbs still adhered to his palm and he wiped his hand on the worn upholstery of one of the chairs. Through an open door he could see into the dining room. He could see a shelf crowded with photographs. He went in and picked a faded black and white picture of a man and a woman, the man in uniform standing, the woman sitting with a baby in her arms. He took the photograph into the hall and held it with two fingers away from his body, then let it fall. It lay face down on the discoloured brown carpet. He returned to the dining room, and examined the decanters and candlesticks on the sideboard. One of the decanters had half an inch of pale liquid in it. He opened the sideboard and found a crystal sherry glass, poured the liquid into it, and placed it carefully beside the now empty decanter.

The next door he opened led into a room that was again lined with books. There was a broad desk at the window, with a neat stack of files and a glass paperweight and an ivory box carved with elephants. He picked up the paperweight and tossed it from one hand to another. It would be so easy to lob it through the window. He put it down again, and picked up a plastic wallet stuffed with papers and strewed its contents across the desk. There were filing cabinets, boxes of books, and in the corner of the room a folding bed. A pile of blankets was on a chair beside it. He lifted his foot and pushed the blankets off the chair. They fell slowly to the floor where they lay in a dishevelled, bluish heap.

He made his way up the stairs, pausing to listen again before he opened the first door he came to. There was a double bed with a flowered duvet, several paperbacks, a radio and a telephone on the bedside table, a copy of the *Bookseller* magazine on the floor. A pair of jeans and a grey cable sweater on a chair. A wardrobe with a broken handle. A second chair, very low, covered in dark velvet. A tall chest of drawers with a bowl of dried flowers on the top. Two pictures on the wall, both landscapes. On the dressing table a dish filled with buttons, paperclips, old receipts, a broken comb, a lipstick. Perfume bottles and a cluster of containers of stuff for the face. Five different colours of nail varnish. An enamel pot of pens and pencils and a small notebook. He flipped through the notebook: a shopping list, a memo to phone Antonia Edie, a calculation of expenses. He stood for a moment regarding his reflection in the mirror.

He picked up the lipstick and pulled off the cover. It was a deep claret colour. He swivelled it up and drew a skull and cross bones on the mirror glass, then closed it and carefully returned it to the jumble of objects in the dish.

The next bedroom had an unmade single bed, a clock and one book on the bedside table. There were clothes everywhere. He knew at once whose room this was. On the only chair there were jeans, skirts, pairs of tights, jerseys, a pink blouse. On the top of the stripped pine chest of drawers there was a dense mass of bottles, jars and tubes, a jumble of strings of beads and earrings, one glove, a hair band, a balled-up pair of socks, a box of tissues. In a corner of the room was a tangled heap of shoes. He poked at the jumble of beads but then spotted a pair of earrings on their own. He recognised them, silver, slim and dangling. He'd bought them in Waverley Market, he remembered, a birthday present for her, before they were married. They'd suit her, he'd thought, suit her pale oval face, and there they were. She must still be wearing them. He picked one up and put it in his pocket.

The next door was slightly ajar and he knew before he pushed it open what he would find. Emma's room was tidier than her mother's. Her floppy-eared rabbit was neatly tucked up under a duvet with a *Magic Roundabout* cover. Where had that come from?

Some toys and books were piled on top of a wooden box, a few clothes were on a chair and one sock on the floor. Her blue dressing gown hung on the back of the door. There were pictures on the wall, some of Emma's but others – a futuristic vehicle of some kind and a rather fine drawing of a stag – were signed 'James Montgomery'. On a shelf were more books and a packet of felt-tip pens. He looked around, stretched out his hand to pick up a book, changed his mind, looked intently at a child's picture of a white house in a green field surrounded by trees dotted with red apples. He wanted to tear it from the wall, but pushed his clenched fists into his pockets and turned on his heel.

There were stairs going up to another floor. He paused at the bottom, listening again, breathing in the smell of paint that drifted down. There were three doors at the top of the stairs. The first one he opened was a cupboard, full of boxes and old suitcases, the second was a large light room, no curtains at the open windows, and a smell of paint so strong it made him cough. There were two easels, a table covered in paints and brushes and blotched with colour. Pictures were stacked upright against the walls. On one easel was pinned a large sheet of beige paper with a few charcoal lines that conveyed nothing. On the other was an apparently finished painting. He stared at it, frowning. He could recognise some of the people in it. There were his daughter and his wife, the woman called Ruth, the bearded man who'd hung around at the back door and the younger fellow, the one with the motorbike. His wife and his daughter were smiling. It was a happy picture, and obviously Christmas, but it was wrong, wrong. He looked at the table in the picture, heaped with food and candles and bottles of wine and decorations, and at the scarred, blotched table with its confusion of colours and brushes. He picked up a tube of crimson lake and unscrewed the cap. Those smiling faces. He squeezed a blob of red over the face of his wife, and was about to obliterate that woman Ruth, the cause of it all, when he thought he heard a sound.

He went to the door. Nothing. He went to the window, which looked to the front of the house. There was nothing on the sweep of gravel, nothing in the paddock beyond, just a few sheep in the field, huddled near the gate. A movement caught his eye. There was something at the top of the track, the gate opening, then a motorbike coming through, the gate closing. He threw the tube of crimson lake across the room and ran down two flights of stairs. He'd have to go out the same way he came in – the motorbike would, he knew, be coming to the back yard. He heard it as he slipped through the French windows. He heard the engine cut out, footsteps, a door slamming. He came round the corner of the house, his car key in his hand. He heard a voice calling, muffled, from inside the house. In seconds he was in the car with the engine started on the second turn, reversing, then down the track, that fucking gate, back in the car, another fucking gate, and away. Nothing in the rear view mirror, no motorbike at his heels.

Of course Peter knew who it was. He looked at his watch – just after five o'clock. Where was everyone? Where was Emma? How had the bastard got into the house? The phone rang. He hesitated, then went into the living room and picked up the receiver. It was a woman's voice, wanting Ruth, but no message. Where was Dixie?

It was nearly six before Peter heard the car, and yes, there they all were, Ruth driving, Larry beside her, Ros and Emma and the dog in the back seat. He watched through his kitchen window as they piled out, laughing, wind-blown, and pulled shopping bags from the boot. He went out to meet them.

'We've been to the garden centre,' Emma said, holding up a bag of seed potatoes. 'And we took Dixie for a walk by the river.'

'We'll put everything in the shed,' Ruth said.

'You said I could plant the potatoes.'

'Not today, though.'

Peter waited until everyone was in the house, milling about in the kitchen, and when Emma dashed next door to switch on the television, he said quietly to Ruth, 'You've had a visitor.'

She was opening a tin of dog food. She stopped and looked at Peter, saying nothing.

'I think he must have got in through the French windows. They weren't locked.'

'A burglar?'

Peter shook his head. 'Not exactly.' He glanced at Ros, who was at the sink rinsing out two dirty coffee mugs. 'Come outside for a minute.'

Ruth fed the dog before following Peter along the passage and through the door into his flat. He closed it behind them.

'Martin,' he said.

'Martin? What was he doing here?'

'Good question. I saw his car when I got back, an hour or so ago. I didn't realise there was no one in the house.'

'He was in the house.'

Peter nodded. 'He must have heard me coming. He slipped out and into his car and off before I realised. I've had a look around downstairs but everything seems okay. I was worried at first he might have taken Emma, but figured she wouldn't have been here on her own.'

'No.' Ruth frowned. 'Maybe I won't mention this to Ros.'

'For a split second I thought I might give chase, but thought better of it.' He grinned.

'Thank God for that. Things are difficult enough without you ending up in a ditch.'

'Better have a good look round, though, just in case.'

'He'd be a bloody fool to take anything. He must have known you saw the car.'

On her way back to the kitchen Ruth stopped and retraced her steps to the front hall. She saw straight away the framed photograph face down on the carpet. She picked it up. A slanting crack in the glass bisected the two figures and separated the baby's head from his shawled body. She replaced the picture on the shelf where a slight disturbance of the dust indicated where it had been. Then she saw the glass and the decanter. She opened the door to the study and instantly saw the blankets on the floor and scattered papers on the desk. She might, another time, have thought that she herself had been responsible, hastily looking for something perhaps, or Emma naughtily curious.

Had he been in every room? She was at the foot of the stairs when a shout came from Larry. 'Emma!' he roared. 'What the hell is going on?'

Ruth ran up the stairs, calling out 'Emma, it's okay, it's not your fault, Larry, it's not Emma,' and out of breath when she reached Larry.

'The little vandal...'

'No, Larry, it's not her, it's not her.' Ruth struggled to get the words out.

'The paint's still wet.'

'Let me see.'

'Someone's been up here. You're not going to tell me it was Peter.'

Ruth shook her head, staring at the red blob in the middle of the canvas.

'It was Martin.'

'Martin? That creep? How did he get here?'

'He got in, while we were all out. Peter told me. He's been all over the house, doing stuff. It must have been him.'

'That figures.'

'Can you fix it?'

'Maybe.' They both gazed in silence at the defaced picture.

'It could have been much worse,' Ruth said at last.

'The twisted bastard.'

'I'm sorry.'

'It's not your fault.'

There was a sound behind them and they both turned. Emma stood nervously at the door.

'It's alright Emma,' Ruth said. 'Larry had a problem but it's okay now.'

'Yeah, honey, false alarm.' They stood side by side, blocking her view.

'Oh,' said Emma.

'Come on, let's go downstairs,' Ruth said.

She said nothing when she went into the kitchen, where Ros was making supper for her and Emma.

'Everything alright?' Ros asked.

'Everything's fine. False alarm.'

Ruth looked warily round the kitchen, but could see nothing out of place. She went into the living room where Emma sat in front of the TV. Ruth scanned the mantelpiece, the table, desk, bookshelves. The cats slumbered as usual. There was a book face down on her desk chair but she thought nothing of it. Later, she picked it up and wondered who'd been looking at *Annals of the Parish*. Maybe Larry, who sometimes idly patrolled the shelves and pulled out books here and there. Then she saw a book on the floor, but that, too, was not unusual. She picked it up and replaced it.

It was more than an hour before she thought of the other bedrooms. Ros and Emma were eating in the kitchen. Ruth slipped upstairs and into their rooms. There was nothing obviously wrong. Then into her own room. She saw the skull and cross bones at once, and felt sick. The thought of him in her bedroom. She sat on her bed and covered her face with her hands.

Several days later Ros could find only one silver earring. She emptied out the box where she kept bits and pieces of jewellery, and got down on her hands and knees to look under the bed. It was easy to lose earrings, and she didn't mention her loss to anyone. She thought it would turn up, at the back of a drawer probably.

'He wants her over Easter.' Martin had phoned Ros at the school, where she had to speak to him in the office with the secretary and the head teacher both present. He would have known that there would be no privacy. She could do nothing but reply in dull monosyllables.

He arranged to pick Emma up on the first Monday of the school holidays. As he had calculated, there was no motorbike parked in the yard. Peter was at work. Emma was ready, with her bag packed and her rabbit and her bike. There was no sign of Ruth or the guy with a beard, just Ros, shoulders hunched in spite of her efforts to look unconcerned. He looked at Ros on the doorstep and couldn't help smiling. As if she could keep him out, as if he didn't know what lay inside, all the rooms, all the little messages he'd left. She doesn't realise, the stupid cow, and he found himself almost regretting that he hadn't left a sign that no one could possibly have missed. That bastard with the bike, he must have kept it to himself.

It was while Emma was away that quite late one evening Ros knocked at the door of Ruth's room and slowly opened it. Ruth was sitting at her desk in front of the computer screen. Ros apologised. 'I didn't think you'd still be working.'

'That's okay.'

'I didn't mean to interrupt.'

'Hang on a tick. I just need to enter this correction... and mark where I've got to. There. Now. What's up?' She sat back in her chair and looked at Ros with a smile.

Still standing, Ros was staring at her feet.

'Have you got a minute?' she finally asked.

'Sit down.'

She sat on the edge of the sofa, upright, her hands clenched on her lap. 'I'm pregnant.'

'Good grief. How did you manage that?'

'I met someone.'

'So I assume.'

'He's nice, I like him, I can talk to him about things, about Martin...'

'Does he know?'

'He's been offered a deputy head's job. It's hopeless. That's how it happened, we went for a drink to celebrate.'

'You can get a divorce.'

'Martin won't, I know he won't.'

Ruth got up from her desk and went to her capacious, cat-filled chair. She heaved the cats to one side and sat down.

'Ros, there's no doubt about his cruelty.'

'It's his word against mine.'

'I'm really sorry.'

'My life is such a mess. I don't know what to do.'

'Do you want the baby?'

'We always meant to have another child, me and Martin. That was the plan – he had it all worked out. A two-year gap, he said. But I couldn't. I told him I'd stopped taking the pill but I had them hidden in my underwear drawer. I did want another child but I couldn't. It got worse after Emma started school. Sometimes I thought he was punishing me for not getting pregnant.'

'Do you want the baby, Ros?' Ruth repeated quietly.

'How can I?'

'I'd help you out – we all would.'

'He'd kill me.'

'I don't suppose you've seen a doctor?'

Ros shook her head.

'Make an appointment. If you're going to have a termination, the sooner the better. If you're not, you need proper care.'

'I know.'

'Don't hang about, Ros. You'll only make things worse.'

'I know.'

'I'll come with you, if you like.'

Ros bit her lip and tears began to spill down her face. 'I have to leave here. I can't go on expecting other people to prop me up. I must learn… I really need… to be independent, to look after myself. How can I look after Emma if I can't look after myself?'

'Look, Ros,' Ruth said briskly. 'Let's take things one step at a time. Let's get the immediate problem sorted out first and then think about the future. Apart from anything else, how can you think straight at the moment?'

'I can't. But I have to. How can I take a decision like this if I'm not thinking straight?'

She leant her head against the back of the sofa and dabbed at her eyes with a scrap of tissue. 'I'm not sure I've ever been able to think straight. There's always been somebody else pulling the strings. I married Martin to please my mother, I know that now. I went to bed with Stuart because he was nice to me. It wasn't even all that great but the niceness was lovely. But for a child to come out of that…'

'Why not? Kindness is a good start.'

'Yes, but… it's not love, is it? It's not two committed parents deciding to have a child.'

'Were you and Martin two committed parents deciding to have a child?'

'I don't know... yes, I think we were. He was alright then. The first time he... lost it was after Emma was born, when she wouldn't stop crying, and he grabbed me, not her, thank God, he was always good with her, but me, and shook me so hard I bit my lip, because I couldn't keep her quiet. He yelled at me, that I was a rotten mother, useless. My mouth was bleeding, he said I was a freak.' She shut her eyes and pulled at the shredded tissue in her lap. 'That's how it all started.' She opened her eyes and stared up at the ceiling. 'It was a while before he actually hit me. But in a way the shaking was worse. There was such anger, so... so fierce, so intense. His eyes. I've never been more scared.'

'You need to decide, Ros.'

'Do you think Emma will grow up with this notion, a loving partnership, a family, a nice house?'

'It's very persistent. She probably will. We collude in keeping that illusion alive, in spite of ourselves.'

'You don't, Ruth.'

'I wish that were true... but if I'm honest, what do I want for my sons? I want them to settle down. I want them to have warmth and happiness and security. I want to be a grandmother. It's hard to add all that up and not come up with a pretty conventional image of their future. They've been brought up in a so-called broken home with unconventional, maybe unreliable, role models, but it's difficult to get away from an idea of fulfilment that isn't a stereotype.'

'I imagine a world without Martin. I imagine him dead. I imagine a phone call, a knock on the door, and a voice saying, "He's been in an accident..."'

There was a long silence.

'And Emma. What's she going to think? I'll end up one of those mothers with a load of kids, each with a different father. She's more likely to grow up cynical, or repeat the pattern.' Ros's voice was a tearful drone.

'It's Easter Sunday,' said Ruth.

'So what?'

'Regeneration. New life.'

'So you think I should have the baby?'

'I'm not saying that, only that whatever you decide, think of it as a new beginning.'

'Killing a baby isn't a beginning.'

'If that's how you think of it, you'd better not do it.'

'That's the point, Ruth. Can't you see? I don't know how I think of it. I don't feel anything except fear. When I found I was pregnant with Emma I felt transformed.'

'Yes. Me too, with the boys. But the circumstances were completely different.' Ruth got up from her chair. 'I'll make some tea.'

'I don't want bloody tea.'

'I'm not going to offer you a glass of wine.' Ruth sat down again. A cat stretched out a paw with open claws, which snagged on her sweater. It started to purr loudly. 'Ros, I'll do whatever I can, but I can't decide for you.'

'I just want someone to tell me I'm doing the right thing.'

'You have to make the decision first.'

'Emma often says she'd like a little brother or sister.' She pushed her hair back from her face. 'I'd have to find somewhere to go, somewhere safe. Not my mother's.'

'Why not?'

'I'd be another failure. I couldn't live with her disappointment.'

'What about your sister?'

'Waste of time.' She crushed small scraps of damp tissue in her fist. 'And a job. I'd need a job.' She looked up helplessly at Ruth and began to shake her head. 'I can't do it. It's no good. It's just a fantasy. I can't do it.'

Three weeks later Ruth drove Ros home from the clinic. Her face was thin, cheekbones like ridges, and sitting next to Ruth in the car her legs were trembling. It was a bright, warm spring day, the leaves not yet fully out on the trees but the Lothian hills freshly green. Ros had her eyes fixed on the road ahead, and appeared not to notice the lambs or the pink splash of rhododendrons by the canal bridge. At Netherburn the apple blossom was out.

Peter was packing and he only briefly wondered why Ros was emerging from Ruth's car in the middle of a Thursday afternoon. His living room was full of boxes. He and Russell would soon be moving into their Dalry flat. Ros got unsteadily to her feet and held onto the car door for a moment before stepping carefully to the house. Ruth carried her bag. She would explain to everyone that Ros had flu. She'd be fine in a couple of days.

Ros had said nothing to Stuart, and did not invite him to Netherburn or introduce him to her daughter. She had agreed that she and Emma would move into the flat when Peter left, but probably not for long, she said. She examined the map and made a list of places where she'd look for jobs – Campbeltown, Wick, Stornoway, Kirkwall, anywhere so long as it is far away.

The Saturday that Peter moved out it rained and a gusty wind scattered the apple blossom. Peter and Russell filled their borrowed van with boxes, hi-fi equipment, television, a rucksack, bin bags packed with clothes and bedding. Ruth and Emma made coffee and sandwiches, and they all ate lunch in the big kitchen. Ros was still pale with little appetite. 'We've scrubbed the flat from top to bottom,' Peter told her. 'It's all ready for you.'

Emma prised apart a sandwich she had helped to make and peered suspiciously at the contents.

'I want to sleep in my new room tonight, mum,' she said. Ros didn't reply.

'Shall we move your stuff down before we leave?' Peter offered.

Ros didn't seem to hear. 'Oh yes please,' said Emma.

'It's okay, Peter,' Ruth said quickly. 'There's no rush. We can do it gradually. You and Russell concentrate on getting yourselves settled.'

'But I want to sleep in my new room tonight.'

'That's fine, Em. You get together what you need and we'll sort you out.'

After Peter and Russell left Ruth went into the empty flat, and it was indeed clean, every surface spotless. But it was dingy, the walls in need of fresh paint, the curtains faded. There was a cracked window pane in the bathroom and the carpet in the small living room was stained and shabby. She went from room to room, absorbing the emptiness, the absence of Peter's magazines and records, the posters gone from the walls, leaving pale rectangles. The small bedroom, the room that would be Emma's, with only a bed and chair, but the bed was made up and two boxes were neatly stacked beside it. On the pillow was a blue bear, its head askew as if it were trying to see out of the window, with a tartan ribbon. It made the room seem all the more cheerless and threadbare.

Footsteps clattered down the uncarpeted back stair. It was Emma, of course. She burst in with an armful of clothes and books, and came to a sudden halt at the door when she saw Ruth standing by the window in the empty room.

'There's nowhere to put things,' she said, disappointed.

'We need to sort out some more furniture,' Ruth said. 'But look, look on the bed. There's something for you.'

Emma opened her arms and let their contents tumble onto the bed, and reached for the blue bear. She sat down, saying nothing. She untied the ribbon and tied it on again, turned the bear's head, straightened its legs and stood it on her knee.

'Is it from Peter?' she asked.

'Must be.'

'I'll call him Blue.'

Ruth wasn't prepared for the sudden loss that engulfed her. Her own daughter appeared, distant, fugitive, as if a curtain had been blown aside at a window to reveal a shadow, then fallen into place again. A vanished baby. Ros. Emma kissed the blue bear.

14

ANTONIA EDIE REQUIRED Ruth to come to her flat in Glasgow's Woodlands Drive so she could hand over in person the completed revision of the life and times of Millie Anderson. Ruth could tell that Antonia wanted to meet on her own ground. Ruth had a book on her lap, but stared out of the window as the train rattled through the Lothian countryside, lit by pale sunshine after morning rain. Cattle, sheep, a knot of Shetland ponies, a tractor labouring up a sloping field. At Falkirk two young girls got on, shouting, screaming for no apparent reason, and threw themselves into seats across the aisle from Ruth, where they collapsed into giggles. She read a page of a short story about teenagers in Craigmillar. Soon they were passing Glasgow's outlier tower blocks.

She was curious to glimpse how Antonia Edie lived. She had learnt at least something of how Millie Anderson had lived. Both women had entered her life. She had thought often of them, as she waited for her author to complete her task.

Ruth climbed the stairs to Antonia Edie's first-floor flat and was ushered into a faded but spacious front room. She was wearing a soft pink sweater and pale grey trousers and looked leaner and no less severe than before. She held her head back, her chin up. Ruth had made an effort to dress the part of a professional, but felt disadvantaged by Antonia's elegance. There were two armchairs and a low table by the window from which there was a glimpse of trees just breaking into leaf. Antonia gestured towards a chair and disappeared to make tea. She returned with a tray of bone china, a silver teapot and a plate of Florentines. A neat pile of typescript was already on the table.

'There it is,' she said, pouring tea. 'I have tried to accommodate your comments, most of them at least. Some were just not acceptable.'

'Fair enough,' Ruth said. 'I hope it wasn't too much work.'

'It was a great deal of work, but if it means that the world will appreciate the life and work of Millie Anderson, it will have been worthwhile.'

Ruth smiled. 'I don't know about the world, but Scotland would be a start.'

There was no answering smile from Antonia. 'In my view, she has world stature.'

'Lorna Hunter is still interested in an edition of her poems.'

Antonia nodded. 'I have, as you suggested, removed some of my original quotations, on the understanding that the collected poems would be published. The love poems must be made available, and the poems she wrote as war approached – the second war, I mean. The ambivalence she expresses, the premonition of loss, alongside her hatred of fascism.'

'No easy answers,' said Ruth.

'There never are,' said Antonia, pressing her lips together and regarding Ruth with an expression that suggested disapproval that she could have for a moment entertained the notion of easy answers. She poured tea into white cups patterned with pale green. With her teacup in her hand she leant back in her chair. 'Millie Anderson was an inspiring figure.'

'That's why we're keen to get your book out,' Ruth said, smiling again. She glanced down at the page at the top of the heap in front of her. The opening hadn't been changed. Millie Anderson still made her way through the dusk along a rainy street not so very far from where they were sitting. She was going to marry Archie. She was going to share everything, her hopes, the poems she had begun to write, her body, all the ordinary everyday things, with Archie. That high-cheekboned face, the light brown hair, the grey eyes, the low but sturdy voice, his desire to heal, would be with her for the rest of her life. And that's what happened, in spite of later loves.

As war approached for the second time she wrote poems about his eagerness to go to France, to face, he said, 'the real thing'. That was the title of one of her most striking poems, 'The Real Thing', where she suggested that the reality was Archie's conviction, his commitment to healing, rather than the putrescent wounds and butchered limbs he had to deal with. But in other poems she retrospectively reproved him. The torn bodies of soldiers were, she said, no more real than the diseased bodies in Glasgow's hospitals. There was just as much reality at home. And in one of her poems, written a quarter of a century after the fact, she tries to persuade him: *The need for healing here is just as great.*

The line had stayed with Ruth. *The need for healing.*

Antonia was speaking. 'I don't think she ever forgave the war, the first war. She never forgave the circumstances that took Archie to France. There is anger as well as loss in those poems. Yet she knows you can't hold circumstances responsible, or individuals. I thought I'd make that clear.'

Ruth nodded. 'It's a coalescence, isn't it? Time, place, events, people. Which is why "what if" never gets you very far, fascinating though it is.'

The tension pinching Antonia's face softened. She herself was not sure if she could forgive the intrusion into her book, the interference, but she wasn't stupid, this oddly insubstantial woman who sat in her front room drinking tea. She pushed the plate of Florentines towards Ruth.

'She falls in love with a married man but she continues a conversation with her first love for the rest of her life.'

'Perhaps it had to be a married man, a man who could never be hers. Perhaps Archie was always in the way. She could love another man, sleep with another man – you don't suggest that there was ever sex with Archie – but she could not in the end set aside her commitment to her first love. I think a couple of her poems might be about that.'

Antonia said, after a long pause and as if the words came with difficulty, 'It's hard to hand it over.'

'I know. A lot of authors feel like that. They want their books to be read but they don't want to relinquish them.'

'I suppose it's what's called an "empty nest" feeling,' Antonia said with an acerbic laugh. 'Not that I have children, but I think I know what it means.' Her voice had softened. She ate a Florentine, meditatively. 'Do you have children?'

'I have three sons.'

'You're lucky there are no wars to take them away from you.'

'Yes. There are other things, of course, but no war, thank God. At least not now, not yet.'

'Millie has a poem where she thanks God for having no sons. Loss is worse than absence, she says.'

'Do we know anything about Archie's parents?'

'Only what's there in the book: that his father was also a doctor, and he had an elder brother who was wounded at Gallipoli. But I wasn't able to find out what happened to him. They were an Ayrshire family.'

'Lorna will send a contract,' Ruth said as she was leaving, 'sort out all the details. If all goes smoothly publication could be next spring.'

Antonia Edie inclined her head as she stood, tall and upright, with one hand on the door. She remained there until she heard the outer door bang shut.

Ruth travelled back on the train in the early evening. The setting sun lit up the fields between Falkirk and Linlithgow, but she didn't notice. She was reading again about Millie Anderson. It was better. There were still some heavy passages of explanation and background, but most of the obstacles to the narrative had been removed and Millie's story was to the fore. Ruth read the first chapter, then went to the end, to Millie's last years, when she was ill, when Charlie Reid's wife Frances was also ill. There were no more walks in Alexandra Park or visits to Arran. Frances Reid died almost exactly a year after Millie, and Charlie spent the last twelve years of his life alone. His daughter discovered letters from Millie, which he had unwisely left on the coffee table in the room that was exactly as his late wife had arranged it. He wrote in a sporadically kept journal: 'Catherine has read Millie's letters, which I stupidly left lying around. I had to tell her everything.' His daughter never saw him again; his son had gone to Canada in the 1950s.

Ruth found herself thinking about Antonia Edie, the sort of life she had led, what had driven her to write about her not-so-close relation Millie Anderson, what it was that connected them, other than probably much diluted blood. The flat in Woodlands Drive was well appointed, comfortable, but slightly dingy, genteel but faded. Yet Antonia herself was not faded, and less genteel than Ruth had at first thought. She found herself thinking, to her surprise, that she would like to get to know her better. No doubt she would, as she steered *The Life and Times of Millie Anderson* through the press. She hoped that Antonia would grow less hostile to Ruth's intervention – there were signs that she was already relenting.

But Ruth knew she would have to be careful. She normally did not find it hard to keep her distance from the books she edited, however engaging the subject or compelling the writing. Millie Anderson was different. The life of a dead and forgotten woman, whose poetry she had never known existed, had in some way got under her skin. And perhaps Antonia Edie realised that. It was her achievement, but at the same time Ruth knew she could feel threatened. It would not do to allow the author to feel that ownership of the book was shared. It's your book, she had wanted to say, but didn't. It's your book. I'm just helping it along. It was getting dark when she got off the train at Linlithgow and walked briskly to where the car was parked. She got into the car and sat for a few moments before turning the key in the ignition. Dead and forgotten. How easy that was, and how unlikely that someone would come out of the future and rescue the dead from oblivion.

Who now remembered Andrew Cameron, apart from his three children, and two of them with some reluctance? Who in fifty years would acknowledge the work of Professor Fay Cameron?

Ruth had not realised how accustomed she had grown to the sounds of Ros and Emma in the rooms next to hers. She no longer heard them getting up in the morning, the murmur of their voices, the flush of the toilet, drawers opened, a shoe dropped, Emma running down the stair. They were no longer in the kitchen when Ruth went down. When she opened the back door to let Dixie out she would see signs of activity in the flat and acknowledged that it was better for Ros and Emma to cope on their own, but the silent space first thing in the morning was hard to get used to. The house seemed to expand, the furniture to shrink. Larry in his attic seemed a great distance away.

And now, with so much of the house to herself, Ros and Emma would not be aware of footsteps on the stair late at night or in the early morning. She would have no need to be furtive in her own home. She watched Ros leave for the early bus and a few minutes later Emma was at the kitchen door ready for school. Ruth and Dixie still walked her up to the top gate. Ruth left her tea half drunk. She was slow that morning.

Altogether slow. It was over a week since Ros and Emma had installed themselves in the flat. Ruth realised she had expected Larry to seek her out, to appear some evening with a bottle of wine, to entice her all over again. But she'd hardly seen him. He'd been out a lot, with his camera, taking advantage of the May sunshine, walking or on the bus, she wasn't sure. He hadn't asked to borrow the car. She ambled slowly back down the track. A group of cows were clumped in the far corner of the field. The house stood white and solid in its green space, a swathe of withered daffodils in front and a deep purple lilac at the side. Her bedroom window was open and a breeze stirred the curtain. Dixie ran in front and waited for her to open the lower gate. The bright sunshine exposed the flaking paint on the window frames and the discoloured varnish on the front door.

She didn't know she was being watched. Larry was at the attic window. He had seen the three of them walk up to the road, and the school bus stop, and then Ruth and the black and white dog making their way back down. He had seen Ruth pause and scan the front of the house and had stepped back from the window, but not so far that he couldn't still see out. She reached the gate and opened it for Dixie, closed it carefully behind her, and paused again.

It seemed a long time since that night in the snow, and that second night they had taken the sledge out under the stars, when they'd all been intoxicated by Emma's shrieks of laughter, when Lisa left, and late, when everyone else had gone to bed, he and Ruth had for the second time stretched out on cushions in front of the fire and made love, with the cats on the chair and the dog lying quietly a few feet away, and listening all the time for footsteps or the sound of an opening door. But he had felt safe.

Perhaps too safe. Now he knew that he worked best when some inner fear throbbed like a half-healed wound, and the temptation of Netherburn, the lure of its sturdy if decrepit walls and its hearth and food on the table, the temptation of Ruth, were things that perhaps he had to resist. If he gave in, if he accepted that comfort was possible, it would be a denial of his past, a past that he did not know, that he did not think about, but had driven him from the time when his mother and Aunt Rosa had overheard him telling his pal Bernard that his daddy was coming on a big ship and they would all go to meet him at the Statue of Liberty and bring him home. He had this notion, as a small boy, that the Statue of Liberty was the arrival point of everyone who came to the United States of America, that she welcomed them, bent down to take them into the safety of her embrace. And then his daddy would be safe, released from the arms of Liberty into the arms of his family, his child and the mother of his child.

And they had argued fiercely, his mother and aunt, behind the closed kitchen door. He has a right to know, said one. It will only upset him, said the other, there is no need.

He was eleven before he summoned the courage to ask his aunt (not his mother). What happened to my father? And she told him that they did not know for sure, that he had not come to the place where they were to meet, Hannah pregnant though she did not know it yet, and Rosa the elder sister, but they must have picked him up as he made his way to meet his fiancée and her sister. They. Hannah had seen him the night before.

'What was his name?'

'His name?'

'What was my father's name?'

Aunt Rosa was sitting at the kitchen table spread with oilcloth. There was a bowl of pansies on the table, and two blue cups. Larry always remembered that, the white and violet and yellow of the pansies in a glass bowl, and the smooth blue cups. Aunt Rosa looked up towards the window and the grey sky beyond.

'His name was Lev. Lev Eisler.'

He knew a family called Eisler, they lived at the other end of the street. He'd sometimes played baseball with the two sons, who were older than he was and only let him play when they needed a catcher. But Aunt Rosa shook her head, as if reading his thoughts. He was relieved, as Mr Eisler was a heavy man with a scowl and dirty fingernails and Mrs Eisler was always shouting at her many children and whenever he passed their house the radio was on very loud.

'Was he killed?'

'Yes, sweetheart, he was killed.'

'How do you know?'

'Because he never came. He never came to America. He never came to look for the girl he was going to marry and the son he didn't know he had. He never came, sweetheart, that's how we know he died.'

'But he might come. He might have... they might have put him in prison or something, by mistake. Or he might have lost his memory. We should go look for him.'

'How can we do that, my love? Do you know how much it costs to go to Europe? No, of course you don't. Believe me, we cannot go to Europe. And your mother... it would be hard, even if we had money. Do you understand? One day maybe you'll understand.'

That was the constant refrain. One day, when you're older, you'll understand, and it left him empty and cheated, as if there was something just out of reach which was denied him. For a while he drew pictures, a man in uniform, a gun in his hand, on the deck of a ship, in a jeep like photographs he had seen of General Eisenhower. He gave him blue eyes like his own. Then he stopped. When he was fifteen he began to draw again, but there were no people in his pictures.

He said to Ruth, as they lay in front of the fire with their arms around each other, 'They always told me that when I was older I would understand, but I don't think I will ever understand. And when I think there were thousands, millions of children whose fathers and mothers disappeared, still are, fathers and mothers still disappearing. When I think that I never see my own daughter. How can that have happened? How can any of it have happened? How can I have been such a lousy father?' Ruth said nothing, but held him close and breathed in the warmth of his skin and the smell of wood smoke.

And now, months later, she tried to remember all that they had said to each other, what she had said to him that might have scared him off, opened up a distance that she did not recognise. Perhaps it was all a mistake, but it was too late now, too late to pretend that she was not filled with a forgotten longing, not just to give, to nourish as she had always done, but to receive, to be cherished.

'I want to marry you,' Ed had said. 'I want to look after you.' How wonderful, to be looked after by a tall, strong man, a man with ambition and energy. And her mother, did she begin by wanting to be looked after? And then learned, in the war years, that that was not, after all, what she needed? They were shocking, those last months, when she was helpless and beyond the reach of independence.

Their wedding photos, Ruth and Ed, she so slight and small and smiling, he tall beside her, his arm around her waist, protective, possessive. She had long ago removed them from the dresser, but had left her parents in the front hall, he in uniform, she in a dark dress and arching hat, holding flowers rather primly, both serious, as if conscious that at any moment a bomb might fall out of the sky. She was glad that Martin had missed that photograph, and chosen the other one, with Michael as a baby, back in the dining room now with the glass still cracked.

Ruth and Larry. She could not help herself. What on earth would they be wearing? Ruth in a smart outfit, Larry in a suit? But the picture that inhabited her mind was Ruth in something silk, wide trousers, a floating scarf, and Larry in an embroidered waistcoat that perhaps came from Hungary, and fiddlers playing gypsy music and Scottish reels and hectic klezmer. Walking in the fields with Dixie, the picture made her laugh out loud, but was seductive nonetheless.

Larry still watched her. She had stopped for some unaccountable reason, before disappearing round the corner of the house, looking at the ground, her hands in her pockets. Then she stooped to pick something up. What did she want, he wondered, what was missing deep inside that self-containment? Probably not anything that he could supply, but the fact that he was painting as never before, half-finished pictures, photographs pinned on the wall competing for attention. Painting people, but uneasy, as if it were some kind of betrayal, as if he was letting go of something essential to who and what he was. A crayoned drawing for a little girl – the first step towards domesticity? Had he drawn pictures for his own little girl? Why could he not remember?

Here he was, not yet nine o'clock in the morning, with a paint brush in his hand. The silent house seemed to buzz with energy, which was odd considering how empty it was. They were leaving, one by one. Ros would go soon, he was sure of that. She was looking more pale and haunted than ever and it was probably best that she should go, a new start. After all, he'd done just that, and in a way it had worked.

He was looking now at the cattle moving in a slow resigned diagonal across the field. Perhaps he should start painting cows. They were strung out in single file, the leading beast with an apparent objective, its head low, dipping slightly. When Larry looked back to where Ruth had been standing by the corner of the house, she was gone.

The whole of the empty house was between them, Ruth downstairs at her desk, Larry in the attic at his easel. She was writing an email to the author of a book on road-building in Scotland. It was a long and dense book, thorough, careful, the product of meticulous research. It could be a better book, she had no doubt of that, but was it worth the effort to make it so? The information would all be there, between two covers. Was it important to make it easier for the reader? At one time she would have said yes without hesitation. Now she began to wonder if anyone, writer or reader, really cared about the way words were arranged on the page. Then she thought of Millie Anderson. Readers would surely care about her words, and the words of the woman who had made her life known.

Larry was painting a face, a folded, lined and melancholy face that resided constantly inside his head. A face he had not seen for three years. The photographs he had were old, a much younger woman in a smart suit, smiling uncertainly. He couldn't remember where it was taken. Going back even further, a woman and a small boy at Central Park Zoo. And two women, both grey-haired, sitting by a window with the light blanking out part of their faces, not white, but a cloudy grey. That was what he was trying to achieve, lined, unsmiling, but also cloudy and obscure. The sense of loss. But how much did she feel it? How much was he projecting onto the flesh that was closest to his own? Why had Hannah and Rosa never married? He had no memory of suitors, except perhaps one, now that he thought of it, an older man with a moustache who sat in the kitchen sometimes and drank tea with lemon and ate with relish the slightly stale cheese kuchen Rosa brought back from the bakery. Which of the sisters did he have his eye on?

Larry had said to Ruth, why don't you write yourself, instead of messing about with other people's words? She had laughed. 'Messing about with other people's words is my profession.'

'Is that what you said when you were small – when I grow up I want to mess about with other people's words?'

'I liked books.'

'That's not an answer.'

'Did you always want to paint?'

'I guess I did, but I didn't always know I did.'

Larry put down his brush and wiped his hands on his jeans. It wasn't right. Maybe he was on the wrong tack after all. Propped under the window was a half-finished picture of the pier at Queensferry, almost abstract, the canvas filled with irregular, misshapen, discoloured blocks of stone with the barest hint of water beyond. He needed to go back to it. He had an exhibition coming up, and that was the kind of picture people were expecting, that was what Larry Segal did. Beside it was one that was ready, a surprisingly neat and elegant signature in the corner, a picture of a cavernous derelict lime kiln with nettles at its entrance and willow herb growing out of crevices in the stone. He could remember the smell, a charred, musty smell. Thirty pictures at least, they were expecting.

Ruth continued to wrestle with whether and how to say that she would like to make the book more readable. She did not know the author, so could not gauge the impact of her comments. It was always tricky, this initial contact with an author, to whom she was a shadowy and insignificant figure whose role was to ensure that every word was correctly spelt. Sometimes she never met the writer of the work she sweated over. It was not always possible to get through, as she felt she had with Antonia Edie, the barrier of suspicion.

She wished that painting was not so silent an activity, that she could hear the sound of Larry working, and know for sure that colour was going on canvas. Her computer's hum and the keyboard's subdued rattle would never make their way upstairs. Larry would not hear the ring of the telephone or the sound of her voice as she answered it or addressed the cats who sprawled as usual on the chair or Dixie who lay on the hearth. He would not hear her go into the kitchen to make coffee. Under the same roof they occupied their different worlds and did not communicate.

15

THERE WAS AN envelope with a typed address and an Oxford postmark. It did not occur to Ruth that it might be from Michael, although she knew no one else in Oxford. Michael did not write letters. She picked it up along with a brown package (typescript, she knew) and a circular from an insurance company. She slit the envelope open with a kitchen knife and pulled out a typewritten sheet of paper. Balliol College, it said at the top, 'Hope you are keeping well. All the best, Michael', it said at the bottom. She sat down to read it.

Michael wrote that he thought it would be a good idea if he came up to Scotland 'to sort out a few things'. If it would suit Ruth, he'd come when term was over, just for a day or two. He would be on his own – Julia was taking the children to her parents for a week.

Michael. She hadn't seen him for – how many years? She couldn't remember how old the children were, her niece and nephew, although she always sent them book tokens on their birthdays. And Michael's eldest, Ruth remembered her birthday too, though she was grown up now, a little older than Sam and probably no longer living with her mother.

But it would be good to see him. She had said that to Alex, and she meant it. She did not like this distance and apparent indifference, and she was pleased that a move to bridge it – if that's what it was – had been made by Michael. She might ring Alex, suggest that he and Sheena came at the same time, a family reunion.

It was early June – the end of term could not be far away. She went into the garden and made her familiar patrol through the vegetable plot. The lettuce were a good size now, the peas and beans growing tall and showing the first flowers, baby turnips ready to pull. And the end of term might bring Ewan home, although he had said nothing of his plans when they had last spoken on the phone. But then there was Larry.

'Why don't we have a night out?' Larry had said, passing her on the stair. 'Go to the movies.'

Ruth looked out of the window at the turn of the stair, at the sky intermittently blue and the shredded cloud. On the first day of the year they had gone through the back gate and down to the burn, edged with ice, and across the shoogly bridge and up the slope leaving parallel lines of footprint and Dixie's meandering trail in the snow. They stood in the light of a three-quarter moon, everything bright and breathlessly still. Ruth moved ahead so she could see down over the sloping fields and past the dark trees to the firth. Larry came up behind her and placed his hands on her shoulders. They stood like that for many minutes, until Larry took a step to stand beside her, and Ruth half turned towards him. Dixie stopped rolling in the snow, scrambled to her feet and shook herself. They had their arms around each other, on the ridge, with the house, white on white, half a mile away on one side, and the broad silver ribbon of water a mile away on the other.

They walked back, their gloved hands linked, their breath feathering the cold air. Inside, Ruth slid off her jacket and knelt in front of the dying fire. She gently stirred it back to life and laid another log on the embers. Larry knelt beside her, his hand on the back of her neck, his fingers slipped inside her collar, cold at first but slowly warming. They made a nest of cushions, the whole of the empty house rose above them. It's been a long time, Ruth could not help thinking, as she explored the familiar yet unknown contours of a man's body, and felt ribs and hip bones beneath the flesh. Seven years since that last brief, bruising affair with a lawyer called Aidan, whose pale, high-ceilinged New Town flat repelled her. How did she do it, with three teenaged boys, Sam waiting for exam results and learning to drive, James morosely in love with a girl called Benita, and Ewan growing visibly, it seemed, crashing into the furniture unable to control his lanky limbs. How did she manage, for five spring and summer months, six months, to have meals in expensive restaurants with Aidan, whose aftershave drifted down the Heriot Row stairwell, and in whose king-sized bed she felt awkward yet needy? To go to the opera and drink champagne? She bought new clothes on Aidan's account. She spiked her hair. She remembered Festival time, driving home at two in the morning, checking that the boys were present and correct before creeping to her own bed. Aidan never came to Netherburn, of course.

The fire was burning now, and warmed a small semi-circle of space where she lay half-naked, remembering Aidan with Larry's breath on her thighs, Aidan whose love-making was quick and slick, and who, on a damp September day when the leaves were falling, the week Sam began his first term at university, when James and Ewan were resistantly back at school, phoned first to cancel a mid-week lunch and then to say he had to work in Inverness. She did not hear from him again. It took months to regain some sort of equilibrium. It's just not worth it, she said to Lorna, who agreed that Aidan was a mistake. But when a well-heeled, personable young man showed interest in an older woman – and that's what she was now, there was no escaping that – the chances were that love was easy to invent. Not so easy, though, to deconstruct. Larry. Another kettle of fish altogether?

And that same September James was sent home from school because he was wearing jeans with ragged tears at the knees and she received a screaming phone call from the mother of a boy Ewan had allegedly kicked. Yes, Ewan eventually admitted, he did, but the other boy had started it. 'If that's all the trouble they get into,' Lorna said, 'you're getting off lightly.' The yelling, the slammed doors. Sam had once disappeared for twenty-four hours. James was set upon by football casuals and Ruth had to take him to hospital at one in the morning. She waited while the gash in his forehead was stitched up. The scar remained. Across from her a young woman with a bruised face sat with her head back and her eyes closed and a sleeping child on her knee.

Lorna did not know about Larry. How could Ruth describe what was happening now? And would happen again, a few days later, with everyone back at Netherburn, love-making again in front of the fire but this time the house not empty, and although it was after midnight and there was no sound, both of them tense in expectation of intrusion. And now months had passed, and the house was almost empty.

'What do you reckon?' asked Larry. 'My treat.'

Ruth was watching the clouds, moving slowly like almost be-calmed ships, and said without looking at him, 'That would be nice.'

Ruth went to meet Michael at the airport. She stood half-hidden by a pillar, watching as people trickled out of the arrivals gate and paused to get their bearings before heading for the baggage claim or spotting a familiar face. The trickle became a solid clump, then thinned out again, then a gap and finally Michael, on his own. If she had had to pick him out of a crowd she might have had difficulty. Tall, though not as long-limbed as she remembered, slightly stooped, and he'd grown a neat beard. His glasses were different, narrow and rimless. His hair was an even iron grey, but the beard was light brown. He was wearing dark trousers and a leather jacket over a pale blue open-necked shirt, and carrying a smallish bag.

She moved away from the pillar and he saw her, walked briskly towards her. She's not changed much, he thought. Some grey in her hair, but still slim, still in her country clothes, still with that hesitant, almost wary smile. He noticed her feet, in thick leather sandals. They didn't embrace, but touched each other on the arm.

'You're looking well,' he said.

'You too. How was the flight?'

'Not bad. I've no luggage except this, so we don't need to wait.'

They walked side by side towards the exit. They asked after each other's families, and the replies lasted until they reached the car.

Michael laughed. 'Is this the same car you had the last time I was here?'

'Probably.' Ruth got into the driver's seat and leaned across to open the passenger door, which required an experienced tug of the handle. The car smelt of dog and earth.

'You can get a perfectly decent, nearly new car, low mileage, for around £5,000.'

Ruth did not reply.

She was glad the sun was out, brightening the white house in the green patchwork of fields. The cattle had settled on the track and she had to slow down to walking pace as they unhurriedly lumbered away. She drove, as always, to the back of the house. It was a Friday afternoon. Emma had arranged her dolls at the back door but was nowhere to be seen. Without a word of explanation Ruth stepped over them and Michael followed.

'You're in your old room,' Ruth said. 'Tea? Coffee? Something stronger?'

'Black coffee. I need to take away the taste of the ghastly stuff on the plane.'

'It's warm enough to sit outside,' Ruth said. She made coffee and took a tray out to the terrace. She noticed that the garden table needed a coat of varnish. Michael would notice too of course, and the uncleaned windows, and the shabbiness exposed by the merciless sunshine. He took off his leather jacket.

'So,' he said, settling back in the faded canvas chair and rolling up the sleeves of his blue shirt. 'You're doing alright.' It was a statement rather than a question.

'Same as usual,' Ruth said.

'Did I tell you I'd been given a chair? Professor Michael Cameron now.'

He hadn't told her, but it was there on his letterhead. 'That's good,' she said. 'Congratulations.'

'Julia likes being a professor's wife. Not that it makes much difference to me – more money of course, but also more admin. The curse of academic life.'

'Well, Professor Michael Cameron,' Ruth couldn't stop herself, 'to what do we owe the pleasure of your company?'

He looked up sharply, put down his mug and shifted in his seat. He took off his glasses and polished them with a clean handkerchief that he took from his pocket.

'It's been quite a few years…'

'Six,' said Ruth.

'We'd be very happy to see you in Oxford, any time.'

'Yes,' she said, 'I'd like to go to Oxford one of these days. San Francisco, too, and Kenya, even London. And Inverness. I'd like to see more of all of my family.'

'What's stopping you?'

Ruth laughed. 'The same as has always stopped me. The house. The garden. Work. Money.'

'Who do the dolls belong to?'

'Oh those are Emma's. She lives in the flat with her mum.'

'I see.'

He picked up his coffee mug again and held it in both hands.

'Michael, let's not mess about. I get the feeling you came here for a reason. You don't like this place, you've never been a great one for family ties. You don't write or phone. I'm pleased to see you, I really am – because I *am* one for family ties. So if you've come here for a reason, I'd really like to know.'

'I've been thinking about dad.'

Ruth was completely taken by surprise.

'It's coming up for thirty-two years since he died. There is something…' Michael took off his glasses again and stared at the blue sky before replacing them and looking at Ruth sitting opposite him. 'There is something that I think you don't know, that probably you ought to know although I promised mother I would not tell you.'

Ruth stared at him, her bronze eyes lit and intense.

'It was Alex who found him, and he was sworn to secrecy too.'

'What are you trying to say?'

'She wanted to protect you, so did Alex. The only time we talked about it, me and Alex, he was insistent that you weren't to be told, there was no need for you to know. Very emotional,' Michael paused again. 'It's probably the last real conversation I had with Alex. He cried, and got furious because he was crying. Very protective of you, Alex was. And it wasn't as if I was going to tell you. It made no difference to me. If that was the way mother wanted it, it was fine by me. I was going back to Oxford. I *went* back to Oxford.'

With the handkerchief he had used to polish his glasses he wiped sweat from his forehead. Ruth felt the sun's heat on her bare arms and closed her eyes to absorb it more completely. With her eyes still closed, she asked, 'When you said Alex found him, what did you mean?'

Michael wiped his forehead again and eased his hips from the chair so he could put his handkerchief back in his pocket.

'Michael, what did you mean? I thought it was mother who found him, in the stable. A stroke, she said. I always thought it was to do with his drinking, I remember Doctor Gunn saying something...'

'Well, so it was...'

'Alex found him,' Ruth said slowly. 'But didn't Alex come home from school at the same time as me? How could he have found him? Mother told me, as soon as I came through the door.'

'Alex had bunked off school. He did that quite often, if you remember. He had some story about study periods... I don't know. But you came back from school on your own that day, Ruth.'

They were both silent for some minutes.

'Right enough,' Ruth said at last. 'I walked down from the bus on my own. You're right. I remember.' She pictured herself walking down the track, downy thistles, red berries on the hawthorn, cattle, or maybe sheep, the sound of a dog barking, a whistling blackbird. Expecting her father to be there, in the garden if he was having a good day, raking leaves, perhaps the smell of a bonfire and smoke blending with a grey sky, or digging up the last of the carrots and beetroot.

'So what did Alex find?'

'He found dad. He went to the stable to practise his guitar – he used to do that.'

'Yes.'

'And he found him.'

'What, Michael, for God's sake, what did he find?'

'He found him hanging.'

She had got there ahead of him, of course, or halfway there, yet she felt sick and she had to clasp her hands together to stop them shaking.

'Ruth,' Michael went on, his voice a dull monotone, 'I'm sorry. He hanged himself.'

She nodded.

'Do you know what day it was?'

Ruth's voice failed her and it was several moments before she managed to say, 'The seventeenth of October. It was a damp, dreich sort of day.'

'I was in Oxford, must have been around the second week of term. Mother couldn't get me on the phone – she had to send a telegram.'

'And you came up on the night train.' Her hands were still clenched.

'The seventeenth of October. It was twenty-one years exactly from the day his pal was blown up on the road to Rome, the man who'd saved his life.'

'Yes.'

'So he told you about that.'

'Yes, he told me.'

'I must have heard the story a dozen times, when he was drunk, of course when he was drunk, at night when everyone else had gone to bed. He talked a lot to me, you know, his first-born. His name was Reggie, did you know that? Reginald David Gray. His pal who was blown up, his best friend. If you'd been a boy, you'd have been called David Gray Cameron. Did you know that?'

Ruth shook her head without speaking. She watched Michael calmly sip his coffee and then place the empty mug on the ground at his feet. She looked away from him and gazed for several moments at a clump of desiccated lilac blossom before saying, 'I don't think dad mentioned his name. He told me in the garden, one afternoon when I was helping him. I was quite little. Only once, he told me only once. I didn't know the date.'

'Well, I know the date and the name. Mother knew the date and the name. I don't know about Alex.'

'All this time and Alex never said anything.'

'He was determined that you weren't to know. Because you were dad's favourite, there was never any doubt about that, and he thought it would be too painful for you. And he thought that our father wouldn't have wanted you to know, though bugger-all difference it made when he was dead.'

'And what did you think?'

'I was happy to agree. I just wanted to get away. It wasn't a problem for me not to tell you because I wasn't there.'

'All this time,' Ruth said again, as if in a dream.

'He used an old rope halter. It had been lying around in the stable for years. I'm surprised it hadn't perished, I'm surprised it held his weight.'

Ruth stared at him, but still dreamy, not fully focused.

'Alex had come home and found an empty whisky bottle in the kitchen. Mother must have been upstairs. Alex didn't think anything of it – it was hardly unusual. He took his guitar to the stable because he didn't want to have to explain why he wasn't at school.'

Ruth remained silent, and then a sound made her turn her head and there was Larry coming across the grass towards them, a battered khaki bag and a camera slung over his shoulder. He had a baseball cap pulled over his eyes and was wearing a denim shirt over a T-shirt that had frayed at the neck. He stopped a few yards away and with his head tipped back surveyed the two figures seated on garden chairs in the sunshine. Ruth looked odd.

'This is Michael, my brother,' she said automatically. 'Larry.'

Larry raised a hand in a vague gesture and continued on his way.

'Who's Larry?'

'He lives here. He rents the attic.'

'I see.'

Ruth's eyes suddenly focused again. No, he didn't see, he didn't begin to see.

'We could have a drink,' she said.

Michael nodded. She went inside, into the cool kitchen, which was exactly as she had left it, but she looked around absently, as if she had forgotten where the whisky was, the glasses, the fridge where beer was chilling, the bottle opener. Through the window she could see Michael on the terrace, leaning back in his chair, one hand hanging down so it almost touched the ground.

He killed himself because of the drink, because of the anniversary of his friend's death, because he lost his mind? Perhaps that was it, perhaps he had never got over it, the whole business of the war. Her mother had said as much once or twice. 'Don't blame him for drinking,' she had said. 'We all thought that growing things was the remedy, but it wasn't enough. We were wrong.'

Ruth watched Michael close his hand into a fist and open out his fingers again. She found the whisky, glasses, some water in a jug. Was her father sorry there was no young David, that she wasn't a boy to carry his name? Was Reginald David himself married, a son of his own perhaps, a son called after him? Back on the terrace Michael sat exactly as before, his hand hanging down, barely moving to take the glass Ruth offered. She didn't sit down, but without a word headed towards the vegetable garden. When she returned twenty minutes later Michael was still in his chair, his head back, his legs stretched out in front of him, the glass on the table in front of him almost empty. She was carrying a wicker basket full of lettuce and rhubarb.

'So you're still content with the simple life, Ruth,' Michael said lazily, as if their earlier conversation had never been.

'Simple?' She put the basket down on the table and began trimming the rhubarb with a kitchen knife. The large, fan-like leaves fell to the ground. 'Surely you remember enough to know there was never anything simple about living here.'

'It's all relative. You've scarcely known anything else. You try the Byzantine convolutions of academia for a while.'

'I suspect there's no such thing as a simple life, unless you're a recluse living on your own and eschewing the materialism of the modern world.'

'As I said, it's all relative.'

'Do you think that going to the vegetable patch to cut a lettuce is simpler than going to the supermarket?'

'Isn't it?'

'Not if you've done the digging and the planting and the weeding that are necessary to produce the lettuce. It's much simpler to pick it up from a supermarket shelf.'

'I wouldn't know. I leave that to Julia.'

'That *is* the simple life. Get the wife to do all the difficult stuff.'

'She likes it. You like it, too – the gardening I mean. Otherwise you wouldn't do it. Or is it some misplaced idea that you owe it to your father?'

Ruth stooped to gather up the rhubarb leaves and looked directly at Michael. 'It's because of dad that I like to grow things, that's true. But it's not an obligation.'

'Isn't it? Don't you feel you have an obligation to keep Netherburn going?'

'It's where I live.'

'You don't have to stay here.'

'I like it.'

'Ruth, why don't you sell the place? Now that the boys have left home. None of them is going to live here. They're probably not even going to make their future in Scotland. Why do you stay? It seems to me it's out of some thrawn sense of duty.'

'So you still use Scots words.'

'Only in Scotland.'

'So not often, then.'

With her armful of rhubarb leaves Ruth walked to the compost heap. The evening sun was still warm and a blackbird was whistling in a corner of the garden. She could feel on the soles of her feet crumbs of earth and grit that had worked their way into her sandals. When she returned to the terrace Michael was sitting forward in his chair, his hands gripping his knees.

'If life is complicated, it's because of Netherburn,' he said.

On the table between them was the architectural pile of rhubarb stalks, two green cones of lettuce and the half-empty whisky bottle. Ruth pulled off a lettuce leaf and held it up. A small, greyish slug clung to it. She tossed leaf and slug under the snapdragons that edged the terrace.

'I should kill it,' she said.

'You're not cut out for this sort of life,' said Michael with a dry laugh. 'I don't think you ever were.'

Ruth sat down and smoothed her skirt over her knees. 'If Netherburn is complicated,' she said, 'it's because of life, not because of Netherburn.'

'Very neat.'

'Families,' Ruth went on. 'All families are complicated. The whole idea is complicated, and we make it more so.' She looked directly at Michael, sitting on the other side of the rhubarb with his glass in his hand. 'You've had two wives and three children. What sort of father have you been to Lucy, I wonder? Or to the other two for that matter. Ed's been distant from his three sons for more than ten years, but now one of them lives down the street from him and none live with me. Alex and Sheena have no children – but not from choice. They'd have welcomed that complication. Is their life simple? For all kinds of reasons I'm sure it isn't. Would it be simple if they abandoned everything and joined the commune at Findhorn? I don't think so. There's nothing simple about communal living. You guys in Oxford may think the north is without subtlety and sophistication, but that just shows your ignorance of human relations.'

'You're dodging the issue – the oldest trick in the book. My circumstances have nothing to do with it. Are you going to live here until you're carted off in a box? Both our parents died here, in this house – or in dad's case in the stable. I don't want my sister to die here. We need to break the curse. This house – I never liked it. It was never the right place, you know, we knew that even as children. We knew it was all for dad's sake but look at what happened – it killed him in the end.'

'Michael, don't be daft. That was nothing to do with the house. And I loved it, I've always loved it, I still love it.' She paused. 'And what you've told me about dad won't change that.'

Michael leant forward, removing his glasses, as if they were in some way a hindrance to speech. 'You don't understand, Ruth. The house, the garden, they gave him the illusion that life could mean something, but he knew it was an illusion and that's what killed him. He couldn't live with the unreality of it all.' He paused, breathed on his glasses, wiped them on his shirt, returned them to his nose. 'And you're suffering from illusions, too. I don't know what you think you're doing, gathering all these people. A kind of security blanket, I suppose. You're afraid to be on your own, aren't you? And I'm not surprised. I wouldn't like to live here alone, isolated, no neighbours, prey to intruders…'

Ruth flinched. Did Michael notice?

'You have to face reality, Ruth,' he went on. 'Accept the facts.'

'Is that why you've come? To persuade me to give up the house? To change my life? Why? You've never taken any interest in my life before. Why?'

'We're all getting older.' He sat back in the deckchair, assuming his dry, sardonic look as if to convey an awareness of cliché and intention of irony. 'Get real, Ruth. You don't really love this place. You've made the best of a bad job, and all credit to you, but there's no need to do it any more.'

Ruth said nothing for several minutes, then, 'I'm going to make dinner.'

While Ruth was in the kitchen Michael walked through the old tennis court and the vegetable garden, and round the back of the house. The dolls were still on the back step. Through a window he caught a glimpse of a dark-haired woman and heard a child's voice and the clatter of dishes. The grass needed cutting. There were weeds growing in the gravelled paths. Beyond the garden wall there was the same jungle of nettles and brambles that had always been there, and a few wild raspberries, nearly ripe. He made a circle round to the front and stopped and gazed at the front door with his hands in his pockets. From the attic window Larry saw him, Ruth's brother, part of Ruth's history, part of the history of the house. A man in his fifties, like Larry, with a neat beard – unlike Larry's unkempt stubble – and expensive shoes. He'd noticed the shoes at the end of Michael's outstretched legs, as he'd walked past earlier. Michael didn't know he was being watched as he stood looking at the front door, which as children they had never used, as if half-expecting it to open and some distant but familiar voice to welcome him.

Michael left the following day. He had someone to see at the university before getting his flight back, so Ruth walked him up to the bus stop. She didn't offer to drive him into town. The sun had vanished. Low cloud dulled the fields and the house, which disappointed her, for she wanted him to look back at Netherburn and regret leaving. She wanted him to see it bright and solid and full of warmth. They did look back, the two of them, as they waited for the bus but he made no comment. Instead he talked of his elder daughter Lucy and her job in customer relations. Children were usually a safe subject, unless they were in trouble. The bus came into view and Michael picked up his bag, looked for a moment as if he might bend to kiss his sister, thought better of it and swung the bag onto his shoulder.

His last words, as he climbed into the bus, were, 'If you decide to sell, let me know. I'll give you a hand with sorting things out.'

'Give my love to Julia and the kids,' Ruth said, not sure why, as Julia and the kids did not know her and had never been to Netherburn.

'So he's gone,' said Larry when she returned to the house. He was in the kitchen making coffee. 'How about our night out?'

16

RUTH AND LARRY had their night out. They drove into town, parked behind the Cameo cinema and had a meal in a Mexican restaurant.

'I have six weeks before my exhibition opens,' he said. 'If I sell enough pictures I'm going back to New York for a while.'

Ruth said nothing, and waited for more.

'Do you fancy a visit to New York?'

She tried to imagine the two elderly sisters, Brooklyn streets, Manhattan, yellow cabs.

'I'll go in the fall. It's a good time of year to be in New York, colours in Central Park, not too hot, not too cold. We could take a trip upstate, the Catskills, or the Finger Lakes.'

'I can't, Larry. For all kinds of reasons…'

'It would do you good to get away. Even just for a week.' He leant forward and reached out for her hand. 'When did you last spend a night away from Netherburn?'

Ruth smiled, shook her head.

'When were you last out of Scotland?'

She was still shaking her head, still smiling. 'I know, I know…'

Larry let go of her hand and reached for the bill. 'Our first date,' he said. 'It's on me.' He pulled out his dog-eared wallet. 'But don't think I'm setting a precedent.'

Later, engulfed by the intimate darkness of the cinema, her arm lightly touching Larry's, Ruth gave in to the figures on the screen and the voices and music that wrapped themselves around her. She had almost forgotten how much she loved it, the enclosure, the closeness. It hardly mattered what the figures said or did. When she was a child, after her rare visits to the pictures she would carry home the magic and shut out any attempt to intrude on the heightened world inside her head. She remembered that feeling, that transfiguration that buzzed through her body like an electric current, but she suspected she would never feel it again.

Yet it was almost the same now, driving home, the people in the streets in the summer dusk, the oncoming cars, the bus stopping on Queensferry Road to let out an elderly couple leaning into each other as if facing a gale, all had a lustre, an effulgence. The magnified reality was unchanged by a walk in the near-dark with Dixie, Ruth and Larry arm in arm, by the prosaic activities of tidying the kitchen and locking up, by the wordless climbing of the stair to Ruth's bedroom, where they embraced and removed each other's clothes and lay down together. And later Ruth woke to find their bodies no longer touching, but the space between them, only an inch or so, vibrant.

It was the last day of school. Ruth was a little later than usual going up the track to meet the school bus. Through the trees, still a hundred yards from the top gate, she glimpsed the bus approaching, but it didn't stop. Damn. Emma can't have been paying attention, but it was odd, as the driver knew where she got off. Maybe it was a different driver. Ruth paused, not sure what to do. Go and collect the car and follow the bus? Ring the school? She continued to the road and looked in both directions, half expecting to see the small figure of Emma trudging along, but of course she wasn't there.

She walked rapidly back down to the house, and picked up the phone but there was no answer from the school. Everyone had left. She got into the car, drove along the bus route for a couple of miles, turned, and drove back to the school. It was Martin, it had to be Martin. But suppose it wasn't? But it had to be. He'd been accommodating at Easter, telephoning Ros to arrange for Emma to visit, probably relishing the memory of his little escapade, guessing that Ros didn't know that he'd been in the house. Ruth sat in the car outside the school, paralysed, staring at the empty, silent playground. But there was nothing she could do but return home.

She waited for Ros in the bedroom, sitting by the window which gave her a view up the track. There were sheep and lambs in the front field now, and gowans and poppies at the fringes. She watched a pair of lambs dive stiff-legged for their mother. Then she saw the bus from the city slow down, stop, pull away and there was Ros on the far side of the road waiting while a van and large truck passed, then crossing and coming through the gate. Ruth met her at the lower gate.

'Ros, I'm so sorry, Martin's done it again.'

Ros went instantly pale, and the chill of her skin seemed to enter Ruth. Ros said nothing. When they got back to the house, like an automaton she went to the phone, but there was no reply. She barely looked at the mug of tea Ruth put beside her. Every five minutes she tried the phone again, her face expressionless and without colour.

'Ros, he's probably there, deliberately not answering.'

'What else can I do?' Ros said at last. 'I know the bastard just wants to make me suffer, but what else can I do? He can't hit me now, so he does this. And I told Emma, I told her...'

'You can't blame Emma.'

The phone rang. Ros jumped, reached out her hand but did not touch the ringing phone. It was Ruth who picked it up.

'Hello... oh, Emma. We've been worried about you... Do you want to speak to your mum? She's right here... okay, I'll tell her. Just so long as you're alright... okay, love.' Ruth put the phone down. Ros stared at her.

'She's fine Ros, but she couldn't talk for long. I don't think Martin knew she was phoning.'

'Did she say when she's coming back?'

Ruth shook her head. 'She said she'd phone again.'

'I'd rather he threw me about than did this. It's torture.'

'That's why he's doing it. The important thing is that she's safe, and you know he won't treat Emma badly, you know she likes being with him, so you really don't need to worry. Don't give him the satisfaction of letting it get to you.' But Ruth didn't add that there was an edginess to Emma's voice, which may have been because she didn't want her father to know what she was doing. She'd said, 'Tell mum not to worry,' as if she knew that Ros would worry, that what Martin was doing was not the way things should be.

Ros was staring bleakly out of the window. 'Stuart wants us to go on holiday together,' she said at last. 'Him and me and Emma.'

'That would be great, Ros.'

'I don't dare. Emma would tell Martin... I can't bear to think what he'd do. I can't tell Emma I'm looking for another job. I can't tell her anything. She'll chatter away to him about our life here, the people here, about you. I feel sick at the thought of what he must know, and the way he'll use it against me.'

'Does it matter if Martin knows about Stuart? What can he do that he isn't doing already?'

'Oh he'll find a way to make things worse.'

'You can't let Martin blight your entire life. I think you should go on holiday. I think Stuart sounds like a decent fellow.'

'Yes. He is.' But then Ros turned suddenly to Ruth, her expression changed, no longer hopeless but with something almost savage in her eyes. 'I could be wrong of course. I've been wrong about almost everything else. I fell in love with Martin – how could I have done that? I like Stuart, but he's probably a bastard too, I just haven't found out yet.'

'There's always a risk,' Ruth said quietly, 'with anyone. Of course you can never be certain, but you can't just give up.'

'Why not?'

'Ros…'

'And I've not been straight with Stuart, have I? He doesn't know he might have had a child. That's terrible, don't you think? His child, and I kept it from him.'

'There are always secrets.'

'That's a pretty massive secret, though, isn't it?'

The phone rang again. This time Ruth picked up the receiver straight away and put it into Ros's hand. She slowly put it to her ear. Ruth could tell that it wasn't Emma at the other end. After a long pause, Ros said, 'I know you're doing this to get at me, but it's not fair on Emma. Tell her, even if you won't tell me.' Her voice was slightly unsteady, but calm. Ruth nodded encouragement. 'Don't mess around with Emma, Martin. If you care about her at all, if you want her to like being with her father…' After another long pause Ros put the phone down.

'He's playing games. He won't say when he'll bring her back. Maybe Saturday, maybe Sunday… Then he said, that school she goes too, village school, not much cop is it? He thinks she should go back to her old school, live with him.' Her hands were trembling.

'He's just trying to upset you.'

'I know that.'

'He doesn't mean it.'

'Maybe he does.'

Hours later Ros was standing at her bedroom window in her nightdress, her bare arms white in the moonlight that flooded in. She looked out into the walled garden, the borders glistening with wallflower and gladioli. The grass was ragged, and weeds grew in the interstices of the paved path that led to a door in the wall at the far end. Ruth, always busy with her vegetables, paid little attention to the walled garden. In the moonlight it was spectral. Ros pressed her fingers against her cheekbones. She could not bear it, this terrible emptiness. She could not go into Emma's room and feel her absence. She could not bear the loss, which only she and Ruth knew of. She could not bear her fear, the clutch at her throat when she thought of Emma and Martin, and when she thought of the child she had chosen not to have. She heard Ruth's voice: 'You have to learn to live with loss, with regret. We all do. It's what life is about.'

She'd lost Stuart too, she knew that. Good-natured, easy-going Stuart, who had been nice to her. She could not keep that going, not now. She had to steel herself to accept his caresses. He seemed unaware that she bit her lip to prevent herself from crying when he slid carefully and thankfully into her. How lucky she was to have met Stuart. 'Maybe another time,' she said, explaining her reluctance to go on holiday with him. 'When Emma's ready. It's too soon.' Liar, she thought, pressing her cheekbones as she looked out into the moonlit garden. Liar, liar, pants on fire. A small creature scuttled out of the flowerbed, paused, looked around, and scuttled back again. A weasel? A rat? She turned and looked around the room, at the empty bed, the chair with its pile of clothes, the untidy sprawl of shoes under the dressing table. She shivered.

Ewan came home for a week at the end of July. He got a lift with friends as far as Leeds, then hitchhiked, arriving late when a haar had come in from the sea. As he walked down the track to the house muffled in mist he could hear the fog warnings booming out from the firth a mile and a half away. His mother was waiting for him. His hair was long and he hadn't shaved for several days.

Sam had phoned: he was hoping to get back to Scotland for a couple of weeks sometime soon, and bring his girlfriend.

James had written to say he'd be home before Christmas, but was considering a job in Nigeria.

Ewan sat in the kitchen that first night, talking cheerfully until one in the morning but without communicating very much. He was sharing a basement flat in Stoke Newington and working part-time in a bookshop. His dad had sent him some money, to help him through his final university year. Ruth was surprised – Ed had never mentioned it. She listened sleepily, propping her chin on her hands, wondering if she would ever have all her sons together again in the same place at the same time. Ewan had got a fish supper in Jedburgh, and then had to jettison his chips because the van driver who stopped for him couldn't stand the smell of vinegar. She remembered coming home from a day on the beach at Gullane when the boys were small, stopping for chips in Musselburgh and eating them by the river with the rain starting. Ewan must have been five then. He looked like his grandmother, Ruth thought then, with his smooth, light-brown hair and blue eyes, but his hair had darkened and she could no longer see the resemblance. She was hardly listening to him now, talking about the bad-tempered van driver who dropped him off at a bus stop in Liberton. Three boys eating chips by the River Esk, Ewan, curly-haired, bronze-eyed James, and Sam, already tall for his age, grabbing chips from his younger brothers and getting kicked in the shins by a screaming Ewan.

She would sit sometimes, after she'd got them all to bed, her mind blank with tiredness, unable to read, or even turn on the television. It was better not to sit down at all, to keep going, sort out their clothes for the next day, walk the dog, tidy the kitchen, and not stop until there was nothing more to be done. But she never reached that point. She had still never reached that point.

Larry sold eleven pictures at his exhibition. He would go to New York in November. His mother, he told Ruth, wanted him home for Thanksgiving, 'that traditional Jewish festival,' he laughed. He tried to persuade her, again, to come to New York 'for the Thanksgiving experience'. When she still refused, he sulked, for three days scarcely emerging from the attic. It was August. Ruth spent the warm evenings weeding. She remembered a dry summer when she was nine or ten years old, and her father snaking the hose from the outdoor tap and letting the water arc over the peas and runner beans, the scarlet flowers glistening with water drops. The tomatoes were ripening. I'd grow tomatoes just for the smell, Andrew Cameron had said once, coming into the kitchen with a flowerpot full of them. She could smell tomatoes now, growing against the back wall still warm from the day's sun. Dixie chased a foolishly bold rabbit from the turnips. The boys used to throw sticks at rabbits but always missed.

Ewan was out every night during his brief stay, catching up with old friends. He borrowed the car. Ruth didn't wait up for him but lay wide awake in bed, listening for his return. She'd hear the car, then the backdoor, Ewan's voice talking to Dixie, and finally the sound of his bedroom door closing.

'I'm careful mum, not drinking, honest.'

He showed little interest in Larry, whom he hardly saw, or in Ros and Emma. It appeared not to occur to him that Larry might be anything other than a lodger. He stuffed his clothes in the washing machine and left it to Ruth to deal with them. She hung them out on the line, jeans, T-shirts, socks and boxer shorts. A couple of hours later she took them in again when it started to rain. He borrowed money.

'Problem with casual work,' he said cheerfully, accepting two ten pound notes, 'if you take time off you don't get paid. But at least they let me take the time off.' Ruth gave him another twenty pounds when he left. 'Thanks, mum, I'll pay you back.'

Stuart went off to Crete without Ros, and she did not tell him that she had applied for jobs in Banff and Invergordon. She got the train to Invergordon for an interview, leaving Emma with Ruth, telling her daughter she had to see someone, a business meeting, Emma would be bored. Ros didn't like Invergordon and didn't get the job. She went back to studying vacancy columns, staring at newsprint and running her hands through her hair. West perhaps. Or south. What about Dumfries? With the new school year approaching vacancies were thinning out, but there, just before the start of term, a job in Dumfries With her red biro she underlined the phone number.

'I've never been to Dumfries,' she said to Ruth. Emma had come into the kitchen and heard her.

'Where's Dumfries?' she asked.

'Southwest,' Ros said. 'Near the border.'

'Near England?'

'Hmm.'

'Are you going there?'

'I might... have to go there for a meeting.'

'Oh.' Emma lost interest and wandered out of the kitchen to sit in her favourite spot on the back step with Dixie beside her.

'You still haven't told her then,' Ruth said.

'There's no point. I'll tell her when I have a job – but only if I'm sure she won't be talking to her father.'

Ros sat on the bus heading southwest from Edinburgh, leaning against the window, watching but not taking in the green of the passing hills. With her forefinger she touched the scar on her lip. It was tiny, hardly noticeable now. It was weeks before Stuart had asked her about it, on the bridge at Ratho, looking down on the canal after a midsummer evening walk. They had held hands. He had kissed her. She knew she was pregnant, and perhaps it was the need to bury that knowledge that led her to talk about Martin, describe for the first time to Stuart how she had acquired the scar on her lip. The way she had put her hand to her mouth and then seen her palm stained with blood. Martin, his hands in his pockets, leaning in the doorway, that chilling half-smile on his face which always followed his outbursts. She tasted the blood, stared at her blotted palm. 'Better get cleaned up,' he said. 'What *will* they say at school tomorrow?'

On the bridge at Ratho, looking down at a pair of swans and a cluster of mallards, Stuart put his arm around her and pulled her close to him and smoothed her hair. 'Why don't we go on holiday, you and me and Emma?'

In front of her on the bus was a woman with a toddler who made non-stop attempts to wriggle off her lap, across the aisle a young man in dark glasses reading the *Herald*. She didn't know this country at all, fold upon fold of green hills, early September rain giving way to pale sunshine. She began to take notice, a river, honey-coloured cattle, a fox trotting across a field, pheasants. In the public lavatory in Dumfries she combed her hair and tied it neatly back, and put on fresh lipstick.

Two days later she told Emma they would soon be flitting. 'But I don't want to leave Netherburn,' Emma howled. 'How can we leave Netherburn?'

They would leave Netherburn, leave Ruth, And Martin. And Stuart. It meant she did not have to spell things out. He was grown-up enough to know that these things happen, that work splits people up, but he would say, of course, that he would come and see her, and she would say yes, it wasn't so very far away, and anyway they would be back at Netherburn from time to time. They would perhaps never see Peter and Russell again, who had twice come back to cut the grass. Emma would no longer climb the stair to Larry's attic and sit with charcoal and a sheet of paper at his paint-encrusted table.

'We'll come back and visit, I promise,' Ros said soothingly to Emma. 'Ruth says we can stay any time.'

Emma glared, confused and hostile.

'It will be a new start, love, and you'll like Dumfries, I promise. It's nice. You'll make new friends.'

'Don't want new friends,' Emma wailed. Dixie, hearing her distress, rushed to her from the next room and pushed her nose into her hand.

Emma sat on the back step with her flop-eared rabbit and sucked her thumb. Dixie sat beside her.

They flitted two days before half-term, but still Ros lay awake at night cold with anticipation of Martin at the school gate, claiming Emma for the holiday. Ruth offered her car to take them to Dumfries, and Larry offered to drive. They would be staying at first in a rented cottage. Emma, stony-faced, refused to help pack or carry the bundles and cases down to the car. She went for walks with Dixie, kicking through the fallen leaves, walking in the muddiest stretches of track. She went down to the burn and threw branches and rocks into the water in an effort to dam the flow. When she came back filthy Ruth made no comment, except to suggest she leave her muddy shoes at the door. She made hot chocolate and they sat together in the kitchen, but Emma refused to talk. Ros found them there when she returned after her last day at school. Emma gulped the last half-inch of cocoa and left the room.

'Don't worry about her, Ros,' Ruth said. 'She'll settle down once you're there.'

When the car was packed and ready to go Emma could not be found. She was nowhere in the house – Ros went from room to room calling for her. Larry scouted outside, and walked as far as the burn.

'She'll not be far away,' Ruth said calmly. And it was Ruth who found her, in the stables, sitting under cobwebs on a musty bale of straw in the half dark.

'I'm not going,' she said. 'You can't make me.'

'Emma, you can't let your mum go by herself. She needs you.'

'What about dad? He needs me, too. He told me. He said he couldn't live without me.'

Ruth hesitated. 'You'll still see him. Dumfries isn't so very far away.'

'I don't think mum wants me to see him. She's taking me away so I can't see him. She shouldn't be allowed to do that.'

'Em, sometimes things have to change, and change is exciting. There will be all kinds of new things to get to know, new friends, a new school.'

'Don't want new things, don't want to go to a new school. I like where I am. I want to stay here.' She sniffed.

'You can't stay in the same place for ever.'

'You have. You've been here always, haven't you? You never go away, so why do I have to?'

'It's for the best, love,' Ruth said lamely. 'I'd love the chance to go away. In fact, we'll come and visit you, me and Dix. And Larry,' she added.

They heard Ros calling for Emma. They heard Larry. 'Come on Emmy, Emmylou. I'll sing all your favourite songs, all the way to Dumfries.'

'Come on, love.'

Larry's voice. '*Way up yonder beyond the sky, bluebird sings in a silver eye...*'

'That's my favourite.'

'I like it too.' Ruth held her hand out to the small hunched figure on the straw bale.

'*Buckeye Jim, you can't go...*'

Emma put a grubby hand into Ruth's.

'*Go weave and spin, you can't go...*'

Ruth pulled her gently to her feet and brushed the straw from her jeans.

'*Buckeye Jim...*'

'Who's Buckeye Jim?'

Ruth laughed. 'I have no idea!'

They emerged through the stable door into October sunshine. Larry was standing by the van with a mug of coffee in his hand.

'Hi, Emma. So you're coming after all. I was just finishing this cup of coffee and then I was going to hit the road without you.'

'Who's Buckeye Jim?'

'Search me. Great song, though.'

Ros was suddenly in the yard with coats over her arm. Ruth shook her head.

'*Buckeye Jim, you can't go...* Come on, Emmylou, all aboard.'

Larry held open the passenger door, and Emma and Ros climbed in. Ros wound down the window and leant out. 'If you ever find that earring, post it to me will you?'

'Of course. I'll have a good look now the room's empty.' But the room had been empty for a while. Ruth knew the earring would not be found.

To Ros's surprise, Larry put his arms around Ruth and kissed her. Ruth smiled and waved as the car bumped down the track and turned to follow the back wall. She and Dixie walked through to the front of the house, watched as Emma jumped out to open and close the gate, and waved again. Ruth waited until the car had turned right into the road and she could no longer see it. There was no one in the house at all now. Its emptiness oozed out through the open back door.

'Come on Dix,' she said. 'Let's have a walk.'

17

WHEN FAY CAMERON was dying, and Sam a baby, it had seemed, in spite of the new life, that all the vitality of the house was seeping through its draughty window frames. Ruth had never felt so solitary, so out of her depth. Sam learnt to walk along the passage to the kitchen, while upstairs his grandmother could not put one foot in front of the other without assistance. She leant on her daughter, but she seemed weightless, without substance, less of her than of the sturdy infant Ruth lifted when his determined staggers brought him low. Ruth had never imagined such frailty was possible, that her mother could be so diminished.

She had to put Sam in his cot when she tended to her mother, and often he stood and rattled the bars and screamed. Fay Cameron seemed not to hear, or not to care. She made no comment, but Ruth saw the resentment in her eyes, that she had to submit to being looked after, that she had no armoury against intrusions into her privacy. It was worse when the doctor came, or the district nurse. And at night, when Fay Cameron and Sam Montgomery slept, the one fitful and emitting low and ghostly moans from time to time, the other wrapped in the soft unconsciousness of infants, Ruth felt disturbingly alone. Television and radio seemed intrusive. She tried to read, but was too aware of the house whispering and skittering. Every night she telephoned Ed. He often was not in.

When Larry, Ros and Emma had gone, Ruth and Dixie walked to the shore, where Ruth sat for a while on a fallen tree and watched eider fussing in the water. The sun had gone, and the low cloud and strengthening breeze chilled the air. Oystercatchers screeched overhead. Larry would be back the next day, only to be gone again in another couple of weeks, to New York to see his mother. It was good that he was going to see his mother, of course, and his Aunt Rosa. She pictured the two survivors in the apartment they had shared for decades, the apartment where Larry had spent his childhood, where he had drawn his first pictures. Old-fashioned, Larry said, but it was he who was upset when Hannah insisted on throwing out the old familiar curtains and replacing them with lighter, brighter fabric. Now Rosa's arthritis was bad, Larry said, and Hannah too was finding the stairs difficult. He bought them cashmere scarves in a little place in the Lawnmarket.

'I'm going to tell them about you,' he said to Ruth. 'But what am I going to tell them, that's the question?'

'So what are you going to tell them?' She was busy at the kitchen sink.

'They'll want their boy married – again.'

'Do they see your daughter?'

'I believe so. Yes, I know so, she visits them, but not very often. Ruth. Don't dodge the question.'

'What question?'

'What am I going to tell my mom and my Aunt Rosa?'

'That's up to you, Larry. But I suggest you don't tell them you're getting married again, unless you've someone else in mind.'

He tipped his chair back and looked up at the ceiling. She had turned towards him but could not read his expression.

'Crack in the ceiling,' he said.

'I know.'

'When I get back I'll take a proper look at it.'

'So you're coming back.'

He let the front chair legs fall back with a thud. 'Of course I'm damn well coming back.'

'You turned up here on a whim. You could disappear on a whim too.'

'I turned up here because someone told me about Netherburn. A good place to paint, he said, you won't get distracted. And the woman who owns the house, she'll just let you get on with it, won't bother you. That's what he said, this guy, can't remember his name, but he knew you.'

Ruth shuffled newspapers and magazines into a pile and wiped the kitchen table.

'But she did bother me. She bothered me a lot.' He tipped his chair back again. 'Don't think it's too serious. Ceiling should stay up until I get back.'

'Well, Mr Fix-it, there's plenty of other things you can do if you're that way inclined.'

'Depends.'

'On what?'

'What am I going to tell Hannah and Rosa?'

'You could try telling them the truth.'

'Don't go all philosophical on me.' The chair thudded four-square again. 'Or do you want me to tell them I'm shagging this great gal who owns a big house and lets me paint in her attic?'

Ruth was leaning with her back against the sink, a dish towel in one hand. She wore faded jeans and a dark blue polo-neck sweater and she hadn't combed her hair since she came in from a windswept walk with Dixie. She was wearing thick socks but no shoes. She looked at him now, silent, quizzical, her bronze eyes wide, and then at last said, 'That about sums it up, I guess.'

'So I'll tell them that.'

'Why not?'

'Don't be exasperating.' He looked genuinely pained. 'Some people think I'm a comedian, an "artist in the garret" act, doing it for laughs. But I thought you understood that I'm serious, serious about what I do, serious about... people. Okay, I've not made too good a job of things so far, but it's not too late.'

Ruth was smiling, in spite of herself. 'Are they going to disapprove, your mother and aunt? Of me? Of you? Are they going to want you to make an honest woman of me?'

'You are an honest woman. I've never known a more honest woman. No man is going to make you honest or dishonest, I know that much.'

'I'm lucky,' Ruth said reflectively. 'I don't have to explain myself to anyone. And you know, I don't think I've ever had to. I'd have liked to have explained myself to my father, but I didn't get the chance. My mother never asked for explanations. Ed maybe, but most often it was me looking for explanations from him. I wouldn't dream of explaining myself to Michael... perhaps to Alex, but he never asks. Perhaps one day to my children, but they're not here.'

'What did you say to Ewan?'

'Nothing. There was no need, he was completely oblivious. It never occurred to him that his mother might be... having an affair.'

'Is that what this is?'

'I don't know what it is, Larry. I didn't expect this. I'd had it with men, really. I didn't expect to find myself... caring again.' She wrapped the cloth around her hands. 'I'll be fifty next birthday.'

'So what? I'll be fifty-four.'

'Guys your age usually go for younger women.'

'So I'm breaking the mould.'

'I can't help feeling... it's because I'm convenient, I'm here, you don't need to go out, on the pull.'

Larry got up from his chair, circled the table and gripped Ruth's arms. 'You have the most beautiful eyes I've ever seen. When I saw you that first time, at the front door, you were so different from what I expected. I was stunned, you know, Jesus, I was stunned. There you were with your amazing eyes, but everything else about you elusive, escaping me somehow. You know what I thought? I thought, there's a woman I'll never be able to paint.' He shook her slightly, slowly. 'But now, now I'm beginning to think I could paint you.'

'You have painted me.'

'No, I put you in a picture. Not the same thing. I mean really paint you, paint the real you. If I can find it.'

Dixie scrambled up from her position beside the Aga and looked warily at Ruth and Larry. He was shaking her again, back and forth, rhythmically. 'Ruth,' he said, each word accompanied by a shake, 'Ruth, I'm going to tell them that I love you. That after all this time I've found a woman I really love, really, really, really love.'

'That's an awful lot of "reallys".'

She had closed her eyes, her hands still wrapped in the towel. Minutes seemed to pass, and she said nothing more. They could hear each other breathing.

'Say something.'

Neither of them moved. Dixie sat, but still watched them. Ruth said, without opening her eyes, 'I'm glad you're planning to come back.'

'Is that the best you can do?'

'For now.'

He let go of her arms and took her face in his hands. He kissed each eye and then her mouth.

A damp, grey November afternoon, Thanksgiving Day, the sky weighted with cloud. Ruth and Dixie walked through unraked leaves into the field of barley stubble by the side of Netherburn. A bullfinch flitted in and out of the hedge. In the centre of the field rooks had descended, and were scrabbling for grain. She locked the house now, whenever she went out, something she never used to do if the house wasn't out of her sight.

The Millie Anderson proofs lay on her desk, but she tried not to think of Millie as she walked, nor of Larry in New York with mother and aunt, contemplating turkey and pumpkin pie. The rhythm of walking and the soft brittle sound of stubble under her feet helped to empty her mind. Dixie ran ahead, lunged at the rooks, followed scents in short bursts with frequent checks that Ruth was still there.

Her eye was caught by a flash of colour. Turning, she could just see through the bare trees something red coming down the track. She closed her eyes. 'Oh God, no,' she said aloud. She opened her eyes again, not moving, and could make out where the car had stopped at the lower gate. Dixie was looking at her, puzzled. 'Dix,' she called softly, and stepped back close to the hedge. The car disappeared behind the house. She could not be seen, she knew, but she felt a need to be hidden. She stood motionless for many minutes, and then began to walk slowly back towards the house. He'll go away, she thought, when he finds no one there and this time all the doors locked. To the west, beyond the house, cloud parted to reveal a streak of pale orange.

She knew as she walked alongside the back wall that the red car had not left. She stopped at the corner, where the track led into the yard, and held Dixie by the collar. He'd parked out of sight. She could hear nothing. She let go of the dog and continued slowly, stepping out of the shelter of the wall into open space. The car was where she expected it to be. She saw at once the scuffs on the back door as if it had been kicked. It took longer for her to notice the broken window into the kitchen of the flat.

She went straight to the door, unlocked it and stepped inside, listening, but Dixie rushed ahead of her and barked. Ruth thought she could hear a voice, then definitely footsteps running down the stairs, the crescendo of the dog's barks, and there he was in front of her with his neat haircut and leather jacket and polished shoes.

'What have you done with them, you scheming cunt?'

His eyes and voice were icy cold. He had known where to go this time, straight upstairs, to find empty rooms, no sign, no scattered clothes or earrings or flop-eared rabbit, no pile of jotters or books or Emma's slippers by the bed. Then he heard them come into the house, the fucking dog.

'They've gone,' Ruth said, gripping Dixie's collar.

'Where are they?'

'I'm not going to tell you.'

'You are going to tell me.'

Ruth said nothing. Beside her Dixie was growling, a low vibration in her throat that Ruth could feel travelling through her hand. But he took them both by surprise, grabbing Ruth's arm with one hand and a stinging slap to the side of her face with the other at the same time as he pushed her hard against the wall. Released, Dixie leapt at him, and sunk her teeth into the arm of his jacket. Without letting go of Ruth he kicked out at the dog, missed, kicked again, made contact, she yelped, letting go of his arm. He slapped Ruth's face again. Dixie went for his ankle this time but he shook her off with another kick.

'I'll kill that fucking dog.'

Ruth put the back of her hand to the side of her mouth, saw and tasted blood. Dixie was crouching and snarling. The scar on Ros's lip. She thought of James, coming home for Christmas, all her sons, but James especially with a rush of longing.

'You're going to tell me where they are.'

With difficulty Ruth said, 'What are you going to do if I don't?' Her mouth felt odd, clumsy, no longer fitting her face. 'Kill me as well as the dog?'

He'd raised his hand again. Dixie quivered with tension, her eyes fixed on the uplifted hand, but then he let it drop.

'She never went to the police, did she?' Ruth said, compelled, not thinking. 'You think you can get away with anything, but now she's got away from you. They've gone. I made a mistake that first time you came, but I'm not going to do it again. We know you were in the house before. It won't take a genius to work out that you made a return visit.' The words came out of her mouth thick and clotted.

His eyes were cold, blank as if sheathed in smoked glass. He had let go of her arm but she remained with her back against the passage wall, nausea welling up, but motionless, and Dixie still quivering and growling very low beside her.

'Get out.' It was almost a whisper.

Minute after minute seemed to pass. There was no movement, no change in his icy stare. And then, at last, he reached out, pulled her towards him and again pushed her hard against the wall. Dixie leapt, but he'd already turned and was out through the back door with the dog snapping and tearing at his trouser leg. He kicked her again as he opened the door of the car. With the engine running he rolled down the window.

'One word to the police and I'll be back.'

He reversed with crunching gears and turned the car abruptly, seemed to aim at Dixie, who continued her frenzied leaping and barking, but missed her and drove fast and precariously round the house with the dog in pursuit. Ruth tried to call her back but her voice had vanished. He'd not bothered to shut the lower gate and the car was away, bouncing up the track. After a couple of hundred yards Dixie gave up.

Ruth went to the telephone, dialled, and immediately put the receiver down again. She sank into a chair, stunned, her head pounding. The house was cold. She put her hand to her mouth again and looked at the blood, and then Dixie returned, trotting in through the open back door, and laid her head on Ruth's knee. A few pages of the Millie Anderson proofs had fallen to the floor and she reached automatically to pick them up, leaving a smear of blood on the top sheet. The movement sent a stab of pain through her shoulder and arm. Dixie licked her hand. She should get up and go and close the lower gate, return and close and lock the back door. Supposing he came back? She put her hand out again, vaguely, hesitantly, and it encountered the dog's smooth head, but continued to reach as if there was something it needed to hold. She had to get on with the proofs, she had a deadline. She looked down at the heap of paper that represented someone else's life. There was comfort in that, comfort in knowing she could open another door, that it was an obligation as well as an escape.

It grew dark but she did not move and nor did the dog. She was still sitting motionless when the phone rang, piercing the silence. She had to get up, slowly and painfully, to answer it and almost hoped it would stop before she got to it. It was Lorna.

'We've got a publication date for Millie,' she said. 'Just thought I'd let you know.'

'Oh... great.'

'Twenty-third of March, her birthday. Means we'll have to get our skates on. Is that okay with you?'

'Yeah... should be fine. I'm... the proofs are coming along.'

'Ruth. Are you alright?'

'I'm fine... been out with the dog... slightly out of breath.'

'You sure? Your voice sounds odd.'

'I'm fine.'

'Okay. Got to run. I'm going to be late home, again. If you can get the proofs back early next week that would be great.'

The room was now quite dark and she was shivering. She went out, not pausing to put a jacket on, into the damp November dark and walked round the house to the lower gate, which she pulled shut. There were no beasts in the field, but she did not like to think of the gate gaping open. Dixie followed her, limping slightly. They walked back and rounded the corner of the back wall. The kitchen lights were on, and Ruth stopped, although heavy drops of rain were beginning to fall, and gazed at the windows as if she were a stranger who had reached a place of warmth and safety after a long journey.

18

RUTH HAD TAKEN Larry to the airport. It was early morning, not yet fully light, but with red spreading in the east. She waited with him while he checked in, with the shapeless hold-all and a small canvas bag that were all he took with him. His paints and half-finished pictures stayed behind. He'd shaved off his beard, which left his face pale and vulnerable. They paused at the departure gate.

The night before they had talked late, sitting opposite each other at the kitchen table. Larry had made fried chicken for their dinner.

'I want you to think of me as a domestic kind of guy,' he said as he stood at the Aga.

But he talked of how he had to paint, how his hands began to twitch if they were too long without holding a pencil or a brush, how he felt compelled to fill an empty surface. He said that sometimes it was hard to live with, because the urge to paint was often without substance, when he would stare at vacant whiteness and not be able to put anything on it, when he could find no meaning in line or colour. He repeated this: 'I'm not the easiest person to live with.' Ruth listened, her elbows on the table beside the dirty plates, her slender face cupped in her hands. Where do they come from, she was wondering, his need to paint and his dark blue eyes?

'You should talk more,' he said.

'I like to listen.'

'Tell me what happened to your father.'

So she told him, remembering word for word, or so it seemed, her father's story in the garden, the story of the bloody landings in Italy, of how he would have drowned, of Reggie's hand and the undamaged wristwatch, of how Andrew Cameron had survived on whisky until he hanged himself in the old stables that still smelt of horse sweat and rotting straw.

'And I didn't know,' she said. 'I didn't know that my father had hanged himself until Michael came in the summer. That's why he came, to tell me something that I might never have found out. And now I have to decide whether to tell my sons the truth about their grandfather whom they never knew.'

'I grew up convinced I was being excluded from the real story of my father.'

'And now?'

'Aunt Rosa used to say I looked like my father. I wanted to make him real, but I still don't know how to do that. Maybe I could find out what happened to him, but would that make any difference? He didn't survive. To know exactly how he died, what he might have suffered... Perhaps I'm just a coward but I'm not sure that would fill the vacancy I've lived with all this time. Besides, I'm used to it now. Maybe that's why I paint, to fill that empty space.'

'Why don't you paint him?'

He looked at her with a half smile, reached across the table and lifted her hand and kissed it.

'Maybe I will. I'll make him up. That's what artists do – they pretend they paint what they can see but actually they make it up.' And then, after a pause. 'And have you decided what to tell your sons?'

'You might say there's no reason for them to know. But Andrew and Fay Cameron are part of the history of this house, and you have to respect the past, I think, don't you? Keep faith with it in some way. This house and the family, they're inseparable, for me at least. One day it will belong to Sam and James and Ewan, and I guess they won't keep it, but sometimes I feel I need to tell them more, not less, more about the things that have happened here.' She paused and smiled at Larry. 'It's just possible that one day, probably when it's too late, they'll wish they knew more about their mother.'

'Like I said, you should talk more.'

'When Michael told me, I was shocked by the fact that I hadn't known, not shocked by the manner of my father's death. So I think that though my sons may feel no connection at all with their grandfather, I can't not tell them. It's part of my life as well as his, and theirs. They used to play in the stables, swing from the same beam that helped my father to his death. '

'Family secrets. We've all got 'em. Skeletons creaking and clanking in cupboards.'

'We're all part of it, the patched together fragments, the creaking skeletons. We can't unpick ourselves.'

'And Michael, he's part of it too.'

Ruth nodded.

'And he kept that information to himself... for how many years?'

'And Alex. He kept the secret too.'

'Do you forgive them for keeping it to themselves for so long?'

'Perhaps forgiveness is simply not seeking retribution,' she said slowly. 'Thou shalt not seek vengeance. I have no wish to punish them.'

Larry took Ruth's hand again.

'Retribution,' he said. 'Where would I go to avenge my father?'

'You can't. You're trapped – there's no retribution but no forgiveness either.'

'And that toerag Martin…You want him punished?'

'He's been punished, for now. He may never see his daughter again.'

'I guess we all have a stake in seeing him punished.'

Ruth shrugged.

'You're right, though,' Larry continued. 'Never seeing his daughter… that's a real punishment.'

'You'll see her? You'll see Hannah?'

Larry nodded. 'It's after midnight,' he said.

'We'll be up again in six hours.'

'Let's go to bed.'

She walked away from the departure gate, scarcely aware of the milling people, the lines snaking back from the check-in desks, the piled baggage. The cars and taxis and airport buses parked outside were no more than a restless blur as she crossed to the car park and paid at the machine. She drove home on the back road, past fields where the winter wheat was already through, under a blue sky shredded with cloud. The white house sturdy amid bare trees and green fields, Dixie at the door to meet her. In the kitchen the relics of last night's meal were still on the table. She saw it all clearly, house, dog, untidy kitchen, the rooms that lay beyond, unoccupied yet layered with the lives that had passed through them.

Larry had held her fiercely, his forearms taut as wire. For a few seconds they were an island in a swirl of people.

'I'll tell them I've got a girl waiting in Scotland,' he said.

'I'll be here,' Ruth said.

Luath Press Limited

committed to publishing well written books worth reading

LUATH PRESS takes its name from Robert Burns, whose little collie Luath (*Gael.*, swift or nimble) tripped up Jean Armour at a wedding and gave him the chance to speak to the woman who was to be his wife and the abiding love of his life. Burns called one of the 'Twa Dogs' Luath after Cuchullin's hunting dog in Ossian's *Fingal*. Luath Press was established in 1981 in the heart of Burns country, and is now based a few steps up the road from Burns' first lodgings on Edinburgh's Royal Mile. Luath offers you distinctive writing with a hint of unexpected pleasures.

Most bookshops in the UK, the US, Canada, Australia, New Zealand and parts of Europe, either carry our books in stock or can order them for you. To order direct from us, please send a £sterling cheque, postal order, international money order or your credit card details (number, address of cardholder and expiry date) to us at the address below. Please add post and packing as follows: UK – £1.00 per delivery address; overseas surface mail – £2.50 per delivery address; overseas airmail – £3.50 for the first book to each delivery address, plus £1.00 for each additional book by airmail to the same address. If your order is a gift, we will happily enclose your card or message at no extra charge.

Luath Press Limited
543/2 Castlehill
The Royal Mile
Edinburgh EH1 2ND
Scotland
Telephone: +44 (0)131 225 4326 (24 hours)
email: sales@luath. co.uk
Website: www. luath.co.uk

Also published by **LUATH PRESS**

Letters From the Great Wall
Jenni Daiches
ISBN 9781905222513 PBK £9.99

You can't run away from things here in China, there's too much confronting you.

Eleanor Dickinson needs to see things differently. To most her life would seem ideal; 33 years old, a professional university lecturer in a respectable relationship with a man who is keen to start a family. But Eleanor is dissatisfied: she's suffocated by her family and frustrated by the man she has no desire to marry. She has to escape.

In the summer of 1989, she cuts all ties and leaves behind the safe familiarity of Edinburgh to lecture in the eastern strangeness of China, a country on the brink of crisis. Basing herself in Beijing, she sets off on an intense voyage of self-discovery. But as the young democracy movement flexes its muscles, Eleanor is soon drawn into the unfolding drama of an event that captured the world's attention.

What freedoms will be asserted in this ancient nation, shaped both by tradition and revolution? And will Eleanor discover what really matters in her life before the tanks roll into Tiananmen Square?

Details of books published by Luath Press can be found at:
www.luath.co.uk